DEATH
OF A
DOLL MAKER
AN AKITADA NOVEL

I. J. PARKER

I · J · P Books

Copyright © 2013 by I. J. Parker.

Published 2013 by I.J.Parker and I·J·P Books
428 Cedar Lane, Virginia Beach VA 23452
http://www.ijparker.com
Cover design by I. J. Parker.
Cover image byOgata Gekko.

Death of a Doll Maker, 1ˢᵗ edition, 2013
ISBN 978-1492765035

Praise for I. J. Parker

"Elegant and entertaining . . . Parker has created a wonderful protagonist in Akitada. . . . She puts us at ease in a Japan of one thousand years ago." *The Boston Globe*

"You couldn't ask for a more gracious introduction to the exotic world of Imperial Japan than the stately historical novels of I. J. Parker." *The New York Times*

"Akitada is as rich a character as Robert Van Gulik's intriguing detective, Judge Dee." *The Dallas Morning News*

"Readers will be enchanted by Akitada." *Publishers Weekly* Starred Review

"Terrifically imaginative" *The Wall Street Journal*

A "mystery with a cast of regulars who become more fully developed with every episode." *Kirkus*

"More than just a mystery novel, (*THE CONVICT'S SWORD*) is a superb piece of literature set against the backdrop of 11ᵗʰ-cntury Kyoto." *The Japan Times*

"Parker's research is extensive and she makes great use of the complex manners and relationships of feudal Japan." *Globe and Mail*

"The fast-moving, surprising plot and colorful writing will enthrall even those unfamiliar with the exotic setting." *Publishers Weekly,* **Starred Review**

"a historical crime novel that anyone can love." *Chicago Sun-Times*

"Parker's series deserves a wide readership." *Historical Novel Society*

"Parker masterfully blends action and detection while making the attitudes and customs of the period accessible." *Publishers Weekly* **(starred review)**

"Readers looking for historical mystery with a twist will find what they're after in Parker's latest Sugawara Akitada mystery . . . An intriguing glimpse into an ancient culture." *Booklist*

CHARACTERS

Sugawara Akitada   governor of Chikuzen province
Tamako   his wife back in the capital
Yasuko, Yoshitada   his daughter and son
Tora   his senior retainer
Saburo   his retainer and major domo

Persons involved in provincial adminsitration:
Fujiwara Korenori   Assistant Governor General of Kyushu
☞ Tachibana Moroe   previous governor of Chikuzen
Captain Okata   police chief of Hakata city
Lieutenant Maeda   his successor
Mori Kiyomi   tribunal secretary
Koji   tribunal servant

Persons connected with the murders in Hakata:
Nakamura   mayor of Hakata
Hayashi   chief of the merchant's guild
Feng   Chinese merchant
Kuroda   shrine priest
Mitsui   doll maker
• Mei   —   his Chinese wife, also a doll maker
Atsuko   their daughter, the shrine priest's wife
Hiroshi   their son, a laborer

Kuroki	a scribe
Yoko	his wife
Mrs. Kimura	a widow who grows bonsai
Naoko and Kichiro	two homeless children
Fragrant Orchid	a ranking courtesan
Umeko	her attendant and trainee
Shigeno	a convict
Ling	Feng's servant
Masashi	Feng's store clerk

The winds of spring
Scattered the blossoms
As I dreamed of you.
Now I waken
To a broken heart.

Saigyo

1

The Parting Gift

Oil lamp held high, he surveyed the nearly empty room one last time. "What a hell hole! May the next governor choke on it!"

His art collection was gone, and so were his carved and lacquered desk and the jade writing set. He had packed up all his treasures. Now the room contained little but a few mats and cushions and the ordinary desk that had been in storage. Let his successor gather his own wealth.

Outside, a horse whinnied, anxious to be gone. He, too, was eager to end it. Nearly three years of having to contend with fools and men he despised. Never mind. It had been profitable, so profitable the government in the capital had taken notice and issued the recall.

As if they weren't greedy bastards all.

But they knew that he knew their venal sins, and that would protect him and get him another good assignment. He smiled. The hard work had paid off. Life was finally beginning for him. With a contented sigh, he blew out the flame, set the lamp on the floor, and walked out.

He was surprised to see only two riders waiting with his horse. He recognized them and asked, "Where are the others?"

"Gone ahead. You took your time."

He swung himself into the saddle. "Just bidding farewell to this pest hole. Well, let's go. The ship's captain is eager to leave before dawn."

"One more brief stop," said the smaller of the two men. "You'll give me the pleasure to accept a farewell cup and a gift at my house, I hope?"

It was the least the fellow could do after all he'd done for him, he thought, but his resentment melted a little. "How very kind of you but not at all necessary."

The other man laughed softly. "You have been generous to my family. We do not forget our friends."

His house was on the way. Why not spare a little time for a last cup of wine and a gift? Surely the present would be well worth it. Yes, the fellow had become very rich through him. At least as rich as he. A man like that owed acknowledgment to his betters. "Just a brief stop then," he replied.

They veered off the main road, passed through some deserted streets, and entered a dark compound.

The smell of cooking hung in the air, and he wrinkled his nose. "Why is it so dark?" he asked looking around.

"I've sent everyone away to make sure we're undisturbed. Your Excellency cannot be too careful. It wouldn't do to be seen in my house before your departure."

"You may be right. Very considerate of you, but it's unnecessary. They know or suspect already, but they cannot hurt me. Well, let's go inside."

They dismounted.

He followed the owner of the house. The large man, a servant, walked softly behind. But his host did not lead the way to the main house. He turned off to the side and took him to a service yard.

"What's this? Are we going to the stables or the kitchen?"

His host chuckled. So did the servant behind him. "To the stables," said his host.

He must be giving me a horse. Most likely a magnificent animal, but there was the inconvenience of transporting the animal all the way back. He slowed down. "Look," he started, but they were already at the stables, and his host swung wide the door. The warm smell of horse flesh met his nose. He had guessed correctly.

"Come in and see," said his host, taking his arm. "Your surprise is waiting. And such a surprise! I can't wait to see your face."

The servant pressed him forward as his master tugged. He gave a little laugh and submitted.

It was an ordinary stable and contained only three horses. By the uncertain light of the lantern near the door, they looked common. He had seen better looking post horses. He stopped again.

"Come," he said, irritated, "if this is a joke, I'm getting very tired of it."

Behind him the stable door slammed shut, and he heard the sound of the bar being shoved across.

Surprised, he turned. The servant, ugly brute that he was, stood there, his arms folded across his chest and a nasty grin in his face. He felt a twinge of uneasiness, then anger. Swinging back to his host, he demanded, "Open this door immediately. I'm leaving."

"No, you're not," said the servant and chuckled.

His host was not smiling. He looked at him coldly. "Unfortunately," he said in his soft voice, "I cannot let you go. You should have realized you know far too much about my business."

An icy fear gripped him. This could not be happening. Where were his people? What could he do? Bluster? Threaten? Plead? Offer the man a deal?

He blustered. "How dare you? I'm an imperial official. You cannot restrain me. My people are waiting for me at the dock."

"We're restraining him?" The servant laughed again. "That's one way of putting it."

His master smiled a little at this. "They have gone on board. Someone sent them a message that you'd found a faster boat and would travel ahead. As for being missed in the capital . . . I doubt you'll truly be missed."

"You fear I will tell our secrets? Why should I inform on you? You have nothing to fear from me. We've always got along well together."

The servant laughed again.

He decided to buy his way out of this unpleasantness. "Look," he said more calmly, "You and I have always worked well together. I have no interest in talking about our business. We've both done well by it. And I can still do much for you in the future. I'm grateful and I'd be willing to share some of my future profits to prove my good will."

The other man's mouth twitched a little. "Tempting, but I'm a simple man. I like to make sure. Promises are like the wind. You can't rely on them. On the other hand, I know you've hidden part of your gold somewhere to collect later. That I'd like to have. Where is it?"

His fury rose again. How did this common creature threaten him? "You heard wrong," he snapped.

"Ling!"

The servant stepped in front of him. To his horror, he saw a thin sharp blade in the man's hand. "No!" he gasped.

Too late. The blade had struck and taken off his topknot. The servant held it up and sniggered before tossing it under a horse's hooves.

He backed away until he was hard against the barred gate. His right hand fumbled for the bar.

The servant was quicker. Again the blade flashed before he could twist away. A sharp pain stabbed his face, and then hot blood poured into his mouth as he screamed.

"Where?" asked the other man again. This time his voice was harsher. "Speak or he'll slice you up alive like a pig."

"No, wait!" he screamed again, his hands pressed to the place where his nose had been. "I'll talk."

The servant moved back a little, but he still held the bloody knife.

He told them. He told the truth because he was much too desperate to think of a good lie. And maybe also because a small part of him still hoped he would get away alive and come back for his revenge.

The other man nodded when he was done. "Good. Very well, Ling won't have to make a mess of my stable after all, and we can go to bed at a decent hour. Ling?"

The servant came to open the gate, and for a moment, he thought it had worked and sighed with relief.

But the brute stopped before him, so close he saw his widening grin as the blow came. He felt a sharp pain in his chest, then a numbness followed by a great cold. And then he was face down in the dirt and couldn't catch his breath. Something inside his chest contracted violently.

And on that agonizing spasm, all went dark

2

The Promotion

Tora was leaning on the ship's rail. "I've been wondering, sir. Why you?" They were watching the approaching shore.

There had been little to do on board ship. Akitada had spent the weeks pacing the deck, searching like Tora for meaning in the past events.

Ironically, the first news about this assignment had been cause for joy in the Sugawara family. It had arrived via Kosehira's New Year's letter. They exchanged family news around this time. Akitada had informed Kosehira he would be a father again in the coming year and wished Kosehira an equal amount of happiness and a long life.

Kosehira had responded with the somewhat puzzling joke about good news being a certainty for Akitada while a long life might require his special talents. Akitada had meant to ask for an explanation, but by then the New Year had arrived, and the house was in a frenzy of decoration and preparation of special dishes. The women were sewing new clothes and the children begged for toys. Akitada went shopping for silk for Tamako and balls, dolls, and games for all the children in his household. There were four of them now. His own two were a girl and a boy, Yasuko and Yoshitada; Tora and Hanae had a son, Yuki; and Genba had a baby girl. His thriving household gave Akitada a deep happiness. The venerable Sugawara residence, though plagued by roof leaks and sagging timbers, was filled with the laughter of children and he was surrounded by people he loved. And now they had also the promise of another child when he and Tamako had nearly given up hope for it. Tamako had thought herself too old, though she seemed to glow with youth and beauty.

The memory of Kosehira's letter did not surface until an acquaintance approached him one morning while he was on his way to the ministry. "My heartiest congratulations, Sugawara. Well done!" he had cried. "Another step in rank. Fortune truly knocks on your door."

Akitada had stopped. "How so?"

"You haven't heard? Your name is on the promotions list."

It was!

Akitada could not account for such a thing. The past year had been so ordinary he had become bored with his work and passed much of it on to younger men. He had felt a strange shiver of premonition.

But sudden and inexplicable promotion was usually an example of the peculiar workings of government. He had decided to enjoy it, along with the other pleasures of the season.

And now they were entering Hakata Bay in Kyushu on an early spring day while gulls danced against a limpid blue sky and a green land beckoned ahead, and Akitada could not shed a sense of foreboding.

Tora said, "Is something going on here that requires someone like you rather than one of their usual picks?"

Trust Tora to see through his subterfuge.

"I'm here to serve as governor of Chikuzen province. I gather you feel that doesn't require special skills," Akitada said, his lip twitching.

Tora laughed.

But of course there was a great deal more to it. His secret orders were to find and arrest the man or men engaged in illicit trade with China. He was told no one was above suspicion. And that made his assignment not only difficult, but dangerous. He had postponed telling Tora and Saburo about this because he was afraid that in their eagerness they would give something away and warn his unknown adversary.

It had all started so innocently. On the fifth day of the New Year, Akitada had presented himself at the imperial palace in full court finery to have his new rank bestowed. The ceremony took place in the Shishinden, the main ceremonial hall of the emperor's palace. The regent himself read out the names and the new ranks, while his secretary added flattering comments on the performance of each recipient. Akitada's turn came somewhere toward the end of the long list. Like those before him, he had approached the front of the great hall, knelt, and touched his forehead to the floor, so overcome he barely heard the rank increase—a mere quarter step, but very welcome anyway—and the praise for his valuable assistance in stopping piracy on the Inland Sea.

They were a mere two years late in their recognition of his work in Naniwa, an assignment that had almost cost his life and those of Tora and Saburo as well. Still, it had felt good to be acknowledged at all, and Akitada had basked in the warmth of official approval, a rare enough occurrence in his long service.

After the ceremony. Fujiwara Kaneie, his immediate superior at the Ministry of Justice, caught up with him and took hold of his sleeve.

"Why didn't you tell me?" he had asked, looking upset. "I would have thought we were on better terms after all this time."

"It was posted a few days ago, sir," Akitada had replied. "I hadn't expected it."

"I don't mean the promotion, which is long overdue and you have my felicitations, of course. No, I meant the fact you're leaving."

"I'm leaving?"

"Yes, you're going to Kyushu. Don't tell me you didn't know."

Kyushu? Akitada had felt an icy chill passing down his body.

When he found his voice, he had said. "Are you certain? Why the promotion if they merely want to get rid of me?"

"Don't jump to silly conclusions. It's a fine assignment. They are impressed with your work." Kaneie grimaced. "Though it will certainly create massive problems at the ministry. I wish they'd think before they make such changes."

"But what assignment? No one has told me anything."

"Oh-oh." Kaneie was looking past him. "I think they are about to correct the oversight."

A pale young man joined them, introduced himself as Akisuki Masanobu, and took Akitada to Fujiwara Kinsada, a major counselor who held the second rank and advised His Majesty on matters of state.

This interview, which took place in the *Dajo-kwan*, a large complex of halls devoted to the important national decisions, had decided Akitada's fate. He still had only a vague memory of it.

He had bowed deeply to an elderly man in a black court robe. Fujiwara Kinsada was middle-aged, on the thin side, and pale. His slightly bulging eyes studied Akitada, but his face gave nothing away.

Nervous, Akitada had barely managed the customary "May I extend the best wishes of the season to you and your family, Your Excellency?"

The answer had been brusque: "Thank you. You may wonder why you are here. I'll come to the point.

No sense in postponing celebrations, is there?" The thin lips had twitched without quite smiling.

"No, Your Excellency." Kyushu was no cause for celebration.

"His Most Gracious Majesty has decided to send a trusted man to Kyushu to look into certain irregularities there. Information has reached the court that someone there may be engaged in secret negotiations with China. Your name was suggested because of your familiarity with trade and piracy on the Inland Sea."

Akitada protested, "I am honored, but I have no knowledge of Kyushu or of the situation there. There must be many men more qualified than I am."

This had angered the great man. "It is indeed an honor, Sugawara. There are reasons why we want to send someone unconnected with anyone there. In any case, you are to take up your duties as governor of Chikuzen immediately. It will place Hakata city and Hakata port under your authority. The *Korokan*, where foreign visitors stay, and the *Dazaifu* will only be a few hours away. A governorship in such an important province is a significant position, and one would hope you are properly appreciative."

Akitada had stammered, "Indeed, I am deeply appreciative, Excellency, and I hope to justify His Majesty's confidence."

"So do I." Kinsada's voice had been cold and the implied threat palpable.

"May I beg for more information?"

"No. It is best that you don't arrive with preconceived notions. And you are to keep our suspicions to yourself. The assistant governor general in Dazaifu has been informed."

Their ship worked its way slowly and cautiously toward land. When the boat traffic increased, the captain took in the sails and they progressed at a snail's pace as the sailors plied their long oars.

Saburo, who had been gathering their belongings, came out to join them. "Magnificent," he said in a rapt voice.

Tora scanned the harbor and the city beyond. "It looks ordinary enough."

"Not really. Look at it. Foreign ships and foreign houses."

Akitada said nothing. His entire youth had been filled with images of wilderness and deprivation as his father had spoken of the suffering of his illustrious ancestor. Now he felt strangely disappointed. It *was* ordinary. Kyushu bustled with life and commerce. Not only was the scene not in the least threatening, the land was positively beautiful. Green fields and forests stretched to many mountains, volcanoes by their shape, and hence home to the many powerful and protective gods of the land. And all around stretched the bay, flecked with small islands. It reminded him of the eastern part of the Inland Sea, but this harbor was much larger, and the city was far more significant than the rapidly declining Naniwa.

But like Saburo, he felt a stirring of excitement. It was certainly an adventure.

When their ship had docked, they saw a reception committee had gathered on shore. A small group of well-dressed men waited in front of a contingent of armed men. Some of them wore official robes and hats, but there were also commoners among them. News must have traveled fast. Akitada had hoped for less advance warning.

As they stepped on land, Tora muttered, "There's an odd-looking fellow for you. The one at the end. What do you suppose he is?"

"Chinese, I think," Akitada said. "A merchant probably. There's a large Chinese settlement here. And a Korean one as well."

"I thought they were our enemies."

"Not any longer, though they bear watching,"

Akitada wore a traveling robe and his long sword. Both Tora and Saburo were armed as well. Tora carried the saddlebag with their funds and valuables, and Saburo had the leather box with Akitada's papers. He had not been given the money for additional staff.

The past three weeks afloat had been at best uncomfortable. The danger of pirate attacks increased the closer they came to Kyushu. Whenever they touched land, warnings were passed on to the captain and Akitada. They had not been attacked, but bad weather had nearly capsized them two nights before.

After he had become accustomed to the motion of the ship, the ground felt unsteady under Akitada's feet; it seemed to rise to meet each step. The group who awaited him watched and whispered, startled perhaps by the fact he arrived with only two attendants, one of whom had a scarred face.

Saburo had been horribly disfigured when he had undergone torture in his murky past as a spy. He had survived the ordeal, but had become useless in his profession. For years, he had eked out a desperate living in the streets of Naniwa, frightening adults and children alike, until Akitada had found him and, somewhat reluctantly since he disliked spies, hired him.

He had since made himself very useful as his secretary. Recently, Akitada's wife had suggested hiding the worst of his deep red scars under a thick paste of make-up, tinted to match his normal skin tone. The result had been amazing. While certainly not handsome—the puckered cheek and permanently scarred lips gave his face a lopsided look—he was no longer frightening children and, what was more useful, could pass in a crowd without attracting stares.

The face of the senior official in the middle expressed disapproval. "Lord Sugawara?" he asked, looking dubious.

"Yes." Akitada stared him down. "And you are?"

His brusque answer convinced the man. He bowed deeply, as did his companions. "Allow me to bid you welcome on behalf of the city Hakata, Your Excellency. I am Nakamura, the mayor."

Akitada nodded and listened to the introduction of the others. By rank, they were the shrine priest Kuroda Omaru, the Abbot Genkai, the head of the Hakata merchants' guild Hayashi, the local police chief, Okata, the oddly dressed Merchant Feng, in charge of the Chinese settlement and his Korean equivalent Yi. Apart from Feng and Yi, whom Akitada noted with interest, it was the sort of welcome he could have expected in any province. But there was a striking difference. Apparently nobody from the provincial headquarters had come to greet him. Neither the outgoing governor, Tachibana Moroe, nor his representative, was present. This was curious, but Akitada did not remark on it.

He turned down an invitation to dinner at the mayor's house and asked instead for horses in order to push on to provincial headquarters. Their baggage could be brought later. The local dignitaries dispersed, looking puzzled.

They stood waiting for the horses and watched their possessions being unloaded. Tora shook his head. "I don't understand it, sir," he said. "If they knew we were coming, shouldn't they have told the out-going governor?"

"Perhaps they did. The provincial authority is in Minami, on the road to *Dazaifu*."

"That's no excuse. He could at least have sent someone. Is this Minami a big city?"

"No. I understand it's not even a city. There are many military installations and forts nearby guarding the road to Dazaifu. Previous governors apparently opted for safety rather than keeping an eye on local business."

Tora pursed his lips. "Sounds cowardly to me."

"The Kyushu coast used to be a dangerous place. Besides, *Dazaifu* is the true administrative center. The governor general stays there. The nine provincial governors report to him."

Tora whistled. "A governor general. A bit like being a king in your own country, isn't it? Doesn't that worry the bigwigs in the capital?"

Akitada chuckled. "Not at all. The governor general is always an imperial prince. As such, he stays in the capital while the assistant governor general does the work here. In our case, it is Fujiwara Korenori, one of the sons of the regent."

"Ah." Tora pondered. "A lot of ships here. More than in Naniwa. I suppose all this protection of the noble officials leaves the locals free to do as they please. The place is crawling with foreigners."

"I expect we'll keep a close eye on Hakata," said Akitada lightly. "Saburo looks forward to exploring the town, don't you, Saburo?"

Their companion's mouth twisted into a grin. "With pleasure, sir. It looks fascinating."

3

An Empty Tribunal

Horses for them and packhorses for their luggage appeared quickly, along with drivers and a guide.

They left the escort and the packhorses behind and passed through Hakata city as rapidly as the crowded streets allowed. The sun was setting, and people hurried from their workplaces to their homes. The market looked large and busy.

Tora sniffed the air. "Their food smells good. I could do with some fried fish or even just a bowl of noodles."

Akitada shook his head. "Later. It will soon be dark. We don't have time. They'll have something to eat when we get there."

"Did you notice those strange houses a while back, sir?" asked Saburo. "They were all plaster and tile, short, ugly, squat little things."

"It must be the Chinese settlement," Akitada said. "I'm very interested in that myself. You'll get your chance to explore, Saburo."

Akitada's own curiosity had been aroused by the size and prosperity of Hakata. Trade must be good, he thought, and remembered the instructions passed to him in the capital.

Riding inland on an excellent road that followed a river and connected Hakata with Dazaifu, they reached Minami and the provincial headquarters at dusk. Minami itself was small and had little or no fortifications. It was essentially a large village. But Akitada had been told there were forts manned with soldiers on the mountains all around.

Still, it was a disappointment after Hakata and the impressive signs of road construction and fortifications along the way. The relatively small and plain walled enclosure of the provincial headquarters seemed to contain little more than a modest residence and stables. A flag hung limply above the gate, which stood open. There was no sign of either soldiers or servants.

They rode into the forecourt, dismounted, and looked about them in consternation.

"Ho? Anybody home?" Tora shouted.

Where were the guards? Where were the servants and the tribunal staff? Where was the outgoing governor? What had happened here? Was the man merely too rude or angry to receive him, or had something happened to him and his people? Akitada put his hand on his sword hilt and scanned the buildings.

Tora had to shout again before a young groom finally appeared to take their horses. The boy looked unkempt and frightened.

"I'm the new governor," Akitada told him. "Where is everyone?"

The boy spoke in a strange dialect. He made out, "Gone. All gone. Old man inside."

"Gone where?" Akitada asked, but the answer was incomprehensible.

Tora muttered a curse and gave the groom a hand with the horses. "Wait for me, sir," he said. "I don't like this one bit."

"It's all right. We'll be careful." Akitada headed for the residence, followed by Saburo, who still carried the small trunk.

"The old man" met them at the door. He was a thin, gray-haired, bent figure with the face of an ascetic. To Akitada's surprise, he had a large bruise on his cheek. "I am Mori Kiyomi," he said, bowing deeply. "The tribunal's secretary. Welcome to Kyushu, Your Excellency."

"Thank you, Mori. Where is everybody?"

"Governor Tachibana left two weeks ago after dismissing his staff."

Akitada raised his brows. "He dismissed his staff? Why?"

"It was thought your Excellency would bring your own people." The secretary peered past Akitada, encountered Saburo's visage and stared.

"This is Saburo, one of my two retainers. The other is Sashima Kamatari, also known as Tora. He's outside putting the horses in the stable. I brought no one else."

"Oh. Oh dear." Mori wrung his hands. "That's a problem. What about baggage? The house is empty."

"Don't tell me my predecessor has also removed all the furnishings."

The old man twisted his hands. "Well, there were some things, but I'm afraid they are gone. They came last night and took everything." He touched his bruised cheek with a trembling hand.

Akitada felt like cursing, but he could not express his disgust with ex-governor Tachibana. Some of the governors were known to enrich themselves during their terms of office, but walking off with the contents of the governor's residence and abandoning the compound to thieves was a bit much. He said, "Very well, Mori. It's not your fault. Take me to my office first. We'll sort out the other accommodations later."

The room designated as the governor's office had been stripped of everything. Pale spaces on the yellowed plaster walls must have held picture scrolls, and darker squares on the wooden floor marked the locations of mats. Akitada saw a small desk, badly worn and of a size customarily assigned to a scribe. It lay on its side in a corner. A rickety bamboo rack held document boxes, but most of them were piled on the floor. Some had been opened and the papers scattered across the room. A bent candlestick lacked its candle, and the cushion near the desk had a big tear in its cover.

Akitada stared at all this and heard a sniffling sound. When he turned around, he saw the old man was weeping. "I'm sorry, sir," he said. "I couldn't stop them. I'm only one old man, and the boy was useless."

"I'm not blaming you. But how could this have happened?"

"After Lord Tachibana left, some of the dismissed servants and their friends came back and helped themselves to things. They hadn't been paid for a long time."

"I see. Saburo, set the box down. Well, we must make the best of it. What about the official seal and administrative funds? Or did they disappear also?"

"No, Excellency. I took those to my room. If you'll allow me . . ." He hesitated. "The money box is rather heavy. Perhaps your er . . ." He glanced at Saburo.

"Right. Saburo, give Mori a hand, please."

Akitada was gathering up the scattered papers and putting them back into the document boxes when Tora walked in with a face like thunder. "They're all gone, and they've taken everything with them. Horses, fodder, carts, everything. And that boy Koji isn't right in the head. That's probably why he didn't run away, too. Should I go back to Hakata for that police captain?"

"No. The former governor's secretary is still here. He says Governor Tachibana left after dismissing his staff. They hadn't been paid, so they helped themselves to whatever wasn't broken or nailed down. I'll have to leave for the Dazaifu in the morning. They should have some answers there. Meanwhile we'll manage. By the way, you will go by your full name while we're here."

Tora nodded. Given the fact that he would have to fill the role of assistant to a governor, his master had decided that he must have an official name. Many years ago Tora had adopted the name Tora, or Tiger, when he had been in fear of being arrested as a deserter and highwayman. He had eventually divulged his given name Kamatari, and they had decided that his family name ought to be that of the district where he was born. So he had become Sashima Kamatari and gained the status of a well-born man, much to his secret satisfaction.

Mori came back, reverently carrying a beautifully carved wooden container in both hands. Behind him, Saburo lugged a large iron-bound chest. Tora went to help him.

"Never mind. It's nearly empty," Saburo told him. They set it down together.

The old secretary passed the box to Akitada. "The seal, Excellency. There is some money in the trunk, as well as papers for properties belonging to the tribunal."

Akitada took out a heavy seal carved from soapstone. "Saburo, please hand me my orders."

Saburo opened the leather box with a key tied to his sash and handed Akitada a document. Akitada compared the seal to the imprint on his orders. "Yes. Thank you, Mori. That was well done. Now let's see what funds we have."

The old secretary unlocked the trunk. Inside were more official-looking papers and a small brocade bag. In the bag were twenty-two pieces of gold and about fifty pieces of silver.

Akitada replaced the money. "Is this all?" he asked, aghast.

"I'm afraid so, sir. It hasn't been a good year, and His Excellency drew some funds for his removal."

Tora grunted. "Bet he travels in style."

Akitada shot Tora a reproving look.

The old man flushed. "It's a long way to the capital from here," he pointed out.

Akitada nodded. "So it is. I take it an imperial inspector cleared the accounts before Lord Tachibana left?"

"Inspector? No, Excellency. The governor cleared them with the Assistant Governor General."

It was certainly against regulation, but perhaps different laws prevailed in Kyushu. Again he felt his lack of experience with a painful stab. He said, "Saburo, go see if you can make some tea. There's some in the saddlebag." Then he asked the secretary to show them the rest of the residence.

They returned first to the reception hall. This, the old secretary explained, also served the governor when he heard court cases. Akitada looked about him in dismay. There was a narrow dais which probably served the governor and his scribes while the accused, his guards, and the populace would all cram into the modest space in front of it. "It's not very large," he said doubtfully.

"His Excellency rarely heard cases. Most are handled in Hakata. And the local population is small."

"There is a jail, I hope?"

"Yes. A room next to the stables. As I said, we don't have much occasion to arrest anyone."

This was ludicrous, given the fact the locals had just emptied the contents of the tribunal, but Akitada said nothing.

The rest of the house held the usual number of smaller rooms under the eaves, most emptied of their contents, four slightly larger, central rooms that could be subdivided with folded screens, and two short hallways separating the central reception hall and his private office from the rooms to either side. The hallways led to a rear veranda which overlooked a tangled garden.

Akitada sighed. They had a roof over their heads, but that was all. He was about to walk down into the garden to see what needed to be done there, when they heard the sounds of voices and horses from the forecourt. Their baggage had arrived. Tora and Saburo were already there to supervise the bearers as they carried boxes and trunks into the house. There was not much of it, certainly no furniture. The trunks contained clothes, a few books, Akitada's writing box, and his favorite sleeping quilt. Tora and Saburo had traveled with much less. All of it was quickly deposited, and the bearers left with their horses.

It was completely dark by now. They walked back through the eerie, shadow-filled reception hall to Akitada's office. Apart from one of the small rooms under the eaves, which the secretary apparently inhabited and which had contained little besides his writing utensils and desk, the building was empty. A scavenger hunt produced some oil lamps and two braziers. The light of the oil lamps somehow made the room seem even more desolate.

Akitada looked around and said, "It will do until tomorrow." Remembering the secretary, who hovered uncertainly, he asked, "Mori, where do you sleep at night?"

"I have a house in town, Excellency. It isn't much, but you are very welcome there."

"Thank you, but we will stay here. You may leave now, but I want you to report for work early tomorrow. There's much to be done."

Mori bowed and started to make more apologies, but Akitada cut him off with a firm, "Tomorrow."

Saburo found a broom and swept the floor. The tea stood on the small writing desk and a candle lit the familiar trunks and saddlebags. A clean cushion lay beside the desk. Suddenly exhausted, Akitada sat down with a sigh of relief. Pouring himself some tea, luke-warm by now, he reached for the provincial documents.

Tora cleared his throat. "Er, food, sir! We haven't eaten since early this morning, and then it was only some cold rice cakes. That storm put out the fire on the ship, remember?"

Akitada remembered. "We can't leave. The place is surrounded by thieves."

Tora grinned. "True, but I saw a restaurant just down the street from us. I'll run out and get us something to eat."

Later, after a rather odd meal of fish and pickled vegetables wrapped into some large leaves, Akitada studied the provincial papers and records. He sighed from time to time and finally closed the last document box. "A sad state of affairs," he said to Saburo, who sat nearby, nodding off. Tora was snoring in a corner.

Saburo jerked upright. "S-sad, sir? How so?"

"There are no funds beyond what we found. And no new payments are expected until early next month. I have a suspicion Lord Tachibana was less than diligent in collecting dues and taxes. Hakata seems a prosperous place. Did you look into the granary when you went to the kitchen to make the tea?"

"No, sir. I didn't see a granary. It was dark outside."

"Well, that too will wait for morning. Go to bed now. It's been a long day."

"What about your bedding, sir."

Akitada gestured to the pile of bags and trunks they had brought in. "I'll put my head on one of those and cover myself with my robe. I'm afraid you and Tora will have to do the same."

Though he was very tired, Akitada could not fall asleep. It was not the unfamiliar surroundings or the unknown problems lying ahead. He was finally at leisure to re-member his family. Nearly every night since he had left the capital had begun this way. His heart contracted with love and longing, and his fear for Tamako's life twisted in his belly.

They had greeted him with such joy when he re-turned with his promotion. Flags waved in the breeze and streamers adorned the eaves. That had hurt almost more than the shock of his assignment. He had paused just inside the gate, put a smile on his face, and expressed his surprise and gratification. The four musicians hired for the occasion plucked and fluted happily on their instruments, the dog Trouble woofed and twisted his crippled body, and the children came running to clasp his knees.

His eyes had met Tamako's. As they made their way into the house and to the fine banquet they had prepared for him, she had drawn him aside.

"What's wrong?" she whispered.

"I'm to be governor of Chikuzen," he whispered back.

"But that's good, isn't it?"

"Chikuzen is in Kyushu."

"Oh!" Her eyes widened and a hand went to her mouth. "Why?"

"Later. Come, we mustn't spoil everyone's pleasure."

It had been a fine meal, eaten by his family and the families of his three retainers. Only the house servants were excluded in order to serve the meal, but their own festivities came later, along with the gift of a gold coin from their "fortunate" master.

When Akitada had finally been alone with his wife, he had not known how to begin with what must be discussed.

She had seen his face and said quickly, "I admit it's bit of a shock, especially just now. But we will manage." Her hand had gone protectively to her belly. Her pregnancy was just beginning to show under the full gown. The child was expected in early summer, four months from now—when he would long be gone. Giving birth was always a dangerous business. She was paler and thinner than she should have been.

"I'm sorry," he had said miserably. "I wish I could be with you."

Her features had sharpened. "You cannot mean to leave me behind?"

"I must. It's far too dangerous for you to travel so far in your condition, and the children are much too small. The climate is unhealthy, and there may be other dangers."

She had looked utterly bereft. "I see," she murmured and turned away.

"It's not a tragedy," he had said, feeling blamed for something that was not his doing. "I will see how things stand, and then perhaps you may be able to join me later."

She said nothing. They had both known this would not happen. She would give birth, and the new child would be unable to travel. Besides, they did not have the money to move an entire household by ship to a distant island and back when his term expired.

Four years!

"Whom will you take?' she had asked tonelessly.

How could he deprive her of the protection Tora, Genba, and Saburo provided? Besides, both Tora and Genba had their own families now.

"Perhaps I'd better go alone."

"No," she had said quickly, turning. "How would it look? You must take Tora and Saburo at least. And perhaps you can get some youngster to be your page."

"I don't know. How will you manage with just Genba?"

"I shall manage. When you're not here, we live very simply and rarely have guests. Besides there's your sister. Their household is quite large. They will surely spare me some servants if I need them."

"Yes. That's good. She'll be by your side when the child is born." He had turned away from her because grief had seized him for a moment, grief that he would not see the newborn, or worse, that he would lose Tamako.

Even here and now, on the hard floor in this godforsaken tribunal, his eyes filled with tears and he wept at his loss, real and imaginary.

Tamako had put her hand on his arm. "My poor husband," she had said half-teasingly. "I'm making this very hard for you. We must be patient about the things we cannot change, and good may come of this in time. Have faith in yourself and in me."

Overcome with love, he had held her for a moment, then left to talk to the others.

And so the matter was settled, and their lives had changed forever.

4

The Doll Makers

kitada slept quite well in the end and woke refreshed. It was another clear spring day. The doors to the outside opened onto a small graveled courtyard. From the narrow veranda, he could see over the tribunal roofs to mountains where the dark green of evergreens mingled with the fresh, bright foliage of new leaves.

His new post no longer seemed quite so discouraging. He was filled with a great energy to get to the bottom of the mystery and set things in order. He would be as good a governor as he could be.

Both Tora and Saburo were gone, and he went looking for them. Tora stood in front of the residence, talking with a messenger. He sounded angry, and the messenger threw up his hands, jumped on his horse and rode off. Tora cursed loudly and volubly after him. In the light of the sunny morning, Akitada was amused.

"What's the matter, Tora?" he called out.

Tora turned, his white teeth flashing in his handsome face. "Oh, good morning, sir," he shouted back. "Just a cursed messenger from that police chief in Hakata. Really, someone needs to teach those yokels who has the authority here."

"Ssh! Not so loud. No need to make enemies before we get started."

Tora loped over. "This reminds me of Echigo, sir. They don't want us here."

"Hmm."

Tora had a point. Echigo had been the province where governors had taken to their heels in a shower of arrows dispatched by the local warlord. Akitada had arrived as a young vice governor and faced incredible difficulties. There like here, he had been without funds, living quarters, staff, or cooperation. But he was older now and more experienced. Besides this was Kyushu. There were no warlords here. He explained this to Tora, then asked, "What did the messenger want?"

"Okata can't be bothered to find the thieves who stripped this place. It seems he's got a murder to investigate." Tora's voice dripped with sarcasm.

"Really? Hmm. While I'm paying my respects to the Assistant Governor General, you ride into Hakata and give the police chief a hand with his murder. I bet you'll get some cooperation from him then."

Tora left Saburo in charge and took one of the horses they had come on. In Hakata, he asked directions to police headquarters. He found them to be nearly the size of the provincial tribunal, well staffed, and busy. The constables eyed him suspiciously when he asked for Captain Okata.

"Not here," snapped the constable at the door. "What do you want?"

The man sat at a writing desk, where he had been making notes.

Tora looked down at him. "You heard me. Captain Okata."

The man flushed, got to his feet, and came to face Tora. Putting his face next to Tora's, he snarled, "Don't mess with me, bastard."

Tora grabbed him by the collar and gave him a sharp push. The man stumbled back and sat down. "Who are you calling a bastard, you dog?" Tora asked. "You are to treat people with courtesy, you hear? Even those who aren't your superiors. Now get up and tell me what I want to know."

The constable shook with fury but he decided to play it safe and called for support. An older policeman, a sergeant to judge by his hat, joined them and stared at Tora.

"He attacked me, Sarge," the constable whined.

"Don't lie," the sergeant told the constable mildly. "Aren't you with the new governor?" he asked Tora.

Tora nodded. "Finally an observant public servant. Greetings, Sergeant. I'm Sashima Kamatari, but you can call me Tora. Senior retainer and inspector to your governor."

The sergeant nodded. "An important man. Did you hear that, Goto? Well met, Tora. I'm Maeda. What can I do for you, or for his Excellency, as the case may be?"

"Well, since we have no staff, there's nothing for me to do, and the governor sent me to help when he heard you're hard pressed working a murder."

The sergeant laughed. "Hard pressed? That's a good one. Though it's true the captain doesn't care much for blood. Or maggots, as the case may be."

"Really?" Tora grinned. "I take your point, Sergeant. Well, I don't mind them. What I can't abide is killers running loose, thumbing their noses at us."

"Or robbers, as the case may be." The sergeant chuckled and studied Tora. "You've been a policeman, then?"

"No, but the master and I have investigated some tricky murders in our day. Anyway, here I am. Where's the body?"

Sergeant Maeda laughed. "Well, let's go see how the captain is managing."

When they stepped outside, the sergeant looked at Tora's horse. "One of ours?"

"I'll need it for a while longer. They took the tribunal's horses, too."

The sergeant stopped. "Not one horse left? Can you be serious?"

"No horse, no ox, no food, no bed, and no staff. The place is empty except for a half-witted boy and an old geezer."

Sergeant Maeda shook his head in amazement. "That would be old Mori. Trust him to stay when the rest took off."

Tora growled, "My master will catch the stealing bastards. They took what belongs to the emperor. Actually, he'd hoped Captain Okata would lend a hand."

The sergeant chuckled and started walking again. "Not a chance."

Tora decided not to pursue the subject. "Tell me about the murder."

"An old woman was stabbed in the merchants' quarter. They say her husband did it."

"He confessed?"

"Not right away. The captain's still questioning him."

They turned down a narrow street of cramped wooden houses. Two red-coated constables lounged around in front of one of the houses, but straightened up and stood stiffly to attention when they saw them coming.

"Lazy lot," muttered the sergeant.

One shouted, "The captain's inside. He's been waiting for you."

The sergeant did not bother to reply. "What do the neighbors say?"

The constable looked at his partner and said, "Not much."

"What do you mean?"

"They heard nothing and they saw nobody."

"You're telling me they were all home and awake during the night?"

The second constable giggled. His partner flushed. "Well no. They were home, but while they were awake they saw and heard nothing." He added lamely, "A bunch of old people."

"So she didn't scream or call for help?"

Both shook their heads.

Have you found the weapon?"

They shook their heads again.

"You *did* look?"

"The captain made us search the house."

"But not outside?" They shook their heads in unison. "Well, get started. First the garden and then up and down the street. Look over fences and into weeds. Pretend you're a killer and need to get rid of a bloody knife where it can't be found."

They looked rebellious. The silent one said, "The captain didn't say to do that." The other tried to get clever. "If nobody can find it, Sarge, there's no point looking."

Maeda just looked at them, and they left.

They entered the house and walked down a dirt-floored corridor past a kitchen and a work room. The house smelled of stale food and dirt. The light was dim because the shutters had not been opened, but Tora stopped to stare at rows upon rows of wooden shelves filled with tiny people, some fully dressed, and others as naked as they were born. "What the hell?" he started, then he realized he was looking at dolls, at least a hundred of them in different stages of completeness. The house belonged to a doll maker.

In the living quarters in back were four people.

An elderly man knelt, his hands tied behind his back. His clothes were stained with blood, and he looked frightened. Two burly constables stood on either side of him. Captain Okata, the fourth man, faced them. He turned and scowled at Maeda. "About time you got here. You can take over now. We made a search of the house and haven't found the knife yet. He has nothing to say about it. Knows nothing and has done nothing." He grimaced. "It's a disgusting mess up there." He jerked his head toward the steps leading to the second floor. Then he stared at Tora.

Maeda said, "We'll take a look, sir. This is Lieutenant Sashima, the new governor's inspector. He's offered to help. He's got experience with murder cases. And he requested assistance with some thieves who cleaned out the governor's place."

Okata eyed Tora coldly. "The murder is solved. And since you have experience, you and your master will surely make short work of the thieves."

Tora controlled his anger. "Normally, we would, Captain, but we don't have any staff. I've always been told we've been given two hands so they can wash each other. Maybe a little cooperation is in order?"

"Coming from the capital, you people may not realize that here we're used to taking care of our own problems. Thieves at the governor's residence are the governor's business, and investigating murders in Hakata is my business. Besides, I just told you we've got our killer." He turned on his heel and walked out.

"That's it?" Tora looked after him. "Where is he going?"

One of the constables snorted. "Home. Case solved. The old guy did it. We're taking him in. Once he's in jail, we'll have the confession out of him in no time, don't you worry."

The prisoner shivered uncontrollably.

Tora asked, "Does that mean he denies killing his wife?"

Sergeant Maeda sighed. "I suppose so. I guess it's my case."

The doll maker looked to be about sixty and in bad health. Thin and stringy, he trembled and stared at the ground. He had large dried blood stains on his clothes and hands. The gray hair of his topknot had come undone and one side of his face was beginning to swell. Apparently the constables had beaten him already without getting a confession.

Tora bent down to the man. "What's your name?"

No answer. The man's teeth chattered. Since it was not particularly cold, he must be in shock.

"Speak up, Mitsui!" The constable kicked him. "The bastard doesn't want to talk, but we'll see if we can change his mind."

Tora gestured to the man's face. "Maybe he won't talk because you punched him. I've always found that the best way to shut up a suspect."

The doll maker came out of his stupor. "I told them! I wasn't here," he wailed. "People can tell you I wasn't. I was in Hakozaki, making a delivery. I got back late. She was dead." He gazed up at Tora. "Please make them understand!"

Tora touched his shoulder. "If you're innocent, you've got nothing to worry about. Sergeant Maeda and I will get it straightened out."

The constables laughed. "Right," sneered the one who had kicked him. "We'll see who gets at the truth quicker. You or us."

Maeda snapped, "It's my case until the captain says otherwise. And you'll leave him alone until we've checked out his story. Or else!"

The other constable pointed. "Look at him. He's covered with her blood. And he didn't report the crime until this morning."

Tora asked, "Why not?"

"He won't say."

The doll maker muttered, "It was dark and I was tired. How was I to know?"

"What?" cried the constable. "You have the nerve to say that you got in bed with a dead woman and went to sleep?"

The doll maker started sobbing.

"You can take him away, but don't touch him." The sergeant turned to Tora. "Come, we'll go up and have a look at the dead woman."

They climbed a steep and rickety stairway to an upper floor with two small rooms. One was evidently storage for the doll making business, the other was the Mitsuis' bedroom. A shutter stood open, and the spring sun shone on a bloodbath. Tangled in blood-soaked quilts lay a woman, her face and limbs white from blood loss, and her dark hair partially covering her face.

She had struggled against her assailant, but probably not for long. The killer had hacked away at her until he had hit her neck and caused her to bleed out. There was blood everywhere, on the floor, on the walls, soaked into her clothes, and into the bedding. Bloody footprints headed out of the room, and there was a bloody handprint near the doorway.

Tora walked around the body, looking at the tangled bedding. He bent to touch the stains. "They're nearly dry," he said. "This happened many hours ago."

"The killer butchered her," said the sergeant, sounding awe-struck. "Looks like he stabbed her at least twenty times. He kept stabbing away in a frenzy." He gave a small snort. "Bet the captain didn't take a very close look. Probably just peeked in or took the constables' word for it, as the case may be. But it looks bad for the husband. Usually only husbands get that angry at their wives."

"I don't know. He had blood on him but it was mostly on his back," remarked Tora, walking around the body to study it from all sides. "How would it get there if he was leaning over her as he stabbed her?"

"Hmm. Maybe he slipped in the blood and fell."

"Maybe. And maybe he really came in after dark and went to sleep next to her." Tora pursed his lips and poked a finger at the bedding beside the dead woman. "As you say, the killer stabbed her many times, but it could have been a woman. It doesn't take much strength to shove a knife into a body." He looked at the floor. "Perhaps we'd better measure the footprints and that handprint, though I'd guess they belong to the husband. Here's a footprint that's bigger though. It's been smudged."

Maeda studied the smaller prints, then measured them by laying his hand next to them. "You're right," he said. He looked at Tora's boots. "The big one's about your size."

Tora placed his right foot on the print and nodded. "It's mine. You got me, Sarge."

They laughed and went downstairs again. The murder weapon had not turned up.

"Strange," muttered Maeda.

Tora said, "If the doll maker told the truth, the murderer came from outside, killed her, and took the knife away with him."

Maeda grunted. "Well, we'd better talk to the next-door neighbors. I don't think those constables asked the right questions.

The house to the right belonged to a man who worked in the harbor office and was at work. Mrs. Kubota was middle-aged, hard-featured, and not fond of policemen.

"I told those yokels I know nothing," she snapped. "Go away and bother other people. I'm busy. Talk to the slut across the street. She has nothing better to do than ogle men."

Tora eyed the slut's house with interest, but Sergeant Maeda said firmly, "There has been a murder. It's your duty to answer questions."

She glared at him. "The constables took old Mitsui away. You've got your killer. So why bother me? Mind you, I could have told you as much a long time ago."

"Why do you say that?"

"Because they were always fighting, that's why."

Tora did not like the woman. He said, "Mitsui claims he was away making deliveries and found her dead."

She snorted.

Maeda said, "Did you see Mitsui yesterday?"

She shrank away from him. "Well, he left in the morning with his cart packed high. But he could have come back. When was she killed?"

"Late yesterday. Did you hear any noise from next door?"

"No. I went to bed early and I sleep like the dead." She gave an awkward laugh. "I mean, you know, real deep."

Tora asked, "What about your husband?"

"Him?" She snorted again. "He came home drunk. Passed out before me. I had to shake him awake this morning. If Mitsui didn't do it, who was it? It's getting so a person isn't safe in their own house. The police are useless."

The sergeant glowered at her, but something had occurred to her. "Maybe it was one of her own people," she said. "They are violent by nature, as we all know. They don't believe in the teachings of the Buddha."

Tora asked, "Her own people?"

Before she could answer, Sergeant Maeda growled, "If that's the best you can do, Mrs. Kubota, we'll be on our way."

Outside he said, "Mrs. Mitsui was his second wife. She was Chinese. There's a large Chinese ward, *Daito-gai,* in Hakata. It's pretty old and they speak our language, but some people still don't accept the Chinese. Mostly, they keep to themselves, but some like old Mitsui have married Chinese women. Personally, I've never seen much difference between the Chinese and us. We're all doing the best we can for our own."

Tora decided he liked Maeda.

The sergeant headed for the door of the neighbor on the other side. "A friend of mine lives here," he said and called out, "Lady Kimura, my pretty! Are you home? It's me."

From inside came a soft cry and a giggle. Then the door curtain parted and a tiny, ancient woman peered out. "Is it you, Love?" she asked, bright black button eyes moving from Maeda to Tora. "And you've brought me a gorgeous youngster. Bless you, you generous man."

Maeda laughed and drew Tora forward. "This is Sashima Kamatari, known as Tora. He's fresh from the capital. Feast your eyes, my dove!" Tora grinned and made her a bow. "Mrs. Kimura practically raised me when I first came here as a raw youngster and took a room in her house. How are you, my dear?" he asked the tiny woman.

"Good as ever. I've been working outside. Come on back, both of you."

They followed her through the little house and out onto a narrow veranda overlooking a tiny garden filled with miniature trees in all sorts of containers. Tora had seen such things before, but in the capital these little marvels, trained painstakingly for years to remain as small as a child's toy, belonged to the wealthy.

She perched herself on the edge of the veranda and they joined her.

"You admire my little trees, Tora? It gives me something to do," she said. "Before my husband and the children died, I never had the time for gardening. Now I have too much time, but most of my strength is gone. Sergeant Maeda looks after me like a son."

The sergeant blushed. "You're no trouble, Love. But I'm here on business today. Mrs. Mitsui is dead. Stabbed. We think it must have happened last night."

"Oh no!" The bright eyes widened with shock. "Oh, poor Mei! Someone stabbed her? How terrible!" She twisted her hands together. "Mei never had any luck. That grumpy husband and those unpleasant children, and now this." She sighed deeply. "I wish I'd known. Perhaps I could have helped her."

Maeda looked at her affectionately. "I take it you heard or saw nothing. I'm glad you didn't tangle with a killer. When I heard about a murder in your street, I was afraid for you. You shouldn't live alone. At least when I was here there was a man in the house."

She gave him a sad smile. "The men aren't exactly looking for old ladies like me."

Tora thought about women alone. The murdered woman next door had also been alone, though not as frail and ancient as this one. "Have there been attacks on women around here?" he asked. "Do you think it could have been a thief? Perhaps she had money in the house?"

Mrs. Kimura thought about it. "No, this is a very safe neighborhood. I'm not a bit afraid." She gave Maeda a sidelong glance. "I don't know if they kept money in their house. Poor Mei." She sighed again. "Her name means beautiful plum, you know. She told me that, chatting over the fence. I think she was pretty once. She said her husband had become unkind, though she was a very hard worker. It was her business, too, you know. He makes the dolls' bodies, and she painted them and dressed them. Even so, they were very poor. Their children moved away and hardly ever visit. When the doll business was bad, Mei had to go clean the Hayashis' house."

Maeda said, "Mitsui left yesterday to take an order of dolls to Hakozaki. Maybe his business was getting better?"

She looked surprised. "I didn't know. I really don't pay much attention."

"You didn't see him come back by any chance? It would have been after dark."

She shook her head.

Tora asked, "What sort of person was she?"

"I liked her, but we didn't talk much. She kept to herself and was always busy. She didn't have any friends. People are sometimes unkind to those who are different. I think she gave up trying to be nice to people, but she was always pleasant to me."

"Was it a bad marriage?"

"Ordinary, from what I saw. There was an age difference, but Mei was no longer young when Mitsui took her as his second wife after the first died. As I said, she was a hard worker. I expect he liked that." She said this a little tartly, as if her sympathies were with his wife.

Maeda got up with a sigh. "I wish we could stay, Love, but Okata will be chewing his mustache if we spend too much time on this. He thinks her old man did it."

She grimaced. "It's foolish to kill your best ox."

"Yes, but people aren't wise when they're in a temper."

She nodded. "True enough. Come back, both of you. A lonely old woman gets bored, you know."

Outside, Tora said, "Nice lady. She's fond of you."

Maeda nodded. "She won't let me do much for her. She sells the little trees and lives on what she earns. She gets good money for them, but it takes such a long time to grow them."

Tora glanced up and down the street. "Seems strange not more people saw Mitsui or anyone else go in or out of the house."

"One person saw him leave early in the morning. There was another who thought Mitsui and his cart had passed him on the main road coming back at night just after the watchman had called the hour of the rat, but he'd been drinking and wasn't sure about it. Besides, that sighting doesn't help him. He could still have done it. It's his word against all the blood on him . . . plus the very suspicious fact he didn't report her dead until day-light."

Tora nodded somberly. "Are you giving up?"

Sergeant Maeda shot him a look. "Not yet. I'll talk to her children next. They have to be told anyway."

"I need to get back to the tribunal. Since Okata won't help, there will be a lot of work."

Maeda slapped his back. "Thanks for your help, Tora. Come back anytime. Oh, and don't worry about your thieves. I'll have a word with some people I know."

5

Dazaifu

Leaving Saburo and Mori behind to put the scattered documents in order and to hire some servants, Akitada got back on his borrowed horse and set out for Dazaifu to report his arrival to the assistant governor general. He hoped to get some answers about the way his predecessor had left things in the Chikuzen tribunal and to have the missing people and supplies replaced.

It was customary for a governor to travel with a retinue but this was, of course, impossible. Akitada had at least no trouble finding his way. The broad well-paved road ran straight south from Hakata to his destination. On the outskirts of Minami, he passed a post station and lodging house for officials. Both were in good repair and busy. The road was busy with official and military travelers among the usual messengers and farmers' carts. He noted the large number of soldiers.

Mountains rose on all sides, but the road followed the valley of the Mikasa River. The distance from his new office to Dazaifu was no more than a single post station, and on the way he marveled at the fortifications protecting the central government of Kyushu against foreign invaders. The mountains on either side of the road had strategically placed forts watching the road. The most amazing sight was the *mizuki*, a huge fortified dam spanning the valley from mountain to mountain. It was a building feat worthy of giants. The only passage was over a bridge across a deep moat and through a narrow, tunnel-like cut through the dam. An enormous gate guarded by soldiers appeared at the other end. Akitada was stopped repeatedly and presented his travel papers. Each time the guards stared at him, then saluted and waved him through. On the other side of the gate, Akitada saw remnants of deep canals which ran behind the earthworks. He had read they could be filled with water from the Mikasa River. The canals had floodgates which could be opened against an invading army.

But these days there was no need for such measures, and he soon saw Dazaifu ahead.

Though much smaller than the capital, Dazaifu resembled it at least in its overall plan. The government center was a walled and gated enclosure to the north of the residential area. No expense had been spared there to erect many large halls and the official residence of the governor general. Like the capital, Dazaifu had a central avenue lined with willows and called Suzako. It took Akitada past offices and dwellings of the officials who oversaw the nine provinces of Kyushu and controlled trade with foreign nations. There was a preponderance of officialdom here. This was not a normal city, filled with ordinary people, and their markets, temples, and shrines. He saw only one pagoda rising above the many roofs.

Akitada felt out of his element. Regardless of the supervision by the capital and the impressive presence of the military, he knew himself in a different world where different rules and laws applied. He could not be more poorly equipped to take on his new duties.

At the main gate to the administrative compound he identified himself again and was admitted and given directions. Once he had reached the assistant governor's palace, he was taken to him rather quickly. In passing the people waiting in the anterooms, he met with curious stares and a buzz of murmurs. Senior officials walked about in their blue or green robes and official black hats. They looked much the way he did himself, yet someone must have passed the word that the new governor of Chikuzen had arrived.

Fujiwara Korenori, a senior Fujiwara noble holding the third rank, was in his late forties and pudgy like most of his family. He looked businesslike enough in his large office, surrounded by secretaries and scribes bent over documents.

Korenori rose to greet Akitada with a smile. "Welcome, my dear Sugawara," he said jovially. "You're early. Had a good journey, I hope? No pirate troubles? Good, good. Let's go into my private office." He waved to a clerk. "Somebody bring some wine." Taking Akitada's arm, he walked him into an adjoining smaller room. It was furnished elegantly with books, paintings, silk cushions on thick mats, fine lamps and ornate braziers. Akitada thought of his own stripped quarters. He also wondered why he had been hustled away so quickly for a private meeting.

As soon as they had sat down, he passed his imperial orders to Korenori, presenting them with both hands and a bow. Korenori received them in the same manner, raised the imperial seal to his forehead and then placed them on a desk.

He said, "I've been informed of your assignment by my cousin, the regent, and also by Counselor Kinsada. You are to take over the administration of Chikuzen while you look into the illegal trading with China."

Akitada wondered how much Korenori knew of his assignment. When you have been told to find a traitor who might be a very high-ranking man, you tend to suspect even the assistant governor general. Akitada confined himself to agreeing with Korenori about his assignment.

When a clerk brought the wine, neither of them spoke until he had gone again.

Korenori poured. "To your health and a long life, Sugawara."

"Thank you, sir, and may you have the same good fortune."

They drank.

Akitada asked, "Do you have additional information for me?"

"Nothing, I'm afraid. Things have been very quiet." Korenori frowned. "Too quiet."

"How so?"

Korenori shook his head. "If I knew, you probably wouldn't be here. I think it will be best if you take things easy at first. No sense in making our man suspicious before we have solid proof."

Akitada cleared his throat. "I agree completely, sir, but I am faced with some unexpected problems. I am to replace Governor Tachibana who was recalled for cause. May I be allowed to make an initial report on how I found the provincial headquarters upon my arrival?"

Korenori raised his brows. "What do you mean?"

"I had expected to meet Governor Tachibana in person but was told he had already left."

"Oh, yes. Tachibana was in a hurry to get home. I let him go. Can't blame the man for wanting to set matters straight. Embarrassing to be recalled before your term is up."

"I see. But it raises the question about how he left Chikuzen affairs. It is customary for the central government to send an inspector general to approve a governor's books before a new man takes over. This apparently did not happen."

"Oh, they dispensed with it. They already knew or suspected the worst and the distance makes it more practical for us to handle the matter here. Tachibana has been properly released, so you needn't worry about it."

Actually this news did not reassure Akitada, but he could hardly say so.

"I'm glad to hear it," he said and took a sip of his wine. "However, when Lord Tachibana left, he seems to have dismissed his staff. His entire staff. Without pay. Apparently the servants returned after his departure and helped themselves to anything of value left behind. I don't know what the former governor may have taken or sold, but at my arrival I found neither furnishings, nor horses, guards, servants, or tribunal staff, with the exception of one elderly senior clerk and a young stable boy. The clerk had the seal and a small amount of gold in his safekeeping, but it is hardly enough to cover expenses."

Korenori had listened with astonishment. "How extraordinary! What shall we do? I suppose you'd better hire people. Perhaps a couple of the clerks and scribes here in Dazaifu won't mind moving. And soldiers. Yes, I can supply those. We've got plenty of soldiers. The rest is difficult. I just don't have ready funds. But Chikuzen is a rich province. You'll raise money there without trouble. Tachibana always did. Just go to the Hakata merchants for a loan."

Akitada gulped more wine. "I rather suspect it may be the reason why Lord Tachibana was recalled."

An uncomfortable silence fell. Then Korenori said, "I did not suggest that you engage in anything illegal. In any case, I cannot supply you with funds." He fidgeted. "I think it will be best if you return to your post immediately. Meanwhile, I'll set things in motion here. You will have your people shortly. Keep me informed about your activities, both the official duties and the unofficial ones."

Akitada cleared his throat again. "Under normal circumstances, a province of Chikuzen's size has a senior secretary and a senior clerk, both of whom hold rank and are appointed by the central government. In addition, there should be an inspector, three junior clerks and a certain number of trained scribes."

"I'm aware of the rules." Korenori frowned. "Kyushu is different. Since most of the administrative duties are handled here in Dazaifu, you will not need so many people. As for appointing ranking noblemen, I'm afraid you are all that is allowed. Appoint your own men. I hope you brought retainers with you?"

"Only two men, sir, but they are capable."

"Under the circumstances, it's a much better solution than using local staff, don't you think?"

Akitada bowed, expressed his thanks, and rose. The issue of funds, he now knew, was not a topic Korenori would entertain now or in the future.

6

Flute Play

Upon his return, Akitada found some changes. For one thing, the barefoot boy in a torn shirt and short pants stood guard at the gate and stepped into his path with a bow.

"Who'll Koji zay, zir?" he asked with a gap-toothed grin.

His local dialect did not help, but Akitada made out that he offered to announce him. To whom was another question. Mori had said he was not right in the head.

His appearance also was hardly appropriate, but his cheerful manner and the way his bushy hair stood up in stiff tufts pleased Akitada nevertheless. "I'm the governor, Koji" he said, returning the smile.

The boy goggled up at him. "Himzelf?"

"Yes."

The boy knelt on the ground, touching his head to the gravel.

"Please get up," Akitada said. "What is your job here?"

The boy stood, still looking awestruck. "Koji's guardin' the gate, zir. Koji's ox herd by perfession. Also good fisherman and growin' melons. Happy to zerve your honor." A wide smile showed off the gap in his front teeth.

Akitada kept a straight face. "Thank you, Koji. You can let me pass now."

"Yezzir." He hopped aside, and Akitada rode in and dismounted. "Take the horse to the stable."

Koji looked at the horse, then back at the gate and at the horse again. "Can't do."

"Of course you can. What do you want *me* to do with the horse?"

Koji twisted in agony. "Maybe you take him?"

It was funny, and Akitada chuckled. Perhaps this new servant was just another example of the many difficulties facing him, but the boy's difficulty over deciding which of his duties was more important made him likable.

And perhaps Akitada's own problem was not so dissimilar. Should he make the administration of the province his first priority or the secret assignment he had been given?

"Koji," he said patiently, "I'm the governor. What I tell you to do must be obeyed before anything else. Do you understand?"

Koji's face brightened. "Very good!" he cried and
came for the horse. "You got it, zir. Very smart, bein' a
governor."

Chuckling again, Akitada walked into the tribunal
hall. The wooden floors shone. The dais held a brocade cushion in its center and two small scribes' desks
on either side, each with its own pillow of plain stuff.

Nodding his approval, he passed into his office.
Here, too, changes had been wrought. New shelves
held document boxes, and two desks faced each other,
each with a cushion and a set of writing utensils. Mori
sat at the smaller desk doing some paper work. He rose
and bowed. Akitada looked around. "What happened?"

Mori was clearly uncomfortable. "I'm afraid you
may not like it, Excellency. They brought back what
they took."

Akitada shouted, "Saburo?"

Saburo, neatly dressed in blue robe, black sash, and
hat came in. "You're back, sir. Sorry. The gate guard
leaves much to be desired. He didn't announce you."

"He will learn. Besides, I made him take my horse."

"Oh. That should have been done by the stable
boy." Saburo frowned. "I'm afraid they're pretty un-
couth still, sir."

"Give them time. I'm amazed by what you and Mori
have accomplished. What about the furniture?"

"People have been showing up all day, carrying this
and that, saying 'We were keeping it safe for the new
governor.'" Saburo grimaced. "They hoped for a reward, but I merely thanked them, reminding them it

was their duty to maintain good relations with the governor and his staff."

Akitada laughed. "You think they were our thieves?"

Saburo exchanged a glance with Mori. "Oh yes. They got worried we'd find out and punish them. Mind you, there are some hold-outs, and we still only have four horses and an ancient ox back, but I thought it best to accept the returns for the time being. Come see your private rooms. They look much better already."

They did indeed. Akitada's study now had some nice reed mats on its floor, and there was another desk and two rather plain old screens to keep out drafts. Bamboo shelves stood ready to receive his books, far more than he had brought with him. A small stand held a brazier and a small iron pot to heat wine or water for tea. Several lamps, both lanterns and pottery oil lamps stood about. His clothing trunks were neatly arranged against a wall.

But there were no pictures. The lighter rectangles on all the walls remained blank. Lord Tachibana had taken all the art. Perhaps the scrolls had belonged to him, but given the many pale rectangles in the tribunal, Akitada did not think so. Three years did not produce such changes.

He took off his sword and placed it on its rack and complimented Saburo on all the work he had done, remarking on how clean the rooms were.

Saburo said, "Oh, the servants have returned to stay. Having handed over the furnishings, they assumed their former positions. There's even a cook now, so we can have hot meals. Mori was opposed, but we needed servants."

"I'm not sure it's a good idea to employ people who'll rob you blind in the blink of an eye, but let it be for the time being. We'll keep an eye on the whole pack of them and fire anyone who doesn't give complete satisfaction."

"Exactly my thought, sir. Do I assume I'm to be major domo then?"

"*Betto* rather. You'll be in charge of the entire tribunal staff. And you'll also continue as my private secretary. Mori will be senior clerk, since he is familiar with the work. Tora will serve as inspector. I suppose he'd better become Lieutenant Sashima. It appears such appointments are left to me. Both of you will receive official salaries."

Saburo grinned and rubbed his hands. "I'm going to enjoy this, sir. Now if you'll excuse me, I have to organize the servants."

He disappeared and Akitada sat down with a sigh. He was quite sure he would not enjoy his assignment. As always when he was alone and at leisure, he thought of Tamako, and his insides twisted with fear for her and brought tears to his eyes. He missed the children, too, and all the others, even the dog Trouble. How simple and happy his life had been, and how foolish he had been to be bored.

With a sigh, he rose and unpacked his books, placing them on the waiting shelves. Last, he laid his flute next to them, wondering if he should feel like playing it again. It had been so much a part of his family life as he had played for the children, or sometimes for the *koi* in the small pond below his veranda. His heart contracted and tears rose to his eyes when he imagined that he would never see any of it again.

He was interrupted in his morose memories by Tora, who walked in, saying, "That's more like it! Did Saburo tell you what happened?"

Akitada nodded.

"It's the work of a nice fellow who's a mere sergeant with the Hakata police. He went behind his chief's back to talk to the people here and threaten them into returning the stolen goods."

"Really? What's wrong with Captain Okata? He seems to have a dislike for governors. Or perhaps only for me."

"He's incompetent. They laugh at him behind his back. All the real police work gets done by Sergeant Maeda."

"Hmm. I wonder if Okata is covering up the shady activities in Hakata. It suggests he's either one of the criminals or too incompetent to be a threat."

"Well, he's incompetent all right, though he may also be a crook." Tora reported on the murder of Mrs. Mitsui and the progress of the investigation.

Akitada nodded. "Hakata and its affairs are part of the provincial administration. Perhaps they need to be reminded of it. Can you keep in touch with developments through Sergeant Maeda? I'd like to know the outcome of this investigation. Perhaps it's merely another domestic crime, but if the Chinese are involved, I want to know about it."

"Glad to, sir. Maeda and I are making friends, and Hakata is an interesting place."

"Yes. Saburo will also do some exploring as soon as his domestic chores are taken care of. You've done well, both of you. By the way, I'm appointing you provincial inspector with a rank of lieutenant. Saburo is to be the *betto* and manage the tribunal staff. Mori will become senior tribunal clerk."

Tora grinned. "Thanks. I'll have to see about a uniform."

But their satisfaction would be short-lived. The big problems still existed. Akitada said, "We must be careful what we say around the local people, even Mori and the stable boy. You will remember, won't you?"

"Saburo said the same thing, but the old man and the boy were the only ones that made us welcome. Surely they can be trusted."

"Someone may have placed them here to find out our plans. At the moment, we seem to have restored some order and sanity, but it can be dangerous to trust too much in appearances."

"Oh." They looked at each other, both serious now. Then Tora walked softly to the door and pushed it open to stick his head out and look up and down the corridor. When he had closed the door again, he said, "We may have to talk outside in the garden."

"At least it's the season for it."

As soon as Tora left, Akitada went back to the tribunal office. Mori was arranging the provincial documents on their shelf.

"Anything missing?" asked Akitada.

"Not so far, Excellency. But what a thing to do! If I find out who is responsible, I'll take his name for punishment."

"I have decided to appoint you senior clerk, Mori."

The old man gaped. "S-senior c-clerk, sir? I was only a junior all these years. The senior clerk is always someone of higher rank and with university learning. I am neither."

"It doesn't matter as long as you're familiar with the work required of a senior clerk. Are you?"

"Yes, sir. I've done it in the past when the senior was not available."

"Very well. You are now senior clerk."

Tears rose to Mori's eyes. "Thank you, Excellency. Thank you very much. I shall endeavor to give satisfaction." He knelt and touched his head to the floor.

"Don't do that," said Akitada. "Remember your new position."

"Yes, of course. Sorry." Mori popped back up, saw the smile on Akitada's face, and chuckled, rubbing his hands.

Afraid of more outpourings of joy, Akitada said quickly, "To work then. I have many questions about the daily affairs of the province. You can be a great help to me. I'm not Lord Tachibana and will probably do things differently, but let's start with the routine you're familiar with."

Mori was eager to explain. As it turned out, the last governor had only spent an hour or two each day in the tribunal office. He had rarely heard criminal cases, leaving this to the judge and court attached to the Hakata police station. During the hours he had spent with Mori, he had gone over the account books and tax registers.

His Excellency was very particular about assessments," said Mori. "He was forever finding reasons to raise taxes, and many a time we set out to inspect rice fields and manors. Almost always he found some reason to raise the assessment."

Akitada frowned. "I see. The content of the granary doesn't show much profit from this."

"Oh, the expenses of the administration are paid in rice. And so was his Excellency's salary."

Akitada nodded. He knew anything beyond the moneys paid out to him in the capital, funds meant to cover travel expenses and his first year's salary, should come from Chikuzen's taxes. It was a reasonable arrangement, given the danger of shipping gold on the pirate-threatened Inland Sea. But the granary had contained a very small amount of rice, not enough to see the inhabitants through a season after a bad harvest or some other crisis. He did not say this, though.

Mori produced the tax registers. They sat together looking at the entries, most in Mori's neat writing with occasional broader and more careless brush strokes marking changes Lord Tachibana had made.

"Did you like your master?" Akitada asked.

This startled Mori. "I . . . I admired him. He was a man of elevated learning, a connoisseur of the arts. He was quite brilliant."

The tax registers were dull work. Akitada closed them and looked at the old clerk. His question had made the man nervous. "It's all right," he said with a smile. "I won't tell him what you said. So he liked art?" He glanced up at the walls where scrolls had been hanging. "I noticed he took his pictures with him."

"Oh, yes. He was very particular about having us pack them correctly. To protect them against moisture on the ship. I was surprised he didn't go with them."

"You mean he sent them on a different ship?"

"Yes. He decided at the last moment to change his plans."

"Why?"

"I don't know. It happened after he left here." Mori frowned. "His captain sent one of his sailors to ask if the governor had really changed his mind, but his lordship was already gone by then, and so the captain had no choice but to leave without him."

Well, Tachibana's travel arrangements were none of his business. Akitada reached for another document box.

This contained papers relating to the various harbors and shipping in Chikuzen province. Hakata and Hakozaki were the biggest ports, but there was another landing stage near the Korokan. Akitada set the box aside. "I shall study these later at greater leisure."

Mori nodded. "Lord Tachibana also took a great interest in shipping and harbor dues when he first arrived."

"But not later?"

"Not so much. I expect he regulated matters so they needed less attention. He spent a good deal of time in Hakata."

"No doubt," said Akitada dryly. "Are you from Ha-kata yourself?"

"No, Excellency. I came here many years ago with another governor. I was a single man then, but I married a local woman and stayed."

"So you have family here in Minami?"

"Not any more. My wife died, and so did my three children. I live alone now."

Akitada's thoughts went to his own family, and his fears rose again. He said, "It must be a lonely life."

Mori smiled a little sadly. "It's quite all right, Excellency. I need little and my life is here."

Akitada could not afford to trust anyone, yet this old man had proved his loyalty to the provincial administration. He said, "I'm sure you will do very well, Mori. And I'm sorry about all the work falling on your shoulders now. The Assistant Governor General has promised to send us more staff, including some clerks."

They worked past the middle of the night. When a guard outside struck the gong and shouted out the hour of the ox, Akitada stretched and closed the last document. "Tomorrow is another day. Thank you for your help, Mori."

Left alone in the office, Akitada felt again the amorphous threat of the place. The darkness and silence of the night outside seemed to close in on him. He sat quite still and listened. Mori's steps had long since receded, but somewhere a door closed, and a small draft set the candle flickering. He got up quickly and flung open the office door. The corridor was a black tunnel. He returned for an oil lamp and walked down the corridor, holding the lamp high. Nothing! All was empty and silent.

Ashamed of his panic, he returned to the office to extinguish the candle, then walked to his own room.

7

The Unfilial Child

The next day began with the arrival of a contingent of fifteen armed men led by a middle-aged sergeant with a thick beard and mustache. Tora met them in the forecourt.

Their sergeant eyed him askance and demanded, "Who are you?"

Tora folded his arms across his chest and grinned, "Where are your manners, Sarge?"

The man bristled. "I'm *Sergeant* Ueda and these are my men. We've been assigned to this tribunal. And now who are *you*?"

Tora yawned. "Sorry, Sarge. Late night. You'd best get your men settled and then have them lend a hand in getting the place ready. We'll talk about your routine later."

Sergeant Ueda said coldly, "I prefer to be addressed as *sergeant,* and I don't take orders from strangers. Where's your master?"

Tora sighed. "I serve Lord Sugawara. The name's Lieutenant Sashima. And I happen to be the inspector here. That means you *do* take orders from me. Now get on with it."

It felt good to be an authority figure at last. Tora grinned as he walked away.

It was not until afternoon that he managed to return to Hakata. After wrangling most of the morning with the guard sergeant, he looked forward to seeing Maeda again. He found him in police headquarters, receiving a dressing down from Captain Okata for wasting time on a dead doll maker when he should have been working on the weekly reports due to be delivered to Dazaifu by the captain.

This reprimand took place in front of grinning constables and various locals who were waiting to report whatever had brought them here. Maeda stood at attention, his face a fixed mask.

When Okata paused to catch his breath, the newly appointed inspector of Chikuzen Tribunal said, "Never mind, Sergeant. Get on with the case. As for you, Captain, I'll take those reports. The governor prefers to have them submitted to him first."

Okata's jaw sagged; he stared at Tora with a wrinkled brow. "Who the devil are you?"

This was the second such question of the day, and Tora sighed again. "Bad memory, Captain? We met yesterday at the crime scene. I'm Lieutenant Sashima, inspector for the province of Chikuzen."

Silence fell in the room. Okata goggled and gulped. Then he said, "Nonsense. You have no authority here. We deal directly with the governor general in Dazaifu."

"New governor, new rules," snapped Tora. He turned back to the sergeant, "I came to ask about progress with the Mitsui murder. The governor is interested in the Chinese angle."

"Absolutely not," blustered the captain. "I forbid it. You cannot just walk in here and give orders."

Tora cast up his eyes. "Captain, if you want a quarrel with the governor, let's discuss it in private. You don't want to lose face before half the town."

Okata turned beet red. He turned and walked away, followed by Tora who glanced at Maeda and winked. In Okata's office, Tora did not wait for the captain to speak. As soon as the door was shut, he said, "You cannot win this game, Okata. Lord Sugawara is your superior, and I have authority here. If we don't get co-operation and obedience from you, you will lose your appointment. In fact, from what I've seen so far, you're incompetent as a police officer. I have so informed the governor. Your post hangs by a mere spider's thread. Now sit down and finish those reports while your sergeant and I clear up the murder."

Okata's face had lost all its color. "Y-you . . . I'll file a complaint. This is outrageous!"

"By all means. Just remember what I said."

Tora returned to the front of the building. "Let's go, Maeda. There's work to be done."

Maeda gave him a mock salute, and they walked out together. "So that's why they call you Tora? Because you snarl like a tiger?"

Tora grinned. "It felt good. By the way, I'll send your horses back. Seems the inhabitants of Minami have been looking after them for us. And here we thought they were thieves."

Maeda laughed. "They're not bad people, you know. The last governor treated them like scum. They were owed for many months of work and then he dismissed them. Either anger or desperation drove them to it, as the case may be. I had a word with the headman. Did they offer to come back to work?"

"They did, and my master approved. But we are to keep an eye on them."

Maeda laughed again. "I like your boss. I like you, too, for getting me out of doing the reports. Shall we go see the Mitsui children?"

"Why not?" Tora looked forward to the visit. "Do they know what happened?"

"Oh, yes. Word travels fast. But I thought I'd better talk to them myself, and the longer we wait the more time they'll have to make up lies." Maeda grinned. "The daughter's called Atsuko. She married a shrine priest. The son is Hiroshi. He's working as a porter at the Hakozaki harbor and may have met his father on the day of the murder. We'll see her first. Her brother will be at work."

"Who benefits from the mother's death? Did she have any money or property?"

"You saw their house. They're poor. In fact, I've been wondering why the children haven't helped their parents out. My friend with the tiny trees said Mitsui's wife had to take a job cleaning a merchant's house."

"Yes. That's right." Tora thought about it. "Atsuko means 'kind child', but this daughter doesn't seem to live up to her name. Children should honor their parents. It's unfeeling to ignore them."

Maeda nodded.

Tora was looking about him as they walked. "Mitsui's wife was Chinese," he said. "Are there many rich Chinese here?"

"Oh no. Most of them are as poor as our people, just scraping by like old Mitsui and his wife. But some have found good fortune here. They're silk merchants or deal in spices, medicines, religious objects, and art. All of it brought here from China or Koryo, as the case may be. There's great demand for such things."

"I thought trade with China was illegal."

"Not all of it. The last governor was a good customer of Merchant Feng. Feng's shop is over there. He sells silk and paintings from China."

They were walking along Hakata's main thoroughfare. To their right was a long one-story building with a tiled roof and ornately carved window screens. The name "Feng" was inscribed in a large black character on the red lacquer sign above the door. The open shutters revealed dim spaces inside, and two brawny men stood guard on either side of the entrance.

Tora eyed the place with interest. He noticed that the guards and several people on the street wore strange clothes—long narrow pants under slender belted robes that had slits up the sides. On their heads they had square black cloth caps unlike those worn by his own people. He asked, "Are you sure they don't sell smuggled goods?"

"The harbor police deals with smugglers, but Chinese ships come right into the harbor. There are smugglers, but mostly in Satsuma and Osumi provinces."

The shrine priest's house was on the outskirts of Hakata in a neat and substantial compound. Presumably, Mitsui's daughter had no need for her parents' money or property. They were admitted by a woman servant.

The priest, a gray-haired man called Kuroda, received them in his study. "Ah, Maeda," he said with a sigh. "I've been expecting you. How are you? The maid says you wish to see my wife also?"

Tora recognized the priest, who had been part of the reception committee, and the priest recognized Tora. They bowed to each other. "I'm honored," said Kuroda, looking from Tora to Maeda and back but sounding not in the least honored. "Has what happened to Mitsui's wife attracted the attention of the governor?"

"Not quite," Maeda said gravely. "Perhaps your lady had best be called, sir."

The priest shot him a suspicious glance. "If you insist, but this is very unusual under the circumstances." He sent for his wife.

The woman who came was quite beautiful, many years younger than her husband, and dressed in the full Japanese robes of stiff silk, but over them she wore an embroidered Chinese jacket which would have tempted an imperial lady. She did not look particularly distraught.

"Sergeant Maeda and an, er, official from the governor's office want to speak to you," her husband told her.

She eyed them placidly.

Maeda looked uncomfortable and cleared his throat. "It's about your mother, Mrs. Kuroda. I'm afraid it's complicated." He paused.

She stared at him with a frown.

"Perhaps you should sit down. No? I'm sorry to tell you that she died from a very violent attack."

The news had little effect on the beautiful Mrs. Kuroda. She nodded and said, "The woman who died is not my mother. My father married again. It was some hoodlum, I suppose. I take it my father is seeing to the arrangements?"

Tora cleared his throat. "I'm afraid your father has been arrested for her murder," he told her bluntly. "We're here to ask you some questions about your parents."

The priest gasped, turned pale, and sat down abruptly. "Arrested for murder? How terrible! What happened? A quarrel? An accident?" He gasped again and put a hand over his eyes. "My dear, some water. I feel faint."

His wife turned on her heel and left the room.

Tora and Maeda exchanged looks.

"Did the Mitsuis have frequent quarrels?" Maeda asked the priest.

"How should I know? I rarely saw them. This is dreadful. A shrine priest cannot afford scandal."

The wife returned with a cup and handed it to her husband. "What happened to my father's wife?" she asked Maeda.

"She was stabbed many times while she slept. Your father claims he's innocent. He says he wasn't home, and someone must've broken in."

"Then why is he in jail?" she demanded.

"There's no sign anyone broke in, and he was covered with her blood."

She shuddered. "Horrible. It doesn't feel real. Such things happen to other people."

"Did you visit your father's house regularly?" Tora asked.

"What do you mean by that?"

"You're his daughter. Surely you visited. Maybe they both came here to visit."

"No."

"No?"

The priest put his cup down and struggled to his feet with his wife's help. He said, "The Mitsuis lead very busy lives, and so do we. Different lives, I mean. If he says someone else murdered his wife, it must be so. You must find that murderer."

Tora frowned. "You mean to tell us neither of you had contact with them at all? Didn't you know they were badly off?"

The priest blustered. "If they were in want, they should have come to us. They didn't."

Maeda asked, "Was there perhaps a disagreement between your families?"

"Of course not," snapped the priest.

"But your wife doesn't seem particularly troubled," Tora pointed out. "What about her relationship with her father? Or her father's wife?"

She glared at him. "You have no right to judge me. I left home when I married, that's all. I went to see them a couple of times at the New Year, but she was always busy with those dolls. She had her life, and I have mine. And my father favored by brother."

Tora was troubled by this lack of feeling. "When did you see her last? Did she tell you she had to clean other people's houses?"

Mitsui's daughter exchanged a glance with her husband. "Yes, I knew. She went on and on about all the fine things in Hayashi's house. She and her friend enjoyed working there." She paused and bit her lip. As if it explained everything, she added, "They were Chinese."

Before Tora could voice an opinion on a daughter's duty to her parent, Maeda asked, "This friend of hers? She worked there also? What's her name?"

This baffled her. "I don't remember the names of maids."

Maeda ended the visit, practically pulling Tora from the shrine priest's house. Outside, he said, "Tora, you must curb your tongue. It's best to make people feel at ease when you want information."

"Sorry. You're right, but I couldn't help it. That woman is a she-devil, and her husband's not much better. I'll watch myself in the future. Let's go find the friend next. Something isn't right about this."

The Hayashi house was a fitting residence for an important guild official. It had its own compound and small garden behind. Maeda got his information from a servant.

Yes, a Chinese woman by the name of Mei worked there, but she hadn't shown up for work. They also had another Chinese woman by the name of Suyin, family name Zhou, but she couldn't be spared during working hours.

Maeda did not press the issue. They headed back and entered the Chinese quarter. This was near the harbor but had its own moat and dirt walls. They passed through a substantial gate and found themselves in a warren of streets and houses built so closely together Tora could not tell where one began and another ended. He thought the many walls, some dirt and some wood or bamboo, enclosed other dwellings within them. Each unit seemed to enclose a small village of houses.

When he commented on this, Maeda said, "They have large families, and all stay together."

The Chinese men wore tight, slit robes with narrow sleeves. The women put their hair in braids or buns on the back of their heads and some piled it high on top. Most struck Tora as plain, with flat, coarse faces and round bodies, but there were one or two young girls who were charming and graceful. The cut of the women's clothes was straight and narrow like the men's, but they wore skirts under the slit tunics. Their language sounded harsh and animal-like to his ears. He walked and stared, and once he laughed out loud, and Maeda gave him a look.

Tora sniffed the air. "It smells delicious. And it's past time for the midday rice. How about sampling the local fare? I'll pay."

Maeda chuckled. "Either you've won a wager or your pay's better than mine, as the case may be. Though come to think of it, your pay must be better. You're the governor's executive officer."

Tora snorted. "As for that, I've yet to see a copper of it."

They ate in a large Chinese restaurant called Golden Dragon near the harbor. To Tora's surprise, the guests occupied wooden chairs like those of Buddhist abbots. Tora sat down, shifted his bottom around a bit, and grinned. "I could get used to this. It feels a little stiff, but you don't have to worry about getting up and down and it keeps your robe out of the dirt."

He was even more enthusiastic when the food arrived and he sampled. The noodle soup was particularly rich and delicious. "What's this?" Tora asked, raising a pale succulent sliver with his chopsticks.

"Chicken."

"May the Buddha forgive me for eating an animal." He chewed and smacked his lips.

"Wait until you taste the pork dumplings." Maeda held one out between his chopsticks.

"Are you sure it's safe?"

"Taste it."

The dumpling was the best thing Tora had ever put in his mouth. "Oh, I know I'll go straight to hell for this. How do they manage all this killing of animals when it comes to their souls?"

"Buddhism isn't very popular with the Chinese. They're mostly devout followers of Master Kung-fu-tse."

Tora ordered another plate of dumplings. "My master will like this. He's not altogether convinced the Buddhist priests are right. By the way, how's your prisoner?"

"Mitsui's weeping and shaking like a leaf. He's sure he's going to the mines for the rest of his life. Or worse, as the case may be."

"What's worse than working in the mines?" Tora recalled conditions in the penal colony of Sado and shuddered.

"You know about mines?"

"Yes. My master was in one on Sado Island."

Maeda stopped chewing. "You're pulling my leg. He's a nobleman, isn't he?"

"Yes. But it's the truth. I swear. He was pretending to be a convict to check into a murder there. He escaped. Barely."

Maeda shook his head in amazement as he thought about this. "He must be a very brave man. You may have a point about mines being worse than a quick death. Here it's cheaper to lose a prisoner while rowing him across the bay to the convict boat. Being chained hand and foot hampers the swimming."

"That's horrible. Is there a lot of crime in Hakata?"

"Not so you'd know. But plenty of bodies wash up. Okata enters them as accidental drownings."

"What? Doesn't a coroner look at them first? You *do* have a coroner?"

"Yes, a good one. Doc Fujita's a trained physician. That reminds me. He had a look at Mrs. Mitsui. She had twenty-four stab wounds, most to the chest and belly, but also several to the face. Some cuts were very deep. Fujita says the knife was sharp and more than the length of a hand. She bled to death."

Tora nodded. "It sounds either personal or the work of a madman. A husband might've done it in a fit of anger."

"I took him back to the house and made him check if anything was gone. He said their big knife is missing. It's about the right length. He insists the killer must've got in and used the knife to kill her."

"Any signs of someone breaking in? She'd gone to bed."

"No, but he says she would've left the door unlocked for him."

"Careless. So what now?"

"Hmm. If he's innocent, I suppose we are left with a madman."

"Oh well, that narrows it down." Tora looked disgusted and poured himself some more tea. It was sweetened with honey, and he thought it a very acceptable substitute for wine.

Maeda waved a waiter over to order another dish, which appeared in the form of fluffy objects like tiny hairy pillows.

"Golden Dragon's Beard," said Maeda. "Try it. It's sweeter than honey."

Tora eyed the hairy objects with a shudder. "Thanks, I'm too full."

Maeda picked up a pillow, tearing it into sticky pieces before putting them into his mouth. He rolled his eyes and rubbed his belly. Tora decided the hairy things couldn't be too bad and took a small bite from another pillow. The sticky strands separated and stuck to his chin.

Maeda laughed and reached across to wipe Tora's chin. "Tigers don't have beards in my experience."

They finished the sweet with sticky fingers and faces, but the waiter brought bowls of warm water to wash off the remnants of the meal.

Tora burped with satisfaction. "Best meal I've ever had. I'm beginning to like our Chinese neighbors."

Maeda grinned. "They say most devils live near a temple."

Tora sobered. "Or marry shrine priests," he said.

8

Father and Son

They located the modest house belonging to the Zhou family and asked for Suyin. Her family received Maeda with the greatest respect in a large room which served as living quarters for many Zhous of all ages. Parents, wives of sons, unmarried daughters, and grandchildren all seemed to live together amicably.

This family togetherness was customary, and it struck Tora he had rarely known anyone as lonely as the dead woman, who seemed to have had no one except Suyin to confide in. In his own country women were supposed to be cherished by their families, protected by fathers, husbands, and brothers, and surrounded by other women in the household. He knew his wife Hanae spent many happy hours with his master's wife and Genba's new bride.

As it turned out, Suyin did not have a husband or children, but she, too, was part of this large family. She was plain to the point of ugliness and past middle age, which explained why she was still unmarried and tended many small children belonging to her brothers' families. The Zhous were not well-to-do. They were able to feed their large family, but had little beyond that. Maeda and Tora talked to Suyin in the same room where most of the Zhous spent the day. She was surrounded by other women, busy with assorted chores, and a startling number of small children ran about, many of them bare-bottomed.

They all listened as Maeda told Suyin about her friend's death. She wept. Several toddlers clinging to her skirts joined in, and it was a while before everyone calmed enough for Tora and Maeda to ask their questions. And finally new facts emerged.

"She was happy for once," sobbed Suyin, "really happy. She had earned some gold; she showed me five coins and said she was going to spend it on herself. She'd never been able to do such a thing before. She was going to buy some green silk at Mr. Feng's store and sew herself a fine new dress. And there were some embroidered shoes she wanted, and then she said she and I were going to take a trip together. We were going to visit a mountain shrine and bathe in the hot water sacred to the mountain god. She believed it would cure the pains in her hands and legs." Suyin looked at them tearfully, then wailed, "Oh, poor Mei. She never had any luck."

The listening family murmured, nodding their heads. A child started to bawl again.

"She had gold?" Tora asked, flabbergasted. "Where did she get it?"

Suyin sniveled and turned away to blow her nose. "She sold some of her dolls for quite a lot of money and decided not to tell her husband. He never gave her anything, even though it was Mei who did most of the work. He just fired the clay dolls and delivered them when they were ready. It was Mei who painted them and made their clothes."

"Who gave her the money?" Maeda asked.

"She didn't say. She just smiled and said she could sell as many dolls as she wanted."

Tora asked, "When did she get this gold? I suppose her customer paid after she delivered the dolls?"

Suyin looked vague. "I'm not sure. She showed me the coins when she came to work with me at the Hayashi house. That was the day before she was killed. She smiled and sang all day as she worked. After work, she bought some sweets for both of us."

"Then she must have gotten it at least two days before the murder." Maeda said. Suyin nodded and burst into tears again.

"Why didn't she want her husband to know about this money?" Tora asked.

"He wasn't nice to her because she was Chinese. He told her it was her fault they were poor. I told her she should ask for some of the money for herself because she did most of the work. She did, but he gave her a black eye. After that she was afraid of him."

Tora and Maeda exchanged a glance. Tora asked Suyin, "What about his children? Did she mention them?"

Suyin shook her head. "I asked her after he struck her that time, but she just shook her head. Something wasn't right with them. I know he had a grown daughter and son, but both married and moved away." She glanced at her eagerly listening family and drew a small child with a snotty nose and a thumb in his mouth closer to her. "Poor Mei," she said again, shaking her head.

The sun was setting when they left the Zhous. Tora squinted at it. "Well, now you've got your motive. Mitsui must have done it. A man who beats his wife because she asks for a bit of money for a new dress is going to do a lot more when he discovers she's kept five pieces of gold from him."

"Maybe. Time to go to Hakozaki. Let's see what the son has to say."

They asked for Hiroshi at Hakozaki harbor. This was not as large or as busy as Hakata's, but here, too, some large ships anchored, and the shore was covered with bundles and boxes of goods which had either just arrived or were to be loaded. Tora wished he had time to look around, but Maeda headed straight for the office of the harbor master. There he got directions to a warehouse much like the ones in Naniwa. Tora suppressed a shudder climbing the steep stairs. The memory of that terrible night of fire and of the burning body falling down still haunted him.

"Hiroshi?" The warehouse manager shook his head. "I got rid of the lazy bastard. He's always either drunk or half asleep."

"When was that?" Maeda asked.

The man scratched his head. Let's see. Yesterday? No, the day before. He didn't seem to care. Sorry I can't help. But when he wasn't working, he used to head straight for the wine shops."

They walked the streets near the harbor, peering into various evil-smelling dives to ask for Hiroshi. They found him in the fifth, enjoying life in the company of friends.

Hiroshi was a big young man with a deep tan from working in the open, but his face was puffy from too much drink. Like the others, he wore only a dirty loincloth and a ragged shirt, but he had wine before him and was shooting dice with three or four other porters.

When Maeda and Tora approached, he looked up, and for a moment they thought he would run, but he relaxed.

"You're Mitsui Hiroshi?" asked Maeda.

"Who wants to know?"

One of his friends supplied the answer. "Hoho! The police want you, Hiro! What have you done?" They all laughed.

Hiroshi flushed. "Shut up!"

Maeda said, "Would you mind stepping outside to talk to us?"

"Yes, I mind. I'm finally winning."

Maeda said, "We'll wait."

Hiroshi cursed but decided to leave the game. Outside, he asked, "What the hell do you want? If it's about my father, I know you bastards arrested him."

Maeda raised his brows at this. "I would have thought you'd be more upset that he's in jail for having killed your stepmother."

"A lot of good that would do. You got the wrong man but what else is new?"

"Do you have proof he's innocent?"

Hiroshi heaved a sigh. "The one hundred questions of a fool! You've got the wrong man because the police are idiots, that's how." He looked from Maeda to Tora. "Who's he?"

Tora said, "I work for the governor. Your father claims he found your stepmother already dead. He says he was here in Hakozaki that day, making a delivery, and got home late. Is this true?"

"Sure. He was here. We didn't talk much. He delivered his goods and left."

"So then he would have gotten home when?"

"How should I know? I was working all day."

Maeda frowned. "When did *you* last see your stepmother?"

"Weeks ago. It's a lousy job. I don't get much time off."

"Did she mention having money of her own?"

"Are you kidding? How would she get money?"

"Maybe from your sister?"

Hiroshi made a face. "You must be joking. Atsuko is a stuck-up bitch who won't have anything to do with her poor relations. Especially when they ask for money.

She's too good for the likes of us." He suddenly looked angry. "Life's easy for women. They just spread their legs for some old rich guy."

It was crude, but having met the shrine priest's wife, Tora could understand the brother's bitterness. Still, why had Hiroshi not done better for himself? He said, "You're married?"

"Am I? To a lazy wife with six brats. All of them eating like hungry wolves. How's a man to feed a family like that on fifty coppers a week?"

Tora did not point out that drinking and gambling were bound to reduce his wages even more, but Maeda was sarcastic. "You have my sympathy. Especially since you're out of work again. Your master says he fired you for drinking, and we found you gambling just now."

Hiroshi flared up, "The son of bitch! I told him what I thought of him and his job. He didn't like it. And I'm trying to earn a few coppers playing dice."

"Right." Tora grinned. "Did you ask your father or sister for help?"

"No. My sister set the dogs on me last time."

"Yours isn't a very close family, is it? Let's go back to your stepmother's murder. What did you do the day of the murder?"

"What, me? I worked."

"And after work?"

"I met some friends and went home. What business is it of yours? Are you accusing me of killing my own stepmother?"

"I'm not accusing you of anything. Did you get along well with your stepmother?"

"Sure. She's my father's wife."

"Be a little more specific."

"Look, I told you I haven't been home in weeks. I've got nothing to tell you."

Maeda nodded. "Very well. Can you think of anyone who might have had a reason to kill her?"

Hiroshi narrowed his eyes. "What sort of reason?"

"I was hoping you'd tell us."

Hiroshi lost his temper. "Fuck you, Policeman! You're too lazy to find her murderer so you're trying to pin it on me or my father. You're not going to get me to do your dirty work. If I knew, I'd have told you from the start. You'd better start doing your job."

Tora cleared his throat. "Your stepmother was Chinese. Did your parents have any problems with their neighbors?"

"Not that I know of, but my sister doesn't want people to know. Me, I couldn't care less. I've got friends among the Chinese."

"Who do *you* think killed your stepmother?"

Hiroshi shook his head. "How the hell should I know? I wasn't there."

Maeda said through clenched teeth, "If you think of anything else, get in touch," and turned away.

Hiroshi snorted. "Don't hold your breath." He glared at Tora. "My stepmother's dead, her killer's loose, and the police have nothing better to do than harass the family. I'm glad I'm not a policeman."

"So am I," Maeda called over his shoulder.

Hiroshi spat and went to rejoin the gamblers, and Tora caught up with Maeda.

The sergeant muttered, "He's worse than his sister. They were well rid of them."

"He wasn't exactly helping his father, was he? I bet the old guy disapproved of the son's life. Maybe Mitsui wasn't a good husband, but he earned his money with hard work."

"Whatever the case may be, the father could have gotten home earlier than he said."

"What about the witness who saw the old man after dark?"

"Unreliable. He was drunk."

"There's too much drinking going on. The son does a lot of drinking himself. He seems to be a regular in the "Auspicious Cloud.""

Maeda just grunted. He was in a sour mood.

"Maybe we should go back and talk to Mitsui's neighbors again. Someone must have seen something that day."

"The crime probably happened after dark. Most people were in bed and asleep."

"Maybe not all. What about the woman Mrs. Kubota called a slut?"

Maeda started laughing. "Yoko? I thought you'd forgotten about her. Very well. We'll talk to her tomorrow."

They were passing an elaborate two-storied gatehouse, and Tora stopped. "Look at the size of the gate. What's behind it?"

"The Hachiman shrine. Sacred to Emperor Ojin, Empress Jingu, and Princess Tamayori. You want to go in?"

"Well, I could ask the god to help us."

Maeda stopped and grinned. "Why not? Nothing else comes to mind."

9

Akitada Goes Sightseeing

A kitada spent every free moment, mostly after hours in his private study, going through the document boxes pertaining to shipping and trade in Hakata harbor. He paid special attention to trade with China and Koryo.

The government controlled and restricted all contact with foreigners by law. The fear of invasions had caused the court to deny foreign ships the right to land their people and goods on Japanese soil. Visitors were supposed to stay at the *Korokan,* the government's lodge for foreigners. But noble families who owned coastal land allowed the foreign merchants to dock there and engage in trade. The court permitted this, because these families acted as intermediaries who funneled costly goods directly to the courtiers in the capital. Thus, an abundance of luxury goods entered the country from China in spite of the laws.

The *Korokan* was part of Chikuzen province, and therefore under Akitada's authority. The noble families dealing with Chinese merchants, and perhaps with the Chinese government, were not. They traded under the protection of powerful men at court.

That left the Hakata merchants, both Japanese and Chinese. The presence of the Chinese settlement encouraged Japanese merchants from other parts of Japan to deal directly with the Chinese. And this trade was very rich indeed. As he read through his predecessor's documents, Akitada found Chinese goods unloaded in Hakata harbor included perfumes, make-up, their ingredients, such as aloe, musk, clove, sandalwood, oils, and salves. Medicinal imports involved herbs and animal parts as well as betel nuts. Exotic objects, such as tiger and leopard skins and glass utensils, apparently were also in demand. In addition, of course, large amounts of silks and brocades made in China were brought into the country.

Akitada wondered how all these goods were being paid for, but the documents did not concern themselves with this. They noted only the harbor fees in aggregate as collected each month. Given the number of ships listed, these seemed very modest to him, and he searched for individual assessments. Certain ships seemed to have paid considerably less than others. In each case, a notation read "special cargo." Akitada glanced up at the lighter rectangles on his walls and decided the special cargo might well have been art objects collected by Governor Tachibana.

At this point, he yawned and put the documents back into their boxes. He pulled out the letter he had been writing to Tamako, reread his last words, then added the line, "I'm as lonely as the pine on the sea shore, looking homeward, longing for the embrace of the wisteria vine."

The next morning, another day of clear skies and bird-song, he was sipping his tea after the usual bowl of rice gruel, when Tora came in.

Akitada offered tea, but Tora shook his head. He poured himself some wine instead. Akitada said, "I don't know how you can drink wine early in the morning. It just makes my head fuzzy."

Tora drank deeply, smacked his lips, and poured another. "It makes *my* blood move faster," he said with a grin. "That guard captain is a bastard. Teaching him his manners has worn me out." He sat down. "I thought you might want to hear how the murder investigation is going."

"Please."

With considerable satisfaction, Tora described the sights and sounds of Hakata and outlined the case and the statements of the son and daughter. He was voluble about the shrine priest's wife.

"Hmm," said Akitada. "In my experience such behavior by children, though reprehensible, is often the result of something the parent has done. What about the son?"

"Oh, he's a loser. He gambles and was fired for drunkenness. He claims he hasn't been home for a long time, but he sees his father regularly when the old man delivers goods in Hakozaki. Apparently, they don't get along. He made no effort to defend him and implied the father might have left early."

"Hmm. What's this about Hakozaki? What was the father delivering?"

"His dolls. There's a shipping harbor there."

"Yes, it's privately owned. Can you find out what sorts of things are being traded there?"

"Maybe, though Maeda may not want to go back there. Hiroshi made him angry. He's got a nasty mouth."

"This investigation and your acquaintance with Sergeant Maeda are useful. You may as well continue."

Tora looked quite happy about this. He quickly quaffed another cup of wine and departed with an airy wave of his hand, wishing his master "a fine day."

Akitada pushed his tea cup aside and reached for the document box he had worked on the night before. Carrying this to the tribunal office, he felt sorry for himself. Tora was off to Hakata on the trail of a killer, and Saburo had plans to explore the city after dark tonight. He was the only one tied to dusty documents and government files, exactly the sort of thing he had hoped to escape in the capital.

Mori rose and bowed when he entered. Two strangers also rose from behind desks, bowing deeply.

"The scribes sent from Dazaifu," Mori explained and introduced them. Akitada saw two nondescript middle-aged men he hoped were up to the work. They needed more staff, but there was hardly any money or rice to pay them. He nodded to the newcomers.

Mori seemed to have taken pains with his costume today. His robe looked new, and a formal small, stiff hat had replaced the soft one he had worn before. Akitada guessed Mori had dressed for his new position and to impress the scribes. He suppressed a smile as he sat down with his document box.

"Perhaps you can answer a question, Mori," he said. "I see we unload all sorts of goods in Hakata harbor. What happens to these?"

"Oh, they are transferred to other ships, or taken overland by porters or ox carriage, or they are warehoused."

"Hmm. In other words, they already have buyers? How are the Chinese merchants compensated?"

"Why, payment is in other goods, or rice, or gold, sir."

"The documents only list taxes collected and names of ships. Who are the buyers?"

"Oh, it could be anybody, sir."

"You mean you don't know?"

"Well, sometimes we know. There was a Nara temple, for example, that bought a whole cargo of religious objects and books. And, of course, the local merchants buy some of the things."

"Does the court in the capital purchase directly from the Chinese merchants?"

Mori looked blank. "I don't think so, sir. The Chinese goods go mostly to local merchants or landowners. They pass them on to Japanese merchants."

"I see."

Actually, he did not see. It seemed to him there must be huge profits collected by local people. The trouble was one could deal with paperwork just so long, and then the facts and figures, those black characters on a white ground, started doing a mad dance, and one was completely lost. He thought again with envy of Tora, who was even now riding happily toward Hakozaki where real people were engaged in the activities he was trying to comprehend on paper.

He got up and walked onto the veranda. Outside, the clear blue sky stretched into the distance. Somewhere to the north was the Inland Sea and Hakata harbor and Chinese merchants. What was to prevent him from going there now? Only his position. Governors did not mingle with the common people. Normally, they travelled with a procession of soldiers and servants. And that, of course, would not get him close enough to the people to learn about their lives.

He remembered the times when he had mingled with the crowds like an ordinary man. In Kazusa province, he had been young and very foolish, and yet it had been wonderful.

Surely nobody would know him here, if he wore ordinary clothes. He had not been in Kyushu long enough to be recognized. Of course, if he were to meet someone who would remember him later, it could be embarrassing. He would almost certainly get a reprimand for not observing proper decorum.

The sun was warm, and overhead sea gulls circled, their wings catching the sun and flashing brightly against the immense blue sky.

He went back inside and interrupted Mori, who was instructing one of the scribes. "I'm going for a ride, Mori. If there are any problems, speak to Saburo."

In his room, Saburo informed him that the boy had brought him a present. "He had a hard time with it, so I helped him. Go outside and take a look."

Akitada stepped on his narrow veranda and saw a small cherry tree in a large tub where there had been nothing but bare gravel before. The little tree was heavily in bud. He did not know what to say. This act of kindness and welcome, delivered belatedly, left him speechless.

"It seems this was one of the things carried away and not returned," Saburo explained. "Koji knew where it was and got it back for you."

"He's a good boy. We must see what we can do for him." Akitada smiled at Saburo. "Maybe things won't be too bad here after all."

In a happy mood, he returned to his room and changed quickly into a plain brown robe and boots. A soft hat replaced the small official cap. Saburo watched in astonishment. Akitada said, "I'm going to have a look at Hakata."

"Shall I come, sir?"

"No."

I. J. Parker

Saburo's face fell. "You'd better take your sword. You never know what might happen."

"I'm going alone and without a sword. Anything else would attract attention. I'll be an ordinary man, strolling about and looking into shops. I may not be back until dark. Meanwhile, you'll be in charge." With a light step, he hurried to the stables, selected a decent but unremarkable horse, thanked the startled stable boy Koji for his present, and rode out of the gate with a lighter heart than he had had in many weeks.

The distance to Hakata was modest and over the same road he had come by before. But this time, Akitada enjoyed the ride and looked about him with less foreboding. The road was still crowded with traffic moving in both directions, but he now noted comforting details. Trees were about to bloom and rice fields newly planted. The farmers with their carts piled with early vegetables were going to the market in Hakata. On the Mikasa River, fishermen worked in their boats. Soon the low roofs of Hakata appeared, stretching out across the plain between the Mikasa and Naka Rivers all the way to the blue sea beyond. The larger islands beyond the distant horizon were the provinces Iki and Tsushima, two of the nine which had given the large island Kyushu its name "Nine Provinces."

He left his horse at the Hakata post station, and started walking. It was good to get some exercise. He had become stiff and lazy on the long boat journey. The people he saw differed little from those at home. They looked like decent, hard-working people. He took courage from this, but those he must discover were no ordinary men. They were almost certainly already on their guard about the new governor.

At Hakata police headquarters, he paused, hoping to see Captain Okata and the capable Sergeant Maeda. But when one of the constables noticed him, Akitada moved on.

The main street was busy. It led to the harbor, and goods were transported in both directions by hand carts, ox carts, and porters bent under heavy loads. At the harbor, he located the harbor master's office and watched as clerks ran about between piles of goods or argued with ship captains and merchants. Each clerk had an abacus tied to his belt and carried fistfuls of lists. Good, he thought, the harbor master must be conscientious.

He turned next toward the market, a more modest version of the markets in the capital but otherwise very similar. It was crowded. The vendors shouted their wares, and the shoppers bargained with farmers who sat amid their produce. These vegetables were still modest at this time of the year, but already some greens and fresh herbs were for sale in this warm climate. He also saw eggs and rice cakes, as well as fish and other creatures from the sea. The abundance and low prices cheered him. The low rice supplies in the provincial store house would not be needed for the coming months.

The smell of the hot foods was tempting, and when he saw a restaurant where guests sat outside on benches in the warm spring sunshine, he decided to go there. He was tired from the walking and would eat his midday meal in comfort while watching the people of his new province going about their business.

Choosing a seat near the street, he ordered noodle soup. He was fond of the sort served as a cheap meal in the capital and encountered it all too rarely at home or during the elaborate formal dinners he had to attend. A steaming bowl arrived quickly, costing only three coppers, and pleased him so much he finished it quickly and asked for another. His aching legs also appreciated the rest, and so he took his time over the second bowl as he watched the people passing by.

He soon noticed a man, a gentleman by his somewhat formal blue robe and small stiff hat. It seemed to him he had passed by earlier and was now coming back. Not only was this his second appearance, but he looked very sharply at Akitada as he passed.

Had he been recognized? Come to think of it, the man looked vaguely familiar. Elderly, though not really old. Given to some corpulence, but still straight-backed and with a firm step.

There were two occasions when they could have met: on his recent visit to Dazaifu or immediately after landing in Hakata. He was still searching his memory, when the gentleman returned a third time with a quicker step and took a seat at a nearby table. He ordered, then looked at Akitada again.

This was becoming awkward. Should he leave or should he confront the man?

The waiter brought the new guest a flask of wine and a cup. The man picked these up and came across to Akitada.

Making a deep bow, he said, "May I join you, Excellency? Forgive me, but I think you must have forgotten me."

It was embarrassing, but at the last moment Akitada remembered. He smiled and returned a slight bow. "Not at all, sir. Please sit down. You're Kuroda, the local shrine priest. We met briefly on my arrival."

Kuroda looked a little disappointed. Perhaps he had expected apologies, or greater respect. He sat, saying rather stiffly, "I didn't mean to intrude on your thoughts, but it seemed improper not to acknowledge the acquaintance."

This was clearly a reprimand for ignoring Kuroda. Akitada took a dislike to the priest, but such men enjoyed considerable respect in their communities. It would not be wise to aggravate him further. He said politely, "I'm very glad you did. Perhaps you can tell me about Hakata. I'm very much a stranger here."

Kuroda seemed slightly mollified and puffed himself up a little at being consulted. "Come, you're not truly a stranger, Excellency. You are, if I recall, a direct descendant of our revered *Tenjin*."

Tenjin was the posthumous name bestowed upon Sugawara Michizane on the occasion of his deification. Akitada's ancestor had become a god, and shrines were built to him all over the country. Miracles had allegedly happened over the past century. Akitada might have felt proud except for one circumstance: all this veneration was due to fear.

Michizane's death from an unjust exile with inhuman conditions had produced a crisis of conscience among his enemies. They had ascribed all disasters befalling the nation to the vengeance of Michizane. An abnormal number of diseases, earthquakes, typhoons, droughts, and imperial illnesses had brought about his deification and veneration. This appalled Akitada, who did not much believe in vengeful ghosts and certainly did not wish to have Michizane remembered as one.

However, in this instance he merely nodded.

"Have you visited his shrine, yet? It's magnificent. We pride ourselves on having made a special effort because Kyushu is the place of the Great One's death."

"I shall give myself the honor as soon as immediate duties permit it. I wonder if you'd be so kind and tell me a little of local conditions?"

"Gladly, Your Excellency. Is there anything special you want to know?" The priest smiled.

Akitada decided smiling was not one of his habits. It was merely an infrequent social gesture. He said, "I'm ill at ease about the large number of foreign persons who seem to be resident in my province. Perhaps you might enlighten me a little about them?"

"Ah. Well you've met Feng and Yi, the two men who administer their respective settlements. They are both most respectable gentlemen. Feng is a very successful merchant, third generation of merchants who have worked tirelessly to further trade between our countries. And Yi is a schoolmaster. He runs Hakata's school and has prepared many a hopeful son of the local gentry for entry to the imperial university. He's a very learned man. Under such men, the two communities are exceedingly well-run and will not give you any problems."

"Thank you. That's good to hear, but what about the trading situation?"

Perhaps it was his imagination, but Kuroda seemed startled by the question. He looked away, clearly gathering his thoughts before replying. "Hakata derives its income from trade, particularly from shipping," he said. "Tax shipments pass through here, and most of the common people are employed in shipping and transport. I'm not sure what aspect you're interested in."

"As there are many Chinese and Koreans here, apparently comfortably and permanently settled, foreign trade comes to mind."

"Ah. But you're aware, I think, that our laws restrict the exchange of goods with China and Koryo. Since the *Toi* invasion, the government in Dazaifu has kept a close eye on this."

"Perhaps, but I'm told the foreign merchants simply take their cargo to landing places belonging to local landowners, thus escaping both restrictions and taxes. Is this a problem in Chikuzen province?"

Now Kuroda was really uncomfortable. Akitada deduced that he did indeed know of illegal practices but would at all costs protect the people involved.

And as expected, Kuroda lied. "I've been told such trading has been legalized with special sanctions. In my position I'm not privy to these activities, Your Excellency. If there are illegalities, they are surely extremely rare."

And with that, he made his excuses and departed. Akitada looked after him thoughtfully. He did not linger either. Paying his bill, he set out for Master Feng's shop.

The building was of an impressive size, and the very handsome carved and gilded panels and shop signs hinted at success. He entered.

The interior was dim after the bright street outside. A strangely exotic smell hung in the air: the scent of sandalwood and lacquer, of paint pigments and strange perfumes, of paper and exotic woods. It took him a moment to adjust his eyes. Then he saw racks upon racks of merchandise: porcelain bowls and dishes in every imaginable shape and color, earthenware vessels with lustrous glazes, carved figures, dolls, metal braziers with ornate patterns, musical instruments of all sorts, stacks of fabrics in many colors, including silks, gauzes, and brocades, embroidered coats and jackets for women, embroidered sashes for men, and a very large number of books and rolled up scrolls. These racks not only covered all the walls, but many were free-standing and divided the large space into smaller ones. He was so impressed by this abundance that he did not notice the slight young man who approached from behind one of the racks on silent felt shoes.

"May I assist the gentleman?"

Akitada jumped. "Oh," he said with a little laugh. "I came in to browse and admire. And perhaps"—he nodded toward the shelf holding dolls in bright clothes—"to buy something for my children."

The young man, who had an unhealthy color and a pimply face, bowed. "Please allow me to show you what we have."

Akitada was given a tour of the store with explanations. His admiration for Feng's collection increased. The young assistant unrolled paintings for him which amazed him with the fine details rendered by the Chinese painters. In one scroll painting of a village, every roof tile and every twig on the bare trees was lovingly drawn. As impressive as such artistic ability and patience was, the scene also showed him life as it was lived in China. He bent closely over the scroll, which the shop assistant unrolled to a considerable length, and saw it took him from the outskirts of a village though its center with a teeming market and out to the last straggling houses before road and river disappeared into hazy mountains.

"This is exquisite," he said. "It seems the work of a divine being."

The assistant nodded. "Master Feng ordered it for the last governor. I'm afraid he won't sell it now."

This startled Akitada, and he looked up. "But surely someone else may want this. How much would such a painting cost?"

"I don't really know, sir, but there is a smaller scroll, not quite so detailed, which I could sell you for forty pieces of gold."

The prices were much too rich for him. Akitada cast one last longing glance at the Chinese village and turned away. While the young man rolled up the precious scroll again, he wandered over to the shelf with the dolls. Surely he could afford two of these. He missed the children, and it would give him pleasure to send them home by the next boat, along with his letter to Tamako. And she should also have a piece of Chinese silk.

The dolls were charming, their bodies made of pale, glazed clay and their chubby childish faces painted with black eyes and tiny rosebud mouths. Their hair was modeled clay, painted a glossy black, but their short bodies were covered with real fabric costumes, sewn from scraps of silk, ramie, or brocade. Several of the girl dolls wore Chinese costumes, and among the boy dolls were a few in elaborate warrior gear, the metal of their armor made of silvered or gilded bits of paper.

He looked at a number of them as the young man hovered by his side. "How charming. Are these made locally?" he asked.

"Yes, sir. Beautiful, aren't they?"

Akitada took up several more and admired them. Eventually, he said regretfully, "These are lovely, but I think a child would soon destroy such fine work. I have a daughter and a small son. Neither, I think, is old enough for these." He looked about and saw another batch of dolls at the end of the rack. These were more simply dressed. The fired clay bodies seemed sturdier. He picked up a soldier. "This should do very well," he started when a very large, very ugly man suddenly appeared at his side.

"Don't touch!" growled the brute, snatching the doll from his hand and putting it back.

Akitada gaped at him. He was at least a hand's breadth taller and powerfully built. His face was flat, with small eyes, a broken nose, and fleshy lips. The hand which had grabbed the doll was missing two fingers. This fact and the broken nose suggested he was either a former soldier or a member of a gang of criminals. In either case, a dangerous man.

The shop assistant stepped between them. "It's all right, Ling," he said with a nervous laugh. "The gentleman is just looking for a present for his children." He touched Akitada's elbow and urged him back to the other dolls. "I'm afraid those dolls are already sold, sir. But we can make you a very good price on two of these."

Akitada looked back toward the plain dolls and the glowering Chinese. "I'd rather order two dolls like those over there."

The young man hesitated a moment. "Of course, but it may take a long time. Look," he said in a wheedling tone, "this charming princess and this ferocious warrior are quite pretty and perfect for a girl and a boy. They are only twenty coppers a piece. Surely a bargain."

They were a great bargain and very pretty. Akitada agreed and bought both. Then, having saved himself some money, he selected a very pretty piece of pale green silk gauze for his wife. The salesman thanked him profusely and bowed him out of the store.

Akitada left with his parcel under his arm and in a thoughtful mood. The sudden appearance of the threatening giant and the pale young man's eagerness to be rid of the nosy customer troubled him. Hiring a powerful guard when the store contained so many precious objects was reasonable, but why had the man interfered so rudely with a customer?

It had probably meant nothing, but he thought Master Feng's business and his employees would bear watching.

10

Tora and the Loose Woman

Akitada was strolling around his little cherry tree and longing for his own garden at home when Saburo appeared silently by his side.

"Good morning, sir. I'm happy to report most of the positions are now filled, and the new and old people seem to be working well together. Possibly the fact I have offered a small award to anyone who reports irregularities encourages them."

"Thank you, Saburo." Akitada frowned. "While we're dealing with unusual circumstances here, I cannot believe spying on your co-workers creates a healthy relationship among the servants. Make sure you relax your rules as soon as possible."

"Of course, sir." Saburo came as close to pouting as at any time since he had started working for Akitada.

"I'm not blaming you. I told you myself to watch them."

"We know they're thieves, sir. And we don't know who our enemies are."

"Quite true, but I've been assured they were mistreated by my predecessor. Let's at least make sure we deal fairly with them."

Saburo nodded, then turned when he heard steps. Tora came outside, grinning broadly. "Beautiful morning, sir and Saburo," he called out. "A great day for great deeds."

Saburo snorted his disgust. Akitada looked at him. "What's wrong, Saburo?"

The maimed man was immediately contrite. "Forgive me, sir. Ascribe it to frustration. After the long journey confined to a ship, I feel confined again. Tora has something to look forward to, and you had a chance to visit Hakata. I feel useless as a house servant."

"Oh!"

A brief silence fell, then Akitada said, "Your work here was more important and more urgent. But if you like, you may leave things in Mori's hands now and ride into Hakata later."

"Ride?" Saburo looked even unhappier.

"You can't ride a horse, brother?" Tora asked, astonished.

"Not very well. And I have no assignment."

Akitada was becoming impatient. At home everything went smoothly, and his retainers and servants knew what their duties were without his worrying about petty jealousies. "We only just got here," he said sharply. "You will adjust and learn in time where your skills are most useful. Now, Tora, what are your plans?"

"Maeda and I will talk to some more neighbors. Someone must have seen something that night." He made it a point to praise Maeda and mentioned his warning to Captain Okata.

Akitada nodded. "You did right. I have no use for men like Okata and want to establish proper protocol from the start. Crimes committed in Hakata are to be reported to me. If the man gives you any more problems, I'll remove him."

Tora grinned. "Maeda would make a good chief. I like him."

"We'll see. I'm interested in the doll maker for another reason. You said someone paid her in gold before her death? Any idea who it was?"

"She was working for Mr. Hayashi. But Suyin says it was payment for her dolls."

Akitada thought. "Hayashi is the head of the merchants' guild. A wealthy man?"

"Oh, yes. Suyin mentioned how fine his house is."

"Saburo, see what you can find out about Hayashi."

Saburo brightened.

"Very well. Now it's my turn." Akitada told of the conversation with the shrine priest Kuroda and his visit to Feng's shop, mentioning the odd incident with the dolls. "It would have been sufficient to tell a customer these dolls were already sold. Perhaps it's just the fact that this big Chinese bully didn't speak our language well, but I got the strangest feeling both the salesman and the servant wanted me gone." He smiled. "I got a very good price on two of the better dolls to send to the children."

"Yuki doesn't play with dolls," Tora said. "Did they have anything a bit more manly?"

"Not really. But you'll surely find something for your son. We'll send our gifts with the next boat. You'd best write to Hanae while there's time."

"I miss them already." Tora looked wistful. Taking a deep breath, he added, "Well, if that's it, I'm off to meet Maeda."

At Hakata police headquarters, Tora was told Maeda was at the jail, questioning the prisoner again. Tora thought it an excellent time to have a look at the conditions there.

It was not up to the standards in the capital, though it was large enough. The cells were dirty and prisoners were chained in airless, dim spaces. The place stank of human waste and sour food. The prisoners sat or lay in the dim spaces. One of them was weeping. In one cell were two women. They came to the door when Tora looked in. Both were young and filthy. One smiled and licked her lips. "How about it, handsome? I'll show you a good time for some decent food."

Tora also did not like the looks of the guards, three in number. They were dirty and brutish. The guard room was decorated with whips, chains, and various *jitte* and other metal instruments used to subdue obstreperous suspects. Some of these still showed traces of blood.

He said nothing, however, saving the information for his master, and instead joined Maeda, who was leaning against the wall of Mitsui's cell.

Mitsui looked, if anything, worse than the day he had been arrested. The bruises had darkened on his skinny body, and his shirt was now torn, bloodstained, and filthy. He was very pale, but otherwise calm, almost listless.

Maeda's greeting was followed by an apologetic, "Sorry about the state of the place. I try to tell the captain, but it doesn't do any good."

Tora nodded. "How are you, Mr. Mitsui?"

The elderly man sighed. "Not too bad," he croaked. "They did beat me terrible at first, but Sergeant Maeda has put a stop to that. It's much better now."

Tora looked at the dim, filthy place with its thin, stained grass mat meant for both sitting and sleeping, at the refuse pail in the corner, and at the earthenware pitcher of water. Mitsui was chained like the other prisoners.

"We've gone over the events of that day and night again," Maeda said. "Mitsui hasn't changed his story. I told him his son couldn't account for the extra hours Mitsui claims he spent in Hakozaki. He has no explanation except to say he had other business to attend to."

"What kind of business?" Tora asked the prisoner.

Mitsui peered up at him. "Talking to people about selling my dolls. I don't know who they were. Ships come and go in Hakozaki."

Maeda frowned. "You see the problem, Mitsui, don't you? You can't account for your time. And you didn't report your wife's murder until the next morning. She was killed at least eight hours earlier. You claim you got home shortly after the evening rice. You must have found her dead."

Mitsui looked away. "It may have been later. It was dark already. And I didn't bother to light a lamp; I went to our room, lay down, and went to sleep."

"You slept next to your dead wife? In her blood?" Tora's disbelief was palpable.

Mitsui's face crumpled. "I can't help it," he cried. "I didn't know she was dead." Tears appeared in his red-rimmed eyes.

"You must have been blind drunk." Tora snarled.

Mitsui stopped bawling and hiccupped. "I did stop for a cup or two on the way," he muttered.

Maeda moved impatiently. "What happened to the knife? We looked. There was no such knife in your house or outside it."

Mitsui's eyes went around the cell as if he could make the knife reappear. "They must've taken it. I don't know where it is."

Tora said, "Your wife Mei had received five pieces of gold the day before she died. What happened to the money?"

Mitsui stared at him. "Five pieces of gold? That's crazy. She got twenty coppers a month for cleaning the Hayashis' house. I told her they'd pay more if she wasn't such a lazy cow."

"Nice!" muttered Tora in disgust, and turned away.

"We'll be back, Mitsui," said Maeda. "You'd better think long and hard about what you did, or the guards will use the whips again."

Mitsui moaned.

Outside, Maeda said, "I'm sorry you had to see the jail. As for Mitsui, I suspect he's stubborn rather than confused about that day."

"He's a bastard of a husband. I wouldn't put murder past him. Are we going to talk to the neighbors now?"

"Yes. We'll see the ones we didn't get a chance to question." Maeda sighed. "It's about as stubborn a case as I've ever seen. We have nothing so far."

They returned to the street where the murder had occurred, but this time Maeda pounded on a gate directly across from the Mitsuis.

Nothing happened for a long time, then a woman's voice asked from the other side, "What do you want?"

"Police. Open up."

There was a short delay, then the bar scraped back and the gate opened, revealing a young woman's face with bright black eyes, red cheeks, and two glossy wings of hair framing it. She smiled at Maeda, and dimples appeared in her cheeks.

Tora gave a silent whistle and grinned. So this was the slut.

Her eyes went to him and widened a little. "How nice!" she said softly, looking from one to the other. "I've been wishing for company. Come in, my dears, come in." She took Maeda's sleeve and pulled him inside. Tora followed eagerly. She slammed the gate shut. "That'll make the old hags happy," she said with a giggle. "They'll talk about it for weeks."

Maeda cleared his throat. "I'm here on police business."

She cocked her head and put her hands at her small waist. "Of course you are, my dear, but they don't know that. They'd much rather think something else."

Maeda shook his head and sighed. "You'll be the death of me yet, Yoko. I'm a married man and a public servant. All right, let's go inside. I want to know what you can tell me about the Mitsuis across the street."

She glanced at Tora. "Who's your friend? Is he a public servant, too?"

Tora bowed. "I'm Tora and always at the service of beautiful ladies."

"He works for the governor and he's married, too," Maeda said with a reproving glance.

She laughed. "Well, so am I. Come in, you two. You'll be safe enough."

Tora doubted it very much as he walked behind her, watching her shapely bottom wiggle on the way into the house. "Where's your husband?" he asked.

She cast a look at him over her shoulder. "At work. All day, every day. He's a city clerk. They keep him busy, and he likes shuffling papers and wielding his brush. I swear the smell of ink turns the man on. The gods know I don't."

Given Yoko's reputation, the large room she took them to was a surprise in its cleanliness. She placed some colorful cushions and brought wine and three cups.

"Not for me," said Maeda stiffly.

"Thanks," said Tora, giving her his widest grin. She rewarded him with a full cup and lingering smile.

Maeda cleared his throat. "About the Mitsuis. I suppose you heard the wife was murdered?"

"Oh, yes." She detached her eyes reluctantly from Tora's. "Your constable told me. He also took some liberties." She put a hand to her bosom and blushed. Both Tora and Maeda looked at her firm, round breasts.

Maeda flushed and looked away quickly, but Tora grinned and let his eyes drift from the breasts to the small waist and the round hips and thighs.

Without looking at her, Maeda asked, "Did you see anyone go into the Mitsuis' house between the hours of the horse and the boar?"

"I don't watch my neighbors," she said. "I did hear Mitsui's cart, I think. It must've been about the hour of the boar. And I heard a door slam earlier. The next morning, all hell broke loose on the street. Constables everywhere."

"Thank you." Maeda was on his feet. "Unless you have any other pertinent information, we'll be on our way."

Tora cleared his throat. "We barely got here, Maeda. I haven't had a chance to question this important witness."

Maeda frowned, but he sat back down.

Yoko giggled. She refilled Tora's cup. "I can see you're much more dedicated to your work than the sergeant," she purred, handing it to him with another melting glance.

Tora returned the glance with interest. "Thank you, but I'm still a stranger. I have to ask more questions than the sergeant. So tell me, what were the Mitsuis like?"

She pursed her lips. "They were dull and crabby. Most people around here are."

"It must be hard for a young, fun-loving girl like you."

"You have no idea how lonely it is for me, Tora."

Maeda jumped up again. "I've got to get back to the station. See you later, Tora. Or tomorrow, as the case may be." And he was gone, slamming the front gate behind him.

"The poor man's henpecked," Yoko said with a giggle. "By his wife *and* by his captain."

"Gossip can hurt a policeman's career. I don't have such worries." Tora emptied his cup and extended it.

"I'm glad." She poured and raised the cup to her lips before passing it to him.

"Ah," he said, his eyes on her moist lips. "Lucky cup."

A short silence fell as they gazed deeply into each other's eyes. She reached across to touch his cheek. "I like you. I want you to come back, but today's not a good day."

Tora set down the wine untasted. "Do you want me to leave?"

"In a little. I'm truly sorry, Tora."

She looked sorry, and Tora was satisfied she had given the gossips cause for their name-calling. But he had a soft spot for sluts and was by no means averse to returning another day. So he nodded and said, "I'd better ask the rest of my questions quickly. What about the Mitsui children?"

She frowned. "I've never seen the daughter. The son comes sometimes to see the father. His stepmother cleans other people's houses when she's not dressing those dolls. They're poor. You'd think his children would help out."

"My thought exactly. Do you have children?"

She shook her head. "No." She sounded sad and a little angry.

"I'm sorry. But you're still young."

She said bitterly, "I'm young, but my husband is old. Like Mrs. Mitsui, I'm the second wife. My husband has grown children and doesn't care much for making the wind and the rain."

This left Tora speechless. He quickly drank down the wine and sighed.

She tossed her head. "Never mind. At least my husband doesn't beat me and make me work for others." She looked down at her pretty dress and smoothed it over her thighs.

Tora got up. "I bet you make your husband happy," he said awkwardly.

She was all smiles again. "I get lonely sometimes. Promise you'll come back, Tora?"

Tora hesitated, then nodded.

11

A Child's Cry in the Night

Akitada closed another document box and rubbed his tired eyes. "Are we almost done, Mori?"

"Only one more," said the old clerk. "It could wait till tomorrow."

"No. Give it here." With a sigh, Akitada delved into another box of tax-grain accounts for the various districts of Chikuzen. Sometime later a scratching at the door interrupted him. Mori shuffled over, opened the door a crack and whispered, "What do you want?"

Koji, newly assigned as houseboy in hopes that he would find it less confusing than gate guard duty or cleaning out the stables, stammered, "Zorry, Master Mori. Very zorry to make a disturbance. Knowin' as I am that it's forbidden to come scratchin' at this door, mornin' or night. Not even to ask questions is allowed. But I'm not askin'. And it's not night yet."

"Spit it out," hissed Mori. "What do you want?"

"Nothin', Master Mori. I'm not askin' questions."

"Come in, Koji," Akitada interrupted this hopeless exchange.

Mori opened the door a little wider. Koji stepped in, grinned widely, and bowed. "How you doin' today, governor zir?"

Mori muttered, "Kneel!" and kicked Koji's ankle.

Koji turned in astonishment. "What you kick me for?"

Akitada asked, "What brings you here, Koji?"

Koji bobbed another bow. "Very zorry about disturbin' you, zir, but zomeone's come. Very important man."

Mori gasped and ran out.

"Did he say who he is?"

"Yes, he's the mayor, beggin' pardon."

"Thank you, Koji. I think Mori has gone to bring him in. You may return to your duties."

Koji grinned more widely, sketched a salute he must have copied from the gate guards, and dashed out.

Mori returned, bringing with him Mayor Nakamura.

"Very happy to find you in, Excellency." The mayor was resplendent in blue silk, fastened across his belly with a brocade sash. "I was passing through Minami and decided to give myself the pleasure of calling on you myself."

Akitada rose to his feet. "You are honoring me, Mayor. Please sit down. Some wine?"

"No, no. I must dash on, and I see you're busy. I just stopped by to extend my invitation to a little entertainment I shall arrange to welcome your Excellency to Chikuzen. Since you couldn't stop when you first arrived, I hope to correct the situation. Would tomorrow night be convenient?"

Akitada heard the implied complaint. He did not relish formal banquets, but they were part and parcel of public administration, and clearly his high-handed refusal to dine with the local dignitaries had upset them. He said, "How very kind. It would suit me perfectly. I regret deeply my rushed arrival the other day. The late hour and urgent state of affairs made it necessary. You may have heard about the chaotic situation I found?"

The mayor relaxed a little and glanced about. "Yes, I heard. Shocking! Thieves stripped your quarters? I did notice the lack of amenities. You must let me know what is needed and it shall be supplied."

Akitada disliked accepting gifts which might obligate him. "Thank you for the generous offer, but we have already recovered most of the furniture. We will manage quite well for the time being."

The mayor studied the room again and shook his head. "Well, I'll look forward to receiving you tomorrow then." He bowed.

When the mayor had left, Akitada returned to his work. But the visit had broken his concentration. The invitation was to make up for a missed meeting between himself and the Hakata notables, and he doubted the mayor had merely been passing by on another errand. No, the man had wanted to see for himself how he was coping, and he had taken pleasure in expressing his disapproval of the new governor's behavior.

When it was fully dark, Koji returned to announce that dinner was ready.

Akitada closed the document box and said, "I'll eat in my rooms, Koji. Thank you, Mori. We'll continue tomorrow."

He was walking down the dark passage toward his quarters, when a stranger suddenly stepped from one of the rooms. Akitada jumped back, his heart in his throat. He reached for the sword he was not wearing. Angry at himself and the stranger who had somehow managed to get into the building, he demanded, "Who are you? What do you want?"

The intruder made a hissing sound, then said in Saburo's voice, "I do beg your pardon, sir. I didn't mean to startle you."

Akitada's relief was instant, but irritation followed, though he was mainly angry at himself. "What the devil are you doing with a beard, Saburo?"

"My disguise, sir. I thought it best if people don't recognize me as your retainer."

"Hmm. Yes. I see your point. Come into my room so I can get a better look at you."

An oil lamp lit his study, making it almost cozy. He had arranged his trunk, his books, his sword stand and sword, and his writing box along the bare walls and on the few pieces of furniture. Now he took up the oil lamp to study Saburo's appearance.

If Saburo had not spoken earlier, Akitada would still not have recognized him. A close-trimmed beard and mustache hid the worst scars of his lower face complete-ly. The one damaged eye still had a cast, but this gave him merely a somewhat rakish appearance.

"I'm stunned," he said. "Saburo, you're quite hand-some."

The compliment astonished Saburo to such an ex-tent that his eye started rolling again. "H-handsome, sir?" he asked, flushing.

"Have you looked in a mirror?"

"Why, yes. I had to, to glue on all this hair."

"Can you control your eye the way you did before?"

"A little. I've been practicing."

Akitada smiled. "Well," he said, "the disguise is per-fect. By the time my four years here are up, nobody in the capital will recognize poor Saburo."

Saburo looked down. "Don't joke, sir."

"I'm not joking. You should consider growing that beard and mustache, but at the moment it's better if you remain two different men."

"Of course. I came to tell you I'm off to Hakata. To check on Hayashi. Anything else you'd like me to take a look at?"

"Well, the harbor. I suspect there are smugglers. And I'm interested in the shop of the merchant Feng. He employs a big brute with a broken nose and two fingers missing on his right hand. He has the look of a thug and made me wonder what sort of business Feng is engaged in."

Saburo decided to check out Feng's store first. It was not quite dark yet, and he wanted a good look at the premises from the outside. He saw immediately that they favored a clandestine visit. There were no living quarters for the owner above the store. Of course, this did not eliminate the possibility of an employee sleeping there at night. And such an amount of costly merchandise would require very careful locking-up at night.

As he strolled into the salesroom, a young shop attendant rushed forward to wait on him. Saburo asked about mirrors. Shown several very elegant items well beyond his means, he picked the best, a bright silver mirror, and checked the looks of his beard and mustache, going so far as to carry it to the door to admire his appearance by daylight.

He was secretly amazed and excited by the change the facial hair made. The horrible, deep and disfiguring scars around his mouth and left cheek were completely hidden. What still showed was nearly unnoticeable under the make-up paste Lady Sugawara had shown him how to mix. Only his left eye still had the disturbing cast in it, and it rolled uncontrollably unless he concentrated really hard. But he was no longer an ogre.

His hand trembled with emotion as he returned the mirror to the shop attendant and left. It took a while before he was calm enough to concentrate on his job.

The Hayashi house was unremarkable except for its large size. Saburo walked all around the property, noting possible means of ingress, then located a small restaurant a few houses away but within sight of Hayashi's gate. There he took a seat outside and ordered a bowl of soup. The sun was setting, and people were going home from work. At the Hayashi house, the small gate in the wall opened, and a middle-aged woman walked out, carrying a small bundle in one hand. Saburo decided she was probably Suyin, the cleaning woman.

A short while later, a familiar figure came down the street. The portly gentleman in a green silk robe and neat black cap walked up to the Hayashi gate and announced himself. He was admitted.

Saburo's memory was excellent. This was the shrine priest Kuroda. There was, of course, nothing suspicious about his visit to the chief of the merchants' guild. Perhaps he was collecting contributions for his shrine.

But Saburo had barely time to consider this when two porters deposited a sedan chair at the gate. Another familiar figure emerged: the stocky person of Merchant Feng with his pointed chin beard, wearing his Chinese robe, narrow black silk pants, and the peculiar low, square hat worn by Chinese men of means or position. Feng paid the porters and also went through the gate.

Saburo pursed his lips. This was beginning to look like a meeting. He wondered who else would show up. For a very long time, nothing happened. Saburo was forced to pay for another bowl of soup. He had barely tasted this, when other men began to arrive and enter the Hayashi compound. He did not know any of them, but by their ages, clothes, and demeanor they appeared to be merchants or shopkeepers. This was then a regular meeting of the guild members. To prove the matter, the shrine priest soon emerged and walked off.

By then, the sun had set, and dusk was rapidly turning into night. Saburo left his soup partially eaten and walked to the harbor. A nearly full moon shone on a sea like mottled silver. The dark land and the black outlines of distant islands seemed to float upon the water. Now and then a cloud obscured the moon, but along the harbor, lanterns and torches attached to walls of buildings shed yellow pools of light. More lanterns suspended on the boats tied up on shore cast dancing beams across the landing as they rocked with the tide. Farther out in the bay, larger ships were at anchor, and there, too, lights gleamed and disappeared, then gleamed again with the motion of the waves. It was almost like looking at a reflection of the stars, Saburo thought. The bay was beautiful even at night.

Saburo had not shared his master's uneasiness about Kyushu, but he had also been well aware of a sense of lurking danger. Perhaps nerves were more refined among the nobility. Or else it was the fact that his master had a lot to lose. He had a family he clearly adored and who adored him. Saburo had no such attachments. He could not recall a time when he had ever been afraid of death.

The torture he had suffered at the hands of the enemy he had accepted as well deserved for having been careless. A spy must never be careless. And whatever had happened to his mind later as the result of having his face permanently and cruelly altered with a sharp knife had not instilled fear in him either. But it had done other things to him that he was only dimly aware of. People's disgust when they looked at him had filled him with anger and disdain for his fellow man. This was doubly true for the women he had met.

Beside the anger there was something else, a weakness he hated to acknowledge. He longed for the sort of human closeness his master had with his family. Tora had it also, and even clumsy, fat Genba had found it.

Saburo would never have it, but he was not afraid.

As he explored the waterfront, Saburo noticed two men, perhaps sailors, meeting with another man beside one of the docked ships. There was a brief argument, then money changed hands and disappeared into the shirt of one of the sailors. Both walked away, heading into town while the other man climbed back on board.

He thought this a promising beginning and followed the sailors. They entered a large wine shop. By the light from lanterns, Saburo saw they were not sailors but thugs, probably Chinese, or of Chinese descent. He deduced this from their tall, muscular build and their flat, broad faces. They wore colorful and new-looking pants and jackets and leather boots on their feet, but they were scum.

Well-paid scum with neatly trimmed hair and beards.

Saburo touched his own facial hair. It itched quite badly, but he didn't dare scratch for fear of losing patches of his painfully glued and trimmed beard. He had confiscated the hair from the stable boy's head, and hoped he did not have to maintain his disguise for very long.

The two thugs entered a large wine shop with the impressive name The Dragon's Lair. Inside, they joined three others, similar types but Japanese.

Saburo was still standing inside the door when the biggest of the Chinese looked up and their eyes met. Saburo had observed before that people could sometimes feel someone staring at them. He let his eyes slide on to another man and so around the room. A waiter appeared by his side, and he sat down and ordered a flask of wine.

Sometime later, he cast another cautious glance at the group and saw the big Chinese reaching for a wine flask. Two of the fingers on his right hand were missing.

It could be coincidence, but Saburo recalled his master's description of the man in Feng's shop. He debated whether to stay where he was and incur further expenses for wine, or go outside to hide in some doorway and wait for the big Chinese to come out.

The door opened again, and two children came in, a slight girl and a much younger boy. They were poorly dressed and each carried a birdcage. Passing among the customers, they were offering to sell their songbirds. When they reached the five toughs, a discussion took place, accompanied by raucous laughter. The girl shook her head violently and retreated, pulling the boy with her. One of the men reached for her, causing the boy to shout something at him. The waiter ran over and pointed the children to the door. When the girl did not move quickly enough, the waiter gave her a rough push that made her fall down and drop her cage. A wild fluttering and twittering came from the cage.

Saburo half rose, cursing the incident, which escalated before his eyes when the boy kicked the waiter's shin and got a loud slap.

The girl scrambled up, snatched the cage, grasped the little boy's arm, and pulled him away. The outraged waiter followed them to the door, shouting after them.

Saburo subsided in his seat and decided not to leave a tip.

Two poor children.

Trying to earn a few coppers by selling birds.

The girl had not been much older than twelve, he thought, and the boy perhaps nine. He wondered what sort of life they led at home. Why did their parents send them out at night into dangerous places to sell their birds?

In the corner, the Chinese suddenly burst into laughter again. Still grinning, they got up, tossed some coins to the waiter, and walked out.

Saburo would have followed in any case, but there was something troubling about their sudden departure after the two children. He paid a few coppers for his wine and went out into the street.

It was still busy, with lanterns bobbing in the slight breeze from the water and men searching for wine, women, or games. At the end of the street, three of the thugs headed toward the dense warren of streets beyond the wine shops and brothels. They were walking fast. Two of them had disappeared. So had the children. The three abruptly turned a corner.

Saburo sped up to the corner and saw a dark tunnel between the walls of two-story houses. The alley was so narrow not even the fitful moonlight penetrated. There was no sign of the Chinese, but he heard a sudden laugh up ahead, and then a shout. Then sounds of running footsteps receded.

Saburo wished he had dressed for spying. Not only were those clothes black and made for climbing and scaling roofs, but they had a series of clever pockets holding assorted weapons of his former trade. He bent to touch the thin blade he carried in his right boot and plunged into the darkness.

When his eyes adjusted, he knew he was in a poor quarter of tenements for sailors and porters. He quickly became disoriented by the way the alley turned this way and that. Dead ends and switchbacks filled with heaps of refuse or discarded building materials slowed him down. Finally he stopped and listened.

In the distance, he heard laughter again, and a moment later the thin high cry of a woman or child. He ran in that direction, stumbled over something and fell, picked himself up, and came to another dead end.

As he turned back, he saw a faint seam of light on the wall of a building. It marked a door in the back wall of this tenement. He pounded on it. When nothing happened, he kicked and the door flew open. He burst into a small room where a man and two women sat at their meal, their eyes wide with shock and fear at his intrusion.

"Quick," he gasped. "Some men are attacking two children. Where's the next street?"

Open-mouthed, they pointed to another door. Saburo pushed back the bar, opened it, and stood in a narrow street. At its end, moonlight fell on some struggling figures. He heard another shrill cry, pulled the knife from his boot, and rushed toward them.

"Halt!" he shouted. "In the name of the governor!" He added a loud whistle for good measure. "Constables! Over here!"

They fell for it. In a moment, all five men had melted into the shadows, leaving behind the slight figures of the two children and their broken bird cages.

The girl was sobbing as she got up and pulled her skirt down. The boy lay unmoving in the street.

Saburo guessed what the animals had been after and was sickened by it. He slowed down, put his knife away, and asked the girl, "Did they hurt you?"

She shrank away from him.

He bent over the boy and found he was alive and breathing, though unconscious. "Don't be afraid," he told the girl, straightening up. "I work for the governor as a sort of constable. I noticed those bullies following you and thought I'd keep an eye on them. Being a stranger in this town, I got lost. I hope I wasn't too late?"

It was a stupid question. The girl was too young to understand. She ignored him and knelt down beside the boy to take him in her arms.

Saburo said. "He's alive," to reassure her, hoping the child was not seriously hurt. He had a bloody nose and would probably have a black eye. He bent and felt the back of the boy's head. It seemed undamaged. As if to prove it, the boy opened his eyes.

"Oh, Kichiro," the girl cried, "are you hurt?"

He blinked at her and then stared at Saburo. Freeing himself from her arms, he cried, "Don't you touch my sister. I'll kill you," and lashed out weakly at Saburo with a balled fist.

"Don't," she cried, catching the flailing hand in hers. "He came to help us."

The boy closed his eyes and fell back.

Saburo stood and looked around. He did not like this place. Neither did he trust the hoodlums not to come back to take out their frustration and anger on them.

"Where do you children live?" he asked. "I'll take you home."

She gestured vaguely down the street. "We'll be all right," she said. "It's not far."

"Your brother cannot walk," Saburo pointed out and scooped him up. The child was not exactly light, and he hoped she had spoken the truth about the distance.

"Thank you," she murmured and went to gather the cages. One was broken and empty. In the other, the bird lay dead. She gave a small moan, removed the limp body and laid it gently in a patch of grass. Carrying both cages, she started off down the street.

Saburo walked behind, the boy occasionally stirring and muttering in his arms. They took a confusing number of streets and alleys to end up in a shrine garden.

The girl passed through this to the back where a ruined building loomed over the trees below. Here, an assortment of bird cages, much like the ones she carried, hung from tree limbs or were stacked against the wall of the abandoned building. There were birds in the hanging cages. Some chirped sleepily.

Saburo stopped and listened carefully. He was still afraid they might have been followed, but all remained still.

The girl walked around the corner of the building to where an open doorway gaped. Entering, she told Saburo, "Wait here, please. There are some boards missing on the stairs. I'll bring a light."

Saburo stood, his arms aching a little, and looked about. It was very dark, but he could see the rickety staircase rising precariously into the darkness above. Below, the blackness was broken here and there by what must be open windows or holes in the roof.

A shimmer of light appeared above, and the girl came down. She carried an oil lamp. Saburo started up the stairs, watching out for missing and broken steps, worrying over whether the stairs would support their weight.

Upstairs, grass mats had been hung from rafters and across windows to make a small space in an empty, open area reminding him of a warehouse. The floor was scrupulously swept. An old trunk, a small bamboo rack with a few chipped dishes, a small pile of bedding, and a bird cage with a bird made up the furnishings.

The bird, a pale green color, woke and sang.

The girl went to spread out some bedding, and Saburo laid the boy down. His eyes were wide open.

"How are you, Kichiro?" Saburo asked.

"My eye hurts. And my head." He looked for the girl. "Naoko?" He sounded frightened.

She said, "This man's a friend who helped us. Thank him!"

Saburo smiled. "No need." He looked around. "How do you manage? Where is your family?"

She looked away. "Our parents are dead. There's no one. I'm called Naoko. Kichiro is my brother. He catches song birds. Bush warblers and white eyes and cuckoos. I make cages for them, and we sell them in the market and on the streets."

"My name is Saburo. As I told you, I work for the new governor and am a stranger here. Those men you tangled with are bad. You shouldn't be walking around at night. And you should really not be going into wine shops."

She nodded calmly. "I know. We needed money, so we decided to give it a try. Sometimes the sailors like a bird to take on their ship with them."

With a sigh, Saburo dug into his sash and extracted a string of coppers. Counting out half of them, he placed them on the trunk. "I think your brother will be all right in the morning. This is for food. I'll be back when I can, but you must be more careful."

She looked at the money. Tears rose to her eyes. "Thank you." Then she looked up at him and added softly, "If you'd like to take your pleasure, I won't mind."

Saburo thought he had not heard right. Then he exploded into a curse, took her thin shoulders in his hands, and shook her. She looked terrified and the boy started up with a cry.

Saburo dropped his hands and said. "I'm sorry. I shouldn't have done that, but you're just a child. How can you even think of such a thing?"

"I'm nearly fourteen," she said, her chin raised defiantly. "And you needn't worry. I've been raped before."

Sickened, Saburo turned away. "Don't ever do such a thing again, do you hear? Now go to bed. Be careful when you go out tomorrow. Those men may be around. I'll be back tomorrow evening, but if there's more trouble, go to Sergeant Maeda at the police station."

12

The Mayor's Banquet

When Akitada woke, Saburo was already moving about his room. Yawning, Akitada sat up. It was light outside, but the long sleep had made him feel rested and energetic. Getting up, he said, "You let me sleep too long," and went to open the shutters. A small greenish bird perched in the cherry tree, singing in sunshine. When he turned around, he saw that Saburo looked tired. He had removed the false beard and mustache and reapplied fresh makeup. It made him seem unnaturally pale.

"You look terrible," Akitada announced and sat down at his desk.

Saburo busied himself with making tea. "I just got back, sir."

"Really? I don't insist you go without sleep completely. Was it an interesting night?"

"You might say so."

"Should we talk about it outside?"

"No. I think your private quarters are safe enough these days. Besides what happened has probably nothing to do with smuggling."

The tea water boiled and Saburo brewed the tea.

"So what happened?" Akitada asked, watching him.

"I found two poor children who'd been attacked by thugs. The girl is only thirteen, and her brother is about nine. There were three of the bastards, and they tried to rape her. I took the children home, if you can call the place home, and then stayed outside to watch in case the men returned."

"Three grown men trying to rape a child? What kind of place is this? And where were the constables?"

"The children made the mistake of going into a wine shop near the harbor to sell some song birds. They live in a bad part of town, and the hoodlums followed them." Saburo presented a cup of tea.

Akitada was too angry to drink it. "Everything that has happened so far points to the complete incompetence of Captain Okata. I think I'll do as Tora suggests and remove him from his post, replacing him with his sergeant."

Saburo nodded. "I told the children to go to Sergeant Maeda. And I'd like to go back tonight if I may."

"Yes, but get some sleep first."

"One of those men was Chinese and had two fingers missing. And he collected something, probably money, from one of the captains of the ships. The missing fingers were on his right hand. The last two. I thought of the man you met at Feng's store."

Akitada sat up. "Aha. Yes, it sounds like him. Ugly, big brute?"

Saburo nodded. "I'd like to have a word with him."

"I don't like this business about collecting money from ships docking here. Better not tangle with him until we have more information. What about Hayashi?"

"Yes. I almost forgot. He had a meeting. First with Feng and the shrine priest. That took about an hour. Then the priest left and others arrived. Looked like a guild meeting."

"Interesting." Akitada finally sipped his tea. "I'm to dine with the mayor tonight. I expect some of those men will be attending. Perhaps I can learn something then."

Tora came in as Saburo poured a second cup. He had little to report but listened with shocked outrage to Saburo's tale about the children. "I'll talk to Maeda," he offered.

"Not today. You've done enough for the local police. Maeda sounds like a good man. Let him work his case. I want you here. Saburo had no sleep last night, and I'm attending the mayor's banquet tonight."

To make up for snubbing the Hakata notables, Akitada had taken pains with his appearance. He wore a fine green figured silk robe and white silk trousers. Behind him rode six soldiers from the provincial guard. Because it was a private entertainment, he had dispensed with the flag bearer, but they attracted attention anyway.

The mayor had arranged to have the banquet on the upper floor of a large restaurant overlooking the Mikasa River. Numerous colored paper lanterns hung suspended from the open gallery and could be seen from a distance. Over the door was a gilt inscription identifying it as the 'Great Happiness' restaurant.

It looks and sounds like a brothel, Akitada thought sourly. He hated these social occasions.

The 'Great Happiness" opened its double doors, and he was greeted by waiters in bright red shirts and black trousers who bowed him in and up the stairs into a large room overlooking the river. Outside was the gallery with the colored lanterns swaying softly in the breeze.

A number of well-dressed men greeted him with bows and wishes for good health and a long life. Mayor Nakamura stepped forward, all smiles and rustling dark blue silk. He made introductions, and Akitada tried in vain to match so many names and faces. He did recognize Hayashi, the fat chief of the merchant's guild, and Feng, the Chinese merchant. He exchanged bows and made polite remarks about Hakata, Minami, Dazaifu, and Kyushu. They requested comparisons to the capital or asked if he had seen the emperor close up. He had not and felt this lowered him in their estimation.

Nakamura eventually led him to a dais where they were to occupy seats of honor. The others took their seats below.

The doors of the room opened to admit a small group of musicians who carried lutes, zithers, and flutes. They took their stand to the side and struck up a light tune. Akitada listened with pleasure to the flute player. He had not played his own flute in many weeks and promised himself to practice soon.

A long line of exquisite young women in colored and diaphanous gowns entered next and dispersed among the guests, each taking her place near one of the men.

Akitada winced when a particularly tall and beautiful creature knelt beside him with a deep bow, announcing softly, "My name is Fragrant Orchid. It will be my pleasure to serve your Excellency tonight."

So it was to be that kind of party, he thought, merely nodding to her. He disliked such affairs intensely and became morose.

His host leaned closer. "Fragrant Orchid is our leading beauty. I'm told she's very talented." He winked.

Words had double meanings. She had offered to *serve* him tonight, and the mayor had called her *very talented.* Even without the wink, it was clear that he had been presented with the services of a prostitute. No doubt they knew he had not brought his family and thought him desperate to lie with a woman. Suddenly angry, he ignored his companion and turned to the mayor. "I'm afraid I have brought my work with me tonight. Being a stranger here, I hope you and some of the other gentlemen will share your views on local conditions and problems with me."

Nakamura looked taken aback, and there was whispering among the others. But then his host smiled and bowed. "Please ask away, Excellency. I hope you will come to enjoy what our city has to offer." His eyes went meaningfully to Akitada's female companion.

"Thank you. I'm sure I will." Akitada did not look at her and continued quickly, "I've been surprised that my predecessor was already gone when I arrived. He must have left in a hurry."

The mayor cast a glance at his companion and said cautiously, "His Excellency, Governor Tachibana was a connoisseur and collector of art. He was anxious about shipping his art home and feared the summer storms. Mr. Feng could tell you more about his collection."

Akitada looked at the Chinese merchant who smiled expectantly. "I had the pleasure of visiting your fine store yesterday, Mr. Feng. A young man showed me an extraordinary painting of a Chinese village. I also found some charming dolls to send to my children."

If Feng was startled by this information, he handled it well. With a bow, he expressed himself deeply honored but devastated that he had not known of the governor's visit. "Perhaps, if you'd advise me of your next visit, Excellency, I'll be able to show you other wonderful things."

"Thank you, Mr. Feng. I look forward to it." Akitada turned back to the mayor. "What sort of administrator was Governor Tachibana? Did you find him easy to work with?"

The mayor shifted uncomfortably. "I don't think any of us experienced any problems while he was governor." He glanced at the other guests. "Does anyone here know of difficulties?" They all shook their heads." Nakamura laughed a little nervously. "This is a peaceful place nowadays, Excellency. Nothing much happens here as a rule."

Akitada raised his brows. "Really? I hear about violent men roaming the streets and attacking children. And my assistant managed to walk in on a murder investigation the very day I sent him to inspect Hakata's police headquarters. For some reason, the chief, a Captain Okata, objected to his interest. He seemed to be under the impression local crime was not the business of the provincial tribunal."

This produced an awkward silence.

Finally, Nakamura said, "Sometimes Okata can be very rude. I've said so myself. The fact is the district magistrate is in Hakata. Police headquarters are under his supervision. The provincial administration hasn't operated as a tribunal for a long time."

Feng added, "Okata is a good officer, a person of rank. Governor Tachibana had every faith in him. Perhaps he misunderstood a question."

Akitada was still digesting the fact that the entire law enforcement for Chikuzen seemed to be located in Hakata and under Captain Okata. He considered Feng's comment and nodded. "It's possible. I shall have a talk with him myself."

A light touch on his sleeve reminded him of the woman beside him. Fragrant Orchid extended a cup of wine to him. Her eyes were downcast, and she was flushed. It occurred to him that he had been unnecessarily rude by not paying her more attention. He said, "Forgive me. You have been very patient with me. It has been a long time since I've had such charming company."

She glanced up with a quick smile and offered the wine with both hands. Her scent was quite heavy, stirring and warming his blood, perhaps because he knew why she was here. Hers was a flawless beauty of large, liquid eyes and full, moist lips. Like elegant women everywhere, she used make-up, whitening her skin and outlining her eyes with black. The paint enhanced her features and gave her an air of mystery. He said more gently, "Business all too often intervenes when we should relax and enjoy the beauties of this world."

She dimpled and murmured back, "How painful that only the wine reminded you of me."

He sipped without looking away from those strange eyes. "Not so. Rather my duties have blinded me momentarily."

The mayor beside him chuckled. "I wondered when your Excellency would begin to enjoy the evening. Here comes the food. I hope our poor fare is not too humble for your taste."

The atmosphere in the room relaxed considerably. The musicians struck up another tune, and the other guests chatted or flirted with the women beside them. Waiters passed around on silent feet, placing tray tables with dishes of food before each guest. Mouthwatering smells began to fill the room. The musicians struck up a new tune, and outside the moon had risen in the night sky, silvering the river below and the roof tops of the city beyond.

Akitada considered Fragrant Orchid's attractions. Her name was apt, but then it was likely a professional one. She was tall for a woman, but graceful, and beneath the diaphanous pale green silk, her breasts were firm and full, her waist surprisingly small, and her hips and thighs softly rounded and inviting. She was a very desirable woman.

It struck him that his physical pleasure in her was stimulated by many different senses. His eyes feasted on her beauty as much as they had on the moon-silvered landscape outside, his ears absorbed the sound of her voice like the very pleasant music, his nose was simultaneously teased by her musky scent and the aroma of the dainty dishes before him, and his tongue yet tasted the sweetness of the wine while yearning to taste her lips. He was strongly aroused.

As if reading his thoughts, she gave him a sidelong smile.

He pulled himself together and asked, "Did you by any chance meet my predecessor?"

Perhaps it was his imagination, but he thought his question upset her. For a moment her eyes left his to glance away. Then she said calmly, "Yes. I enjoyed his acquaintance. His Excellency was a most learned, considerate, and polite gentleman."

He was embarrassed. "And I am not. You haven't forgiven me."

"Perhaps I shall when I know you better."

Boldly, he suggested, "A promise and an offer?"

She nodded, smiling.

He felt ridiculously flattered and excited. Since he did not trust himself to say anything else, he turned to his food. To his relief, nobody seemed to have noticed the flirtatious exchange. The conversation among the guests ranged from an upcoming festival to rumors of the discovery of gold in Osumi province. Akitada listened and asked a question about the gold, but no one seemed to know particulars.

Toward the end of the banquet, the mayor suddenly recalled Akitada's earlier comment. "About this murder, Excellency," he said. "No need to trouble yourself about it. The dead woman was just the wife of a doll maker. The husband did it. Okata has a confession."

Akitada reflected that apparently the murders of women, especially if they were the wives of mere doll makers, were not considered important enough to disturb the peace of mind of the mayor or have an impact on the Hakata community. He became morose again, but nothing else of interest was said, and he was more relieved than disappointed when his beauteous companion and the other females took their leave. Some of the guests were already drunk and snatched at the hands and skirts of the departing women. The musicians packed up their instruments, and the mayor rose to thank him and the other guests for coming. Akitada expressed his own gratitude for the luxurious entertainment, and the others applauded.

And so the evening ended. Akitada walked down the wide stairs first, the mayor behind him.

Waiting at the bottom was a child, a little girl in a colorful silk gown and embroidered jacket, a miniature version of the beautiful Fragrant Orchid except that her hair was only shoulder-length. She looked almost exactly like the doll Akitada had bought for his daughter. For that matter, she was only slightly older than Yasuko but apparently already in the trade.

She made him a very deep bow and held up a folded note on scented paper dusted with flecks of gold. He took it, asking, "Is this for me? Who sent you, child?"

But she only smiled an enchanting smile and ran out of the restaurant. The mayor caught up and chortled. "Congratulations, Excellency. Our most famous beauty likes you. She rarely gives invitations."

Akitada suppressed his embarrassment and left quickly.

Back at the tribunal, Tora awaited with eager questions about the food and the women at the banquet.

Akitada answered curtly, then said, "The doll maker has confessed to the murder, so your case is closed."

"Maeda won't have liked that," Tora commented. "And I think he's right. There was something else going on."

"But you will not have time for it in the future. Your duties at the tribunal are waiting."

Akitada did not open Fragrant Orchid's letter until he was in his room and alone.

It was brief. The message, written in a somewhat awkward hand simply read, "Please come to me. I have something to tell you."

He firmly resisted regret, tore up the scrap, and sat down to add a few lines to his letter to Tamako, describing the banquet and the foods, though not his companion.

13

Disappearances

Temptation can be a powerful force for change.

Akitada brooded for days about the way he had reacted to Fragrant Orchid. Her presence had distracted him from asking more questions about conditions in Hakata and the province; he had felt so strong a physical response to her that he was now filled with shame.

His letter to Tamako and the dolls were dispatched for home, along with letters from Tora and Saburo and other small gifts. They all missed their families. The difference for Akitada was that Tamko was in the last weeks of her pregnancy.

He threw himself into administrative work. Apart from dealing with the two homeless children, Tora and Saburo stayed at the tribunal. Tora was training his guards while Saburo saw to the smooth running of the household.

In Hakata, Mitsui had confessed and now awaited trial.

Akitada began the process of removing Captain Okata from office. This was by no means simple. The odd arrangement by which such appointments had been handled by the governor general's office meant he had to make a case against Okata. He had to gather evidence and prove Okata was unfit for his position. This he hoped to achieve by posting notices in Hakata asking people to report police brutality or malfeasance to the provincial tribunal.

Okata responded with a formal protest to the vice governor general. He, in turn, asked for a written explanation from Akitada. Akitada replied that he hoped to improve law enforcement in the port city, an important first step to dealing with smuggling and treasonable contacts between China and their own country. A populace intimidated by its police was not likely to cooperate with it. Unpleasant though all of this was, a number of serious complaints had already been filed.

Saburo's report about Hayashi's activities was a disappointment. It had not revealed any illegalities. While a long meeting with Feng and the shrine priest Kuroda might be suggestive, it could also be perfectly harmless. He did not send Saburo back for another look at the guild master.

The only bright spot was that the attack on the two children had led to their finding a home. Tora had mentioned their plight to Sergeant Maeda, who had the bright idea to take them to Mrs. Kimura, the old lady who grew the tiny trees. Now the children's birds and her miniature forest coexisted happily in her garden, and the children were company for her.

There was, however, also good news of another kind. A ship finally brought long-awaited letters from the capital. Akitada broke open his packet immediately, scanned the contents, and found Tamako's thick sheaf of pages. She had done what he did, written a little every day about the events of the day, giving him news of the children and the household. She apologized that her news was so trivial, but Akitada devoured every line joyously. Most important was the fact that they were all well. He began to relax. The child would be born in its time, and Tamako would recover as she had before. She was healthy woman.

The two weeks after the banquet passed with only one puzzling piece of news. Among the paperwork sent to Akitada from the Governor General's Office in Dazaifu was a brief note from Fujiwara Korenori to the effect that a strange report had reached his office.

It appeared the former governor had not been seen or heard of for over a month now. He had been expected to touch land in two provinces on his journey home. The ship with his possessions and retainers had arrived and left as scheduled, but there had been no sign of their master.

This was not Akitada's business, but it troubled him. Something had happened to the man, and the peculiar way in which his departure had been handled, meant that no one in Kyushu had missed him. As far as was known, he had left Hakata, and presumably Kyushu, two weeks before Akitada had arrived. He had disappeared somewhere between Hakata and his scheduled first stop.

Akitada and Mori were checking tax reports in hopes of collecting delinquent taxes and shoring up the treasury when Tora walked into the office.

"Maeda sent for me, sir," he said, nodding to Mori. "He says Mrs. Kuroki's disappeared."

"Who is Mrs. Kuroki?"

"She's the Mitsuis' neighbor across the street. It may have something to do with the case."

"I thought the man had confessed and was going to trial."

"Yes. The trial's tomorrow. But I think he made a false confession."

Akitada stared at Tora. "Because of beatings?"

"Maybe, though Maeda hasn't allowed any more mistreatment. People do foolish things."

"True, but you can hardly base an argument on this assertion. I hope this isn't an excuse to spend all your time in Hakata."

Tora was offended. "I haven't started kidnapping women, if that's what you're implying, sir."

Mori looked shocked at such impudence, but Akitada said only, "I think it will be best if you attend the trial. I'd like to know how they are handled in Hakata. Afterward you can see what Maeda is doing about the missing female. I hope he isn't about to make a mistake. The paperwork is almost complete for dismissing

Okata, and the vice governor general is not about to
overlook irregularities."

The Hakata court sessions were held in an annex to
the jail. The courtroom was modest in size, but the
murder of Mrs. Mitsui had attracted an interested
crowd which spilled over into the courtyard outside.

Tora and Maeda pushed through and into the courtroom. Maeda usually attended the trials of his own ar-
rests. Technically, Mitsui was Okata's arrest, but Okata
could not be bothered with token appearances.

The judge, an elderly man with a sparse beard and a
tired expression, was already in his place on the dais. A
scribe sat to one side, and four constables were lined up
below and on either side of him. When the judge
rapped his baton, two jailers brought in Mitsui. He was
in chains, and they pushed him down in front of the
judge. When the dazed-looking doll maker did not
immediately bow to the judge, one of them kicked him
forward making his face hit the floor.

Mitsui looked pitiful. The beating he had received
had left his face badly discolored. At least they had giv-
en him a clean shirt and pants for his trial, and washed
the blood off him. He looked at the judge, the constables, and the crowd pressing in all around him, and his
face puckered up.

"Why does the prisoner's face look like that?" demanded the judge.

"He resisted the police who arrested him and the
guards in jail," asserted one of his guards.

"Hah! Another one of those?" The judge shook his head. "You seem to have trouble controlling your prisoners."

"Not me, your Honor." The jailer grinned and snapped the short whip he carried in the air. The crowd laughed, and Mitsui shrank into himself.

The judge leaned forward and fixed his eyes on Mitsui. "You are the doll maker Mitsui, husband of the dead woman Mei?"

"Yes, your Honor," Mitsui croaked.

"And you have confessed to killing her on the fifteenth day of this month?"

"Yes, your Honor."

"Why did you do this?"

His hands being bound behind his back, Mitsui wiped his nose on the shoulder of his shirt. "I got home late from a delivery in Hakozaki. She called me names and cursed me for being late. She said I was no good and I made her work too hard and she knew someone who would treat her better."

The crowd muttered, and the judge rapped his baton. "Go on. What happened next?"

"There was no food. I complained, but she laughed in my face and told me to do my own cooking. So I got out a knife to slice a radish. Then she showed me some gold coins. She said she got them from her lover and he would give her more. And then she said she was going to get her clothes and leave me that very night."

More muttering from the crowd. Someone shouted, "The bitch deserved what she got."

The baton rapped again.

When silence had been restored, the judge said, "So she left the kitchen. What did you do?"

"I was angry and followed her."

"With the knife still in your hand?"

"Yes. She was upstairs throwing clothes into a large square of cloth. She had a new dress. A green silk dress. She held it up for me to see. 'See, what nice things he gives me?' she said. That's when I went mad and went for her. She dropped the dress and backed away. I pushed her down on the bedding. She spat at me and called me names, and I lost it completely. I stabbed her and kept stabbing until she stopped moving. That's all."

The judge consulted some papers. "Hmm. It seems to fit the coroner's report. The police never found the knife. Or the gold. What happened to those?"

"I threw the knife in the river and kept the gold."

"Attacking your wife of many years, the mother of your children, so violently is a heinous act. How could you do such a thing?"

Mitsui looked down. "She was always a bad wife. It just got too much for me when she was gloating. I wanted her to stop."

"You did not report your wife's death until the next morning. And then you claimed you'd found her already dead. Why was that?"

"I thought I could get away with it."

The judge nodded. "Yes. It certainly sounds like the truth. Very well. Since you have confessed freely to the brutal murder of your wife during a jealous rage, and since there is evidence that you have had prior fits of anger during which you hit her, I find you guilty of aggravated murder. You will serve out your remaining years at hard labor for the government in Tsushima."

Mitsui cried out at this sentence, but the crowd applauded. The guards pushed the prisoner down again, then jerked him to his feet. They dragged him out between them, and the judge rapped his baton and declared the court session closed.

Outside Tora asked Maeda, "What did you make of it?"

"I expected it. He did confess before."

"I still don't like it. What if he was lying?"

Maeda sighed. "Then he must be either abysmally stupid or mad, as the case may be. We can't be held responsible for people's stupidity."

They stopped for a bowl of noodles in the market, and then went on to the Kuroki house. Tora was curious about what could have happened to that luscious bit Yoko. He had ignored her open invitation so far, thinking piously of his sweet Hanae at home, but he was glad his master did not know about Yoko's reputation.

Two constables lounged outside the house; they straightened up when they saw Maeda. Inside Yoko's husband was sitting in the main room, looking distraught. He was a fat man with a large belly and was mopping his red face with a tissue held in one pudgy hand. He stared at them with swollen eyes. Maeda made the introductions.

"I don't understand it," Kuroki complained. "Such a thing has never happened. She wouldn't just stay out all night. You must search for her, Sergeant."

Maeda eyed him and looked around the room. "Perhaps your wife has left you," he said bluntly.

"No," squeaked the husband, waving his hands about. "No, she wouldn't just leave me. She's a devoted wife."

Tora almost laughed. "How long has she been gone?" he asked.

"Since yesterday."

Tora raised a brow. "You found her gone when you got home from work?"

"No. She was here then. We had dinner together. A very nice fish stew. I'm fond of *ayu* and managed to get some very fresh ones the day before. She cooked it with a little ginger, just the way I like it." He heaved a heavy sigh. "This has never happened before. What shall I do?"

Maeda asked, "What happened after the fish dinner? Did you have an argument?"

"Oh, no. We never argue."

"You'd better tell us what you both did." Maeda looked disgusted.

"Well, we ate. Then she put away the dishes and said she had used all the ginger in the fish stew and if I wanted some in my morning gruel, she'd have to run to the market. I do like ginger in my gruel, and a bit of honey. I reminded her of the honey and gave her a piece of silver. I thought maybe she'd find some sweet bean paste and candied chestnuts." He looked at them earnestly. "I have a taste for those."

"So she left to go to the market?"

"We left together."

Tora and Maeda exchanged a glance, and Maeda asked, "You went to the market together?"

"No. She went to the market. I went to the bath house. It was my regular night for a *moxa* treatment. I had my bath and a shave as usual, and then I had a massage and the *moxa* treatment." He made a face and lifted his round shoulders. "It's a bit painful, but so good for the intestines and it regulates the breath. I have a sensitive stomach."

Maeda bit his lip. "Go on. Was she home when you returned?"

"I didn't see her, but the honey and ginger were in the kitchen, so she must have come back."

"What do you mean, you didn't see her?" asked Tora.

"Well, after a *moxa* treatment I'm always quite exhausted. I unrolled some bedding and went to sleep here. I thought she was sleeping in the other room."

Tora and Maeda exchanged another glance. Maeda said, "But you don't know for a fact she spent the night here?"

Kuroki shook his head. "When I got up this morning, she was gone. The ginger and honey were still there, but no gruel." He sounded aggrieved.

"And no message?"

He shook his head again. "She can't write."

Silence fell.

Tora said, "Did you look at her clothes? We need to know what she was wearing."

"Why?"

Maeda said, "She could have had an accident."

"Oh, I hope not. Surely she'd tell people who she was?"

Tora sighed. "Not if she was unconscious."

Kuroki started weeping. "You think she's dead." He made it sound like an accusation.

Tora snapped, "Go check her clothes. She could have decided to walk out on you."

The fat man staggered to his feet and waddled to a door. "She'd never . . .," he mumbled on his way out.

"What do you think?" asked Maeda.

Tora snorted. "If you were Yoko, would you stay with him if you could find another man? He certainly wasn't her idea of a good husband. She said as much to me."

"Really? And what did you say?"

Kuroki came back in. "Only the gown she wore is gone, and her new quilt. The gown was blue with a small white pattern of shells. The quilt was light green with a pattern of cherry blossoms. She loved it, so I bought it for her." He shook his head. "What could have happened?"

Maeda asked, "Could she have gone to visit a friend?"

"No. She had no friends. Or family either." He started blubbering again and wrung his fat hands. "I told you, she was a devoted wife. She had me, and I had her. We were like the two halves of a clam."

Tora looked at him. He was a singularly unattractive man. No wonder his wife invited men into her house.

Maeda got up. "Well, we'll ask around, Mr. Kuroki. You do the same. If you can think of anything, let us know."

Outside, he said to Tora, "She's gone off with a lover. Taking her favorite quilt."

Tora thought it likely, but something nagged at him.

Across the street, Mitsui's son was loading his father's handcart. Now that old Mitsui had been sentenced, the son was in a hurry to sell his property.

Tora said as much, and Maeda nodded. "May he choke on the money," he growled.

They crossed the street to Mrs. Kimura's house. They could hear the children's voices and laughter. When Maeda shouted a greeting, the children came running, smiles on their faces. Kichiro's eye had healed, but he still had an ugly scab on his cheekbone.

"You look like a man who's been in a fight," Tora said, grinning.

Kichiro laughed. "I was. It was nothing. They ran."

The girl, suddenly shy, said, "Kichiro, that isn't true. Saburo made them run."

"Saburo sends his regrets, being busy with work," Tora said. "He may stop by some evening." Saburo wanted to visit them, but the children only knew the bearded man, and he could not wear his facial hair during the day without someone becoming suspicious.

Mrs. Kimura welcomed them and offered fruit juice on her veranda. The garden was filled with bird song coming from the many cages hanging from trees.

"The children are such a blessing to me," she said, watching them fondly as they tended to the birds. "I'm still afraid to let them go out, but they want to sell the birds in the market."

Maeda said, "It should be safe enough, provided they only go there and come straight back, and never after dark. We stopped by on another matter. Mrs. Kuroki, your neighbor across the street, seems to have disappeared and her husband is very worried. Would you happen to know anything about her activities yesterday?"

Mrs. Kimura's eyes widened. "Yoko? Disappeared? So she finally had enough." She giggled, then covered her mouth. "Shame on me. The poor man." But she spoiled it with another giggle. "I'm sorry. He's been so silly about her, and she hates that so much. Some people should never get married." She nodded toward the Mitsui house. "There's proof for you. I hear Mitsui confessed to killing Mei?"

"He did. That case is closed. Now we're looking for Yoko. You don't think Kuroki killed her?"

She laughed. "Oh, no. He doesn't have the strength for anything as strenuous as murder. I expect she's gone off with someone."

"Who?"

"A man. She used to have them coming around pretending to make deliveries. They went inside, stayed a while and came back out whistling." She smiled.

"Can you describe them?" Tora asked.

They got descriptions of several young men, younger than either Tora or Maeda. They had other features in common. They were handsome and well-built. They wore short pants and colorful shirts and sandals on their feet. "Ordinary market porters," she said, "but young and good-looking. Yoko had good taste. I used to wish them joy. Yoko and those young men were positively bubbling with hunger for each other." She laughed.

Maeda was shocked. "How do you get such ideas? Surely it's not proper to spy on a neighbor having an affair with a market boy."

Tora chortled. She said, "Maeda, you have a lot to learn about women, especially old, lonely ones. Those children are a blessing for me. You're right. Loneliness makes people nosy."

"And where would the police be without nosy people," Tora said.

Maeda grinned sheepishly. "I'm turning into a prude. The other day I thought Tora was Yoko's latest victim."

Tora blushed. "Prey maybe, but not victim. Though she's a pretty woman and doesn't deserve a husband like that. Do we look for one of her lovers now?"

Maeda frowned. "I don't know. She has a right to leave her husband. Besides, I don't want to tell the poor besotted bastard where we found her. Assuming we do."

And that was the end of that. On the way back, they stopped to speak to Hiroshi, who glared at them as he flung a last bundle into his handcart. "What now?" he growled.

"Nothing to do with you or your father," said Maeda. "I just wondered if you were here yesterday."

"What if I was?"

"Well, did you happen to see the woman across the street?"

"No."

"Or any visitors to her house?"

"No. Are you after that poor bitch now? What's she supposed to have done, killed her husband?"

Maeda clenched his hands. Tora said quickly, "Nothing of the sort. What are you up to?"

Hiroshi transferred his glare to him. "None of your business, but if you must know, I'm selling some stuff. My father has no need for it now, and my wife and children are hungry."

They walked away, shaking their heads.

14

Spring Rain

The door opened abruptly.

"Captin Okatta, governor, zir." Koji stood aside to let the police chief enter.

Akitada was in the tribunal office, and the captain stood just inside the door. He was a slender man with a narrow face and pinched lips and wore his bright red uniform with the black feathered cap. At the moment he looked irritated. Akitada gave Mori a nod, the secretary did the same with the two scribes. They got up and walked out of the room, closing the door behind them.

Akitada said coldly, "So you finally show up. What kept you from reporting?"

Okata saluted and said in a clipped voice, "Press of business, sir."

"You will address me as 'Your Excellency.' I'm surprised nobody explained simple protocol to you."

Okata flushed. "His Excellency Governor Tachibana was the easy-going type. He didn't stand on ceremony, provided a man did his job well." He paused, then added, "Your Excellency."

He was defiant. Akitada saw that the interview would be extremely unpleasant. Suddenly angered, he decided to make short work of it.

"I'm glad you speak of a man doing his job well, Okata," he said. "I have ordered you to report because I have reason to find fault with the way you are handling it."

Okata raised his chin. "I'm aware of the posters you put up around town. No doubt every man, woman, and child who's ever been in trouble with the law filed a complaint."

So the man was not stupid. His bad performance was due to other reasons. Laziness? Or the conviction he was too good for the job? It did not matter.

Akitada pulled out a sheaf of papers. "Whatever your explanations may be for them, I have here fifty-one separate charges against you or your men. That is an unreasonable number even if they were all from people you've arrested. One of my men had the chance to observe your handling of a murder case." He held up the thick sheaf of papers. "In some of the other cases you refused to investigate charges brought by citizens, you ordered your men to rough up witnesses, you confiscated goods for no good reason, you took two families' homes away from them and bestowed them on friends of yours, you dismissed policemen because they opposed your orders to use cruel beatings in order to get confessions, and the list goes on. This will not do, Okata." He paused. "You are dismissed."

Okata blinked. "Dismissed?" he asked uncertainly. "You mean I can go?"

"No!" Akitada slammed his fist on his desk, making the ink stone and water flask jump and a stack of papers topple. "No," he repeated more calmly. "I mean you are dismissed from your position as captain of the Hakata police force and as chief of police. My secretary has your final pay requisition slip. You need not return to your station. If you have property belonging to police headquarters, you will return it within a week. Now you may leave."

Okata's jaw sagged. He turned red and then purple and choked. Akitada was afraid he was having some sort of fit and would fall down dead before his eyes. But the man caught his breath and snarled, "You don't have the power to dismiss me. I could have you arrested. We'll see what Lord Fujiwara at Dazaifu has to say about this." He flung about and rushed out, shoving Mori, who was waiting with his pay slip, violently aside.

Mori hit the wall with a thud and slipped down. Akitada jumped up to help him, but the old man staggered to his feet on his own. "I can't say I like that man," he commented, coming back into the office.

"Nor do I." Mori's mild comment had managed to defuse Akitada's own fury. "Please draw up a formal appointment for Sergeant Maeda to replace Captain Okata. He will be the new police chief. Make the appointment and the new rank of lieutenant probationary. Tora has nothing but praise for Maeda, and there are no complaints filed against him. I'd like to see how he handles the job before we make it permanent."

Mori smiled. "I know Sergeant Maeda and his family," he said. "They're good people. Maeda didn't attend the university, but he excelled as a pupil in the local school. His people couldn't afford to send him to the capital. This has hurt his chances."

"Well, I could wish he had a better education, but it's certainly preferable to have an honest, capable, and diligent chief of police than a learned one."

The next day the weather turned bad. The world was cast into a gray twilight as the rain sheeted down. An air of hopelessness hung over the tribunal compound where the forecourt remained empty except for a large number of puddles. Everyone kept indoors.

Toward noon, a messenger from Maeda arrived with news. Mitsui had been tried and found guilty of murdering his wife. He was condemned to hard labor in the silver mines of Tsushima. It was a harsh sentence for an old man because he would not survive long. Still, since he had no chance of being pardoned, a quick death was thought to be preferable to years of suffering.

Tora looked uncharacteristically glum when he heard the news.

Akitada asked, "Why are you upset? It was a very violent crime. Surely you don't think a mere prison sentence would have been enough?"

Tora shook his head. "I don't know what I think, sir. Mitsui isn't a likeable man. Nobody in that family deserves pity or respect. But I have an odd feeling we don't know everything in this case. There's something more to find out. And now the woman across the street from the Mitsuis just walked away from her marriage and disappeared. I talked to her a few days ago, and she didn't strike me as the sort who would do such a thing."

Akitada frowned. "Well, the Mitsui case is closed. If it makes you feel any better, go and ask a few questions about this missing woman."

Tora sighed. "It must have been hard for Maeda to work under that bastard Okata."

"Yes. The sins of superiors poison the staff. That is why we have a rigorous system of evaluation. But Maeda will have his reward." He did not mention that his predecessor, Governor Tachibana, had given Okata excellent evaluations, while Okata had always reported mediocre performances for Maeda, listing a number of reprimands for insubordination.

An hour after Maeda's message, a wet and bedraggled messenger arrived from Lord Fujiwara with the order for Akitada to report immediately to Dazaifu. Akitada looked out at the driving rain and then at the dripping soldier, and sighed.

"I have to go to Dazaifu, Mori," he said. "I'll try to be back by nightfall. If there is any trouble, Tora and Saburo will know what to do."

Tora and Saburo offered to go with him, but since none of them knew the tribunal staff very well yet, they were needed here. Akitada changed into his good green brocade robe and white silk trousers. The proper court costume required on this occasion was singularly impractical for a ride through this downpour, but he could not afford to offend Fujiwara. He put on boots over his slippers, tucked his court hat into his sleeve, and covered himself with a straw raincoat and straw hat.

Thus attired, he mounted his horse and, accompanied by the muddy messenger, set out on the highway to Dazaifu.

There were fewer people traveling in this weather, but contingents of soldiers passed now and then, their trotting horses spattering Akitada. He tried to pull the straw coat over his white trousers, but the soaked straw resisted and hung more and more heavily on his shoulders. Since there was nothing to be gained from a slower pace, he drove his horse at a gallop most of the way. Nevertheless, when he dismounted in front of the administration hall and divested himself of the wet straw items and the boots, he found his fine robe wrinkled and water-stained where the rain had leaked through the straw, and dirt spatters on his white trousers. He put on his hat, the only item that had escaped a drenching, and walked to Lord Fujiwara's office.

The servant glanced at his clothes and smirked, but he opened the door and announced, "Lord Sugawara, Your Excellency."

Akitada went in and bowed. As last time, Fujiwara was at his desk, and his clerks and secretaries were at theirs. All stared.

Akitada cleared his throat. "Sorry, sir, but the weather is very bad."

"If this is a complaint, you may forget it," Fujiwara said coldly.

Akitada flushed and glanced at the clerks and secretaries. Such a tone to a senior official was highly improper in front of them. He said, "I beg your pardon?"

"I called you because Captain Okata was here. He claims you dismissed him."

Akitada felt his anger choking him. He had not even been asked to sit down. He was here to be publicly reprimanded like a small boy who had broken a favorite dish. He glared at Fujiwara. "That is correct."

"What possessed you to do such a high-handed thing? It is the function and privilege of this office to make senior appointments to the police and military of Kyushu. You had no right. I have reinstated Okata, who is a fine officer."

The room swam before Akitada's eyes. To be sure, Kyushu was a special case as administrative areas of the nation went, but surely a governor could not permit outside powers to interfere in the administration of his province? He tried to clear his head and review the laws applicable to provincial administrations. Commanding officers of the police were dispatched from the capital to the various provinces, but they served only with the approval of the governor.

Akitada bit his lip. "I regret Captain Okata rushed here before my report could reach you, sir. Okata was dismissed for cause. He has shown gross negligence in the past and is universally despised by the people in

Hakata. There is reason to think he is responsible for a miscarriage of justice in a recent murder case where he suppressed evidence. In addition, he has proved to be impossible to work with, ignoring the Chikuzen tribunal completely and insulting its staff, including myself."

Fujiwara frowned. Disrespect toward higher-ranking appointed officials was clearly a serious charge, more serious than miscarriage of justice, for example. He said, "Well, I expect you provoked him. He *is* rather set in his ways. I'll have him apologize."

"Sorry, sir. I will not work with Okata. He is dismissed. If you do not support me in this matter, I'll resign."

Silence. Everyone in the room held his breath.

Fujiwara woke belatedly to the presence of his staff listening with avid ears to a confrontation between two ranking noblemen. He got up. "We'll settle this in my study."

Akitada followed him. In the private room, Fujiwara finally had the grace to gesture to a cushion. Akitada remained standing. "Thank you, but I prefer to stand. I shall not change my mind and see no point in a long discussion."

Fujiwara stared at him. "You're out of order, Sugawara. I'm your superior."

"My apologies, my Lord, but I hold my appointment from His Majesty, just as you do. I have responsibilities and duties, just as you do. When these conflict, I must choose what most closely applies to my assignment. I would remind you I am evaluated each year. With Okata running the Hakata police, I cannot carry out my duties as governor. I must also remind you that I have received certain secret instructions which a man like Okata would jeopardize. Under the circumstances, I must stand by my decision."

Fujiwara deflated with gratifying promptness. "Ah, well. There is the special assignment. Hmm, yes. I see your point, though I cannot imagine . . . never mind. Very well, have it your way. But the man will be your enemy, and he has friends and supporters. He may give you more trouble dismissed than he would as police chief."

"I shall deal with him if he should be so foolish."

Fujiwara pursed his lips. "If there's trouble, I cannot give you any assistance, you know."

"I know."

A silence fell. Akitada thought bitterly that it was always thus with his superiors: they handed out difficult assignments but refused to become involved if problems arose. His wet trousers stuck uncomfortably to his legs and itched, reminding him of the miserable homeward journey.

He cleared his throat. "If I may be excused then?"

Fujiwara nodded. Akitada turned and started for the door when Fujiwara said, "Wait! I'm somewhat troubled by those reports concerning your predecessor. You received my messages?"

Akitada turned back. "Yes, I did. Since Lord Tachibana left two weeks before my arrival, and everybody seems to agree he took ship for home, I did not consider it my duty to search for him."

"No, of course not. But it's strange, isn't it?"

"Yes. He may have encountered pirates, or perhaps his ship ran aground somewhere."

"Not pirates. We would have heard. And he's been gone a whole month now. Surely someone would've found him if his ship got lost. Besides, there are no reports of missing ships."

"He may have taken a smaller vessel. And there are many uninhabited islands in the Inland Sea."

"Yes. All the same."

"It *is* strange, sir. Is there something about Lord Tachibana that causes this concern?"

Fujiwara chewed on his lower lip. "No-o," he said. "Not exactly. Well, there was gossip. I wondered if he was the reason they sent you."

"I was sent to replace him before his term had expired. It suggests something caused his recall."

Fujiwara peered at him and nodded. "Yes, exactly. What was it? Come on, surely you can tell me." His tone was almost pleading.

"I wasn't told myself, sir. I had hoped to learn the reason from you, or in Chikuzen, but as you know, the customary clearing of provincial accounts was handled by your office. What gossip were you referring to?"

"Oh, it concerned his personal wealth and, er, a certain behavior. But making money while serving as a governor is not uncommon, and his accounts were correct. As for amorous liaisons, he isn't the first nobleman in Kyushu to enjoy a vacation from his family." He frowned. "Well, keep your eyes and ears open, Sugawara."

This time Akitada made him a slight bow.

15

Closed Case

When Tora returned to Hakata the day after his master's visit to Dazaifu, he found Maeda in his office, looking stunned.

"My congratulations, Chief," he said with a grin.

Maeda focused. "Was this your doing? No, surely not. It takes more than a clever wag from the capital to remove Okata from his chosen post."

Tora said modestly, "As provincial inspector, it was my duty to report on conditions in Hakata. My master's the one does the hiring and firing."

Maeda shook his head. "Well, I thank him for his confidence, but he knows nothing about me. Surely this is not the way things should be done?"

Tora raised an eyebrow. "You disapprove?"

"Well, no. Yes, I do. He cannot have known what he was doing. Besides, this won't work. Dazaifu makes those appointments."

"Oh, it has already worked. My master got back from there yesterday. You're confirmed."

Maeda gulped. "I don't believe it."

Tora folded his arms across his chest and frowned. "I've heard better acknowledgments for favors of this magnitude."

Maeda blushed, then chuckled. "Sorry, Tora. Of course I do appreciate your good words, and I'll thank the governor in person. But this is pretty unheard of."

"Oh, you're on probation. And my master says he's been warned Okata will try to make trouble."

"Yes, it's likely." Maeda grimaced. "Well, to work then. There's news about the Mitsui case."

"Yes?"

"The old man was found hanged in his cell yesterday. He was about to be transferred to Tsushima. Apparently he couldn't face it. His son had paid him a visit earlier, and all seemed quiet. The guards paid ignored him or slept, as the case may be. I'll deal with them later."

Tora thought about it. "It means the case really is closed," he said.

"Oh yes. It was closed after the judge pronounced his verdict, but now we don't even have reason to clear a possibly innocent man. The crazy thing is I feel bad about it, confession or not."

"Well, as has been pointed out: why would an innocent man confess?"

"I wish I knew."

They sat in silence, contemplating the vagaries of the investigation which had brought them together.

Finally Tora sighed. "What now? Any news of Yoko?"

"No. We posted notices. I have too much to do today to start talking to people again. Her husband was here this morning. The man's frantic. I tried to tell him she might have gone off with a friend, but he swore she had no friends. Women friends, he said." Maeda gave a snort. "Not surprising, really. Women don't care for other women who are on the prowl for their men. I finally told the poor fool what her neighbors had been saying. He got angry and stormed out."

"I think I'll look in on Mrs. Kimura and the kids. Maybe she's heard something."

"Be my guest."

Tora grinned. "Speaking of guests, now that you're in receipt of a lieutenant's salary, you can pay for the next meal at the Golden Dragon."

Maeda burst into laughter. "Just say when."

Tora stopped to buy some sweets from a vendor and then walked to Mrs. Kimura's house.

He noted that Mitsui's house was inhabited again. Laundry was draped over the rickety fence, and a large number of very grimy children were throwing stones at a mangy dog tied to a fence post. Tora waded in, slapped the boy who had just scored a painful hit, threatened the rest of the children with the same if they tormented any more animals, and untied the dog. The animal sped away, its tail between its legs. The children raised an outcry, and a fat and dirty woman came to the door, cursed Tora, and handed out a few more slaps.

Hiroshi had moved in his family.

Tora shook his head and went next door into a very different world.

He could hear them singing as he walked through the bamboo gate, the children's voices high and clear, and old Mrs. Kimura's slightly cracked but spirited. He smiled to himself and thought their visit to Kyushu had not been completely wasted. Of course, most of the credit for rescuing the children went to Saburo.

They greeted him with shy smiles. He held up the paper with the sweets. "I brought you something," he said, "but I see you've already eaten, so I think I'll keep these for myself."

"Oh, no!" cried Kichiro. "We're quite hungry. Aren't we, Naoko?"

"Hush, Kichiro. We're not hungry. Auntie has cooked a very good gruel for us." She paused, her eyes on the sweets. "But we might manage a sweet."

Tora and Mrs. Kimura laughed, and he passed his present over.

The children made him deep bows and ran outside into the garden, their cheeks bulging with the treats.

"Has something happened?" the old lady asked, eyeing Tora shrewdly.

He flashed her his big smile. "I came for the pleasure of seeing you, Mrs. Kimura."

"Nonsense. I could see it in your face."

Tora sobered. "As it happens, there is some news. Did you know Okata has been relieved of his post and Maeda appointed chief in his stead?"

"Oh!" she cried, clapping her hands. "That's wonderful news! Thank you, Tora. You've made me very happy." She paused. "But there's something else?"

Tora nodded. "Your neighbor killed himself in jail."

Her face fell. "Poor Mitsui, though he wasn't a very nice man. His sentence was too much to bear, I suppose. That good-for-nothing son of his has already moved his family into his parents' house. He looks very smug and goes out drinking every night. His wife fights with her neighbors, and the children are little savages. I'm still amazed that his father doted on the boy. He wasn't a very nice child either."

"I'm not surprised. They had a falling out before the murder, though. I think the old man must've berated him for gambling and losing his job. "

They went out on the veranda. Kichiro was spreading some paste on twigs with a piece of wood. He already had four or five small branches laid out along the edge of the veranda.

"What are you doing?" Tora asked.

The boy looked up. "It's glue I made from bean paste. I put the branches into trees or shrubs. The birds get stuck on them, and I catch them. I only keep the ones that sing."

Mrs. Kimura said softly, "It seems quite cruel. But children don't think about such things. He tells me he learned this from a man in the market. I confess I like all those birds singing in my garden."

Tora looked at the cages hanging from tree branches and the house eaves and listened. The birds sounded quite happy. They were singing their little hearts out. Or maybe they were mourning the loss of their freedom. He asked the boy, "How do you know where the best birds are?"

Kinchiro grinned. "I watch them. Two days ago I heard a warbler in the big cedar in the alley behind us. I was looking up into the tree, when a man digging his garden got mad and screamed at me."

Tora smiled. "Every craft has its troubles." He turned to Mrs. Kimura, "Any more thoughts about Yoko leaving?"

"So you haven't found her?"

"Not yet. Maeda is posting notices. If she sees one or hears about them, she'll show up. Or maybe her boyfriend will."

She shook her head. "Yoko can't read or write. And what makes you think a market porter can?"

Tora sighed. "Why is it people just disappear here? It's weird."

"Who else disappeared?"

"The last governor seems to have vanished."

As he explained that the governor's ship had not touched land since he had left, her eyes grew round. "How strange! I think I saw him the day he left Hakata. He was with two other men on horseback. It was getting dark, but one of them is quite distinctive looking with his elegant mustache and beard and those eyebrows like two small roofs above his eyes."

Tora smiled. "Roofs?"

She moistened a finger with her tongue and drew a pair of slanting lines meeting at an apex on the boards they sat on.

"So you could see his face?"

"Just for a moment before they turned the corner."

Given the way Lord Tachibana had left things for them, Tora did not really care. "Well, I expect he'll turn up eventually unless the fish ate him. I'd better be on my way. Do you need money?" He saw her expression and added quickly, "What with the extra mouths to feed."

"Thank you, but we manage quite well," she said primly. "In fact, the children are a big help to me and I'm growing fond of them. I shall ask them to stay. I have no one else to care for."

16

The Abandoned Well

As soon as he could do so, Akitada sent for Maeda and made his promotion official. He liked what he saw when he met the former sergeant. Maeda was well-spoken but modest about his education. He had a military background, something which would serve him well in his new role, and he expressed a concern about protecting the peaceful lives of the ordinary people in Hakata. He also impressed Akitada with a good knowledge of forensic practices. They parted pleased with each other.

Two days later they found Yoko.

By the time someone came to report a nauseating smell coming from an abandoned well, the rain had stopped and the weather had turned unseasonably warm. The smell and the number of flies around the wooden cover of the well had attracted the attention of some dogs who scrabbled at the wood, releasing more flies. Competition led to a noisy dog fight, which brought some boys, who obligingly moved the lid and looked down the half-filled shaft. Below lay a dead woman wrapped in a pale green quilt covered with cherry blossoms.

After verifying that the body was Yoko's, Maeda sent a message to the provincial tribunal. By the time Tora arrived at Hakata police station, Yoko was already in the capable hands of the coroner, Dr. Fujita. Tora and Maeda went to watch him at his work.

In spite of all the horrors he had seen, Tora's stomach turned. The beauteous Yoko was unrecognizable in the naked, swollen, and discolored corpse that lay on a stained grass mat while Dr. Fujita knelt beside it, probing various openings with a silver instrument which he raised to his nose from time to time.

Tora covered his nose with a sleeve and swallowed hard. He glanced at Maeda, who seemed absorbed in the coroner's probings. "How long?" Tora asked.

"Who knows?" Maeda answered. "Most likely since the day she disappeared."

The coroner looked up. "Deterioration is well advanced. Several days, I'd say."

"What killed her?" Tora tried next.

Fujita snorted and pointed to Yoko's chest.

Holding his sleeve over his nose, Tora stepped closer. Below Yoko's left breast were two blood-stained wounds, two additional openings for Dr. Fujita to probe. He promptly inserted his instrument as far as it would go into one of these. A trickle of foul-smelling liquid appeared. Tora stepped back quickly. The coroner repeated this with the second wound.

"A knife," Fujita said, frowning at the slender probe. "Fairly long and sharp. It went deep. The first one missed the vital organ. The second killed instantly."

Maeda asked, "The same sort of knife as the one used in the last murder?"

Fujita nodded. "Yes, it could be the same. But such knives are common in people's kitchens."

Maeda glanced at Tora and took his arm. "Thanks, Doctor. Let me know if you discover anything unusual." He led Tora outside and closed the door on the scene behind them. Tora gulped a few breaths of clean air.

"Delicate stomach?" Maeda grinned.

Tora glared at him. "Recent large meal."

"I expect seeing the object of your amorous desires in such a state had something to do with it."

"Shut up!"

Maeda chuckled, then sobered. "Sorry. Poor Yoko. You think the husband killed her?"

"No, I think whoever killed Mitsui's wife did." He paused as a memory surfaced. "Hiroshi," he said in a tone of wonder. "It was him. The boy saw him digging a few days ago. I bet he was burying the knife."

Maeda said nothing.

"Well?" Tora turned to him. "You see it, don't you? She was stabbed, and with the same knife as his stepmother."

Maeda shook his head. "Don't be silly. You don't know it was the same knife. This one could have come from Yoko's own kitchen and been used by her husband who finally figured out she was sleeping with everybody but him. Why Hiroshi? What would be his motive?"

"Yoko's husband's not the type to do anything so strenuous as stabbing a fully-grown and healthy female much younger than him. Let alone carry her all the way to an abandoned well to dump her body in. Hiroshi had a cart."

"Why do you keep linking this with Mitsui? He confessed to killing his wife. Case closed."

"So everybody keeps saying."

"Tora, the man confessed."

"I know, but I think he was covering for Hiroshi. A father's love for his son."

Maeda sighed. "Not without more proof. Come on, we've got to start questioning people again."

He selected three constables and sent them to the market to ask about Yoko's shopping on the night she disappeared and about who had made the deliveries to her house during the past weeks. Then he and Tora set out for her home, accompanied by two more constables who started knocking on neighbors' doors again.

Maeda and Tora went to see Yoko's husband again.

Kuroki was a blubbering bundle of self-pity. His face was wet with tears, and so were the rumpled sleeves of his robe. He was barefoot and his sparse hair hung in loose strands to his shoulders. "What have you done?" he cried when he saw Maeda and Tora. "Have you found him? Is he in jail? My lovely Yoko! Oh, that I had to see her like that! What shall I do? I'm lost, quite lost without her."

"No, Mr. Kuroki," said Maeda, "we haven't arrested anyone. We need your help to do so."

"My help? You know who did it then?"

"Not yet."

Kuroki burst into more wails. "This is terrible! The monster killed my wife a week ago, and he's free? Who knows, he may be waiting to shove his knife in my belly next. I want a guard at my door day and night."

Tora gazed at Kuroki's quivering stomach and wondered if even as long a knife as the one that killed his wife would penetrate such a gross layer of flesh and fat far enough to strike at vital organs.

Maeda snapped, "Impossible. Pull yourself together. We have some questions. I want to know which merchants your wife patronized, and whether she ever spent a night away from home."

Kuroki stared at him resentfully. "Of course she didn't spend the night anywhere but here. What are you suggesting?"

Maeda wisely did not answer that. "Where did she do most of her shopping?"

"No idea. That's woman's work. I have my own duties to worry about. A clerk's life isn't easy, you know. I come home exhausted."

He was no help. Tora knew Maeda had already checked with the bathhouse and confirmed the man's earlier account, but he went over the details again. After dark, sometime between the hour of the boar and the hour of the dragon when her husband finally awoke to another day, Yoko had disappeared. This time span included her visit to the market, but since Kuroki had no idea when she had returned to their house, they could not narrow down the early hours, and because Kuroki had not checked on his wife after his return from the bathhouse, they could not be sure what had happened later.

The likeliest scenario was one where her killer caught up with her after she returned from the market but before Kuroki had come home from his massage and *moxa* treatment.

They left Kuroki not much wiser. Maeda's constables returned from knocking at the neighbors' doors and reported that one woman had seen Kuroki and his wife leaving their house together and walking off in opposite directions. The time matched what Kuroki had given for their departure. No one had seen either return or anyone else enter the Kuroki house, probably because by then they had been at their evening rice or asleep.

Tora said, "Let's go question Hiroshi."

Maeda sighed. "Very well."

Hiroshi was not home. His slattern of a wife was cooking something. Some of the smaller children played with vegetable peels on the floor. "What's the bastard done now?" she asked.

Maeda said, "We're just double-checking on the murder of Mrs. Mitsui."

Tora added, "And the disappearance of your neighbor across the street."

She laughed. "That slut? If Hiroshi had ever tried to get anywhere with that one, I'd have killed them both." She swung the knife and sent more scraps flying. The children squealed.

Maeda shuddered. "If you don't mind, we'll have a look out back."

"What for?" she demanded.

"My friend here thinks he's buried the murder weapon." Maeda chuckled..

The woman glared at Tora. "That's just more harassment. The police said he killed the old woman, and that was a lie. Now you're trying to pin something else on him." Tora fled. She shouted after him, "I hope you bastards go to hell."

The big cedar grew just outside the fence between the yard and the back alley. It was easy to see how Kichiro could have surprised Hiroshi digging in that corner.

"There," Tora said with satisfaction, pointing to a patch of disturbed soil. "You can see where he's been digging." He looked around, found the spade among some other tools, and started working.

After considerable exertion on his part, it became obvious that there was nothing to be found. Tora cursed and refilled the large hole.

Maeda wisely only said, "I've got to get back."

At police headquarters, a surprise awaited them. In the front room sat three young market porters, looking extremely nervous. Mrs. Kimura had described their appearance well. One of the constables announced proudly, "These are the porters who made deliveries to the Kuroki house. We have been to every food merchant in the market."

The three youngsters squirmed. The tallest said, "I've done nothing. What do you want from me? I'll lose my job. My master will think I'm a thief or something."

The other two added their own protestations.

Maeda heard them out, then said, "If you've done nothing but your job, you can leave after we've had a talk. And you can tell your employers you were helping the police. Let's go to my office."

They herded the three into Maeda's new office, where they knelt and waited. Tora judged them to be between sixteen and twenty years old. One was quite handsome, and all three were well-built and as muscular as market porters should be. Yoko had had an eye for young men. It would have amused Tora, if he hadn't seen her corpse that very morning.

"Very well," Maeda started after he'd sat down and directed a scribe to take notes. "Give me your names, ages, where you live, and where you work."

They complied.

"You made regular food deliveries for the Kurokis?"

They nodded, eyeing each other.

"Who made a delivery of honey, ginger, bean paste, and candied chestnuts about a week ago?" He consulted his notes. "It would have been the nineteenth day of the month in the evening."

They looked blank and shook their heads in unison.

The constable cleared his throat. "The purchase was made at the Miyagi shop."

One youth said quickly, "I was sick that day."

Tora was leaning against the wall. "It wasn't much," he said. "I think she carried it home herself."

Maeda frowned at the three youths. "We know for a fact that all of you did more than deliver purchases. Were you paid for this other work?"

All three turned beet red and averted their eyes. "Well?"

The tall youth raised his chin. "Why would she pay for a little sex? Maybe she thanked me for the delivery." He glanced at the other two. "I didn't know about them," he added.

The mood in the office had changed subtly. The three had become rivals and glared at each other.

Maeda asked, "And the same true is true for all of you? You all made deliveries and stayed for sex, invited or uninvited, as the case may be?"

They nodded. The handsome one offered an explanation. "She shops at my place regularly. She said she liked me and I liked her. She's still pretty young and looks good, and her husband's old and can't get it up. She was willing."

Tora suppressed a snort.

"Did she tell all of you about her husband's problem?" Maeda asked.

They nodded. The tall one said, "Is she in trouble? Did he find out?"

"I don't know if he found out. She's dead. Murdered."

They gasped and went pale. The handsome youth cried, "Did the fat slug kill her?"

"We don't know yet who killed her, but I think you three had better tell us what you were doing that night."

They stared at each other, perhaps weighing the likelihood that one of the others was a killer. Then they burst into explanations.

Maeda listened patiently and asked for details. It turned out they could not have been at Kuroki's house the night of Yoko's disappearance. He let them go with a warning. "We'll check it out. If you lied, it will go hard with you."

17

A Missing Governor

A sudden spell of warm weather caused Akitada's little tree to burst into blossoms. It cheered him until another summons from Dazaifu arrived.

At least it was not raining this time. He rode under a cloudless blue sky. The sun seemed mercilessly hot, and there was no breeze at all. The road had turned to dust, and passing horses and carts raised clouds of fine dirt that clogged his nostrils and covered his clothes. The weather had turned hot, and by the time he had completed the journey, he did not feel much better than last time. His clothes stuck to his body again, and sweat trickled down between his shoulder blades.

Otherwise, the atmosphere in the vice governor general's office had improved. Akitada was admitted quickly, and Korenori rose and greeted him pleasantly before leading him to his study.

There, however, it became clear that a serious matter had arisen.

"Please be seated," Korenori said. "We have a problem."

Akitada sat and waited, expecting nothing good.

"Your predecessor has disappeared."

"I believe you've already notified me of this, sir."

"Yes, but now I have instructions from the chancellor himself." He held up a rolled document with impressive seals and scarlet ribbons. "They came by a fast ship and express messenger. He has commanded that we make an immediate search for Lord Tachibana. It seems he never reached the capital."

Akitada nodded. He had expected this but did not see how it affected him. Or the vice governor general, for that matter. "But why search here?" he asked.

"They think he never left Kyushu."

"Oh." Akitada absorbed this startling information. It seemed very unlikely. "What makes them think so? I was told he took ship in Hakata."

"Ahem. Yes, but there is no evidence he actually did so."

"Ah."

It meant nobody had bothered to verify a dubious rumor about Tachibana's having chosen to go by a separate ship. In fact, it had seemed to Akitada all along that there had been no very good explanation for this last minute change of plans. But his next thought made him sit up. Unless one assumed Tachibana was hiding out somewhere, it meant he had been abducted and possibly murdered.

Most likely in Hakata.

In Akitada's own province.

And this made it his business.

His curiosity was aroused. Here was a mystery for him to solve, a case of sufficient magnitude, given Tachibana's rank and status, to challenge his best investigative skills.

"I take it you want me to check into this, sir." he said.

Korenori gave him an irritated look. "Naturally. What else would I call you for?"

Akitada did not remind him he had last summoned Akitada for meddling in Okata's investigations. He nodded. "May I ask for your support?"

Korenori' eyebrows shot up. "Naturally you have that."

"I need to know about Lord Tachibana's stay here in Kyushu. And I shall need to see all the documents your office has for his administration."

Korenori bristled for a moment, then gave in. "Very well. What do you want to know?"

"Perhaps we might start with your impression of his personality."

The vice governor general thought for a moment. "Well, I didn't care for him, but he was very efficient. A good administrator. His final reports were perfect, as I told you before. I don't know much about his private life. He did not bring his family." Korenori frowned for a moment. "That's not unusual, by the way. You yourself decided against it. Tachibana was known to be an expert on Chinese art and seems to have collected it quite passionately. I expect he took it all with him?"

Akitada grimaced. "Every last item, unless thieves got what he left."

"No, I think he took it." Korenori shook his head. "I think he was a little obsessive. Talked about Chinese culture constantly, and invited me to his place just so he could show off his treasures. This was probably the most striking thing about him. If you ask me, he was a bore, though rumor had it that he visited a local woman. Not unexpected for officials without their families." He winked at Akitada.

Akitada flushed. "Did he socialize with the local Chinese?"

"I wouldn't know. If you mean, did he invite them to his house, I doubt it. It's not at all encouraged, you know. But I expect he knew the merchants dealing in imported art quite well."

"Was there anything besides the art purchases and the occasional prostitute which might have put him in a financial bind? Was he a gambler, for example?"

"No, not to my knowledge. And as I told you, his accounts were in order."

"Yes. I would like to see those now, and anything else of sufficient significance to have been recorded."

Korenori clapped his hands. The door opened and a clerk peered in. "Gather all the paperwork for Chikuzen province and anything else pertaining to Lord

Tachibana's administration," he said. The clerk withdrew.

"Is this all you require?" Korenori asked.

"Yes. Thank you, sir. If you recall anything else, perhaps you'll let me know?"

"I will. Good luck, Sugawara. The court expects an answer right away." The vice governor general rose. "You may use this room to look at the documents. I'll leave you to it."

Akitada spent the next four hours sifting through the paperwork he had wished to see when he had first arrived. Apart from sending in a servant with hot tea and some rice cakes, Korenori left him in peace.

He finally closed the last document box and stared into space. He was convinced Tachibana had enriched himself from government funds in multiple ways but no more so than most governors. Court nobles tended to consider a provincial assignment a miserable life away from friends and stimulating activities, but they sought out such assignments precisely because they offered a way of rewarding themselves and their families for the sacrifice. This was clearly understood in government circles, and no reprimand would attach to his predecessor for milking the provincial treasury and the rice taxes dry.

He got up and stretched his stiff back. For some time now he had been feeling that Tachibana Moroe was dead and, like the chancellor, he thought it had happened in Kyushu, more precisely in his own province.

He went out into the main office. Korenori was dictating a letter to a young clerk. He looked up and stopped.

"All done, Sugawara?"

"Yes, sir. Thank you. I'll head back now and see what I can find out in Hakata."

The other man nodded. "I take it you found all the paperwork correct?"

"Yes. The answer must lie elsewhere."

"Good. Please find the man. It is extremely urgent."

Akitada bowed. "I'll do my very best, sir."

He rode homeward almost unaware of the blazing sky as he tried to understand what had happened. Tachibana's eccentric preoccupation with Chinese art did not suggest anything, but he promised himself a visit to Feng as soon as possible. Perhaps even more interesting was the casual comment by the vice governor general that Tachibana had visited a local prostitute. Such women were often the recipients of secrets their enamored customers poured into their ears.

The image of Fragrant Orchid passed across his memory. To his own shame, he had allowed the woman to distract him at the banquet. If he had weakened enough to accept her invitation, he might well have become seriously compromised.

Then, like a blinding flash, a thought struck him, and he reined in his galloping horse. He had asked her about Tachibana, and she had admitted she had known the governor. More than likely, she had been one of his lovers. He had been the highest-ranking official in the province and would have been acquainted with its most beautiful courtesan. No doubt, they had been introduced early, as had happened to Akitada himself. The note she had sent by the little girl took on a new meaning. She had asked him to come because she had something to tell him.

And he had torn up the note.

He spurred his horse again. In his vanity, he had assumed the note was an invitation to her bed when all she had done was to let him know she had information about the ex-governor.

As soon as he reached the Chikuzen tribunal, he sent for Tora and Saburo. In his private study, he told them about his meeting with the vice governor general.

"I'd be glad to see this Fragrant Orchid for you," offered Tora. Saburo cast up his eyes.

Akitada said, "Thank you, Tora, but considering that the lady invited *me*, I'd better be the one to pay her a visit. You can find out for me where she lives."

"Gladly." Tora knew his way around willow quarters and looked forward to the excursion.

"Then we will check on shipping departures between the fourteenth and sixteenth days of the second month. I'm interested in any ships carrying passengers bound for the east. Tachibana may have had a secret reason for changing his travel plans. He may have taken passage incognito to an unknown destination. Or he may never have left."

Saburo frowned. "It's all rather vague, sir."

"I know. I'll see Fragrant Orchid as soon as possible. We may know a lot more then."

They exchanged glances and looked at him gravely.

Akitada said defensively, "She has information about Governor Tachibana. I have no idea what kind, but since he seems to have had—er—dealings with her, I need to speak to her."

With a grin, Tora offered again, "I could talk to her for you, sir. It might cause gossip for you to visit her."

Akitada snapped, "Just for once, keep your lewd thoughts to yourself."

They left in accusatory silence.

Akitada paced the small room. He was furious. This was what came of such cursed familiarity with servants and retainers. They took an unacceptable interest in one's private affairs and dared to voice criticism. Tora's level of familiarity had always been a thorn in his side, and now he was even infecting Saburo with it.

But Akitada's conscience was by no means good. He *had* been tempted by the beautiful woman. He *had* wanted to see her again. He *had* thought with desire of her during the lonely nights away from home.

He bit his lip and stopped pacing.

18

Fragrant Orchid

aeda was in the chief's office when Tora
arrived. He looked very much at home in
the place previously occupied by Okata.

Tora looked around and admired the neatness with
which Maeda had arranged document boxes, writing
utensils, loose paper, and assorted weapons. Hanging
from one wall were swords, clubs, chains, knives, arrows, daggers, axes, truncheons, and ropes. On shelves
rested jars and vials and paper twists. Each item had a
small wooden tag attached. Document boxes, paper,
and ink and brushes rested on his desk, lined up perfectly with the corners.

"What's all this?" Tora asked, nodding at the ar-
mory and peering at some of the tags. They bore names
and dates.

"Murder weapons," said Maeda with a grin.

"Your cases?"

"No. Things aren't that bad here in Hakata. I found them in a shed and thought they should play a more prominent role. People like to see them. What do you think?"

"Very impressive! Pity we never found the knife Mitsui used on his wife." Tora paused. "Some day when I have more time, I'll ask you about some of those. Today I'm on an errand for my master. He wants to know where a courtesan called Fragrant Orchid lives."

Maeda's jaw sagged open. "F-fragrant Orchid? He wants to know about Fragrant Orchid?"

"Don't look so shocked. It's not what you think. The beauty has some information about the last governor. The master is looking into problems concerning his administration."

Maeda still gaped, shaking his head. "I don't believe it," he muttered.

"What do you mean?"

"The lady is dead."

"Dead? You don't mean she's been murdered?"

Maeda uttered a humorless laugh. "No. Not that. She killed herself."

Tora digested this. "When and how?" he asked.

"Nearly three weeks ago. She took poison."

Tora shook his head, baffled. "That's strange," he mused. "It must have been right after the mayor's banquet."

"Unlike you, I wasn't invited. When was the banquet?"

"I wasn't invited either. The master went. That's why he's asking about her. It was the day after you and I talked to Yoko."

Maeda reflected and nodded. "Yes. That sounds right."

Tora asked, "How sure are you it was suicide?"

Maeda said unhappily, "It can't be anything else. There was a letter she left, and the poison was hers. Some of the other women said she'd had a disappointment recently, a love affair . . . or whatever. Maybe the rich man she'd had her eye on decided against marriage. It certainly looked like suicide." He paused. "But you're going to investigate anyway, right?"

Tora sighed and got to his feet. "Where did she kill herself?"

"She shared a house with a young girl she was training. Here, let me draw you a map." Maeda rubbed some ink and dipped his brush in it. He drew lines for streets and a river, marking the spot with a miniature house.

Tora took the drawing. "Didn't know you're an artist, too."

"Let me know what you find out. I'd hate to look like an incompetent fool so early in my new job."

Tora took the news of Fragrant Orchid's suicide straight back to the tribunal. An hour later Akitada arrived at Fragrant Orchid's house accompanied by Lieutenant Maeda, Tora, Saburo, and a scribe belonging to the police headquarters. Two constables walked ahead.

The courtesan had lived in a quiet residential part of the city not far from the center of town. Her house was small and hidden in the back of a lovely garden. Cherry trees bloomed and birds sang. A small fountain splashed water from a bamboo pipe into a basin and thence into a narrow pebbled stream which lost itself among the shrubbery. The air was cool and scented and birds sang in the trees, but the house lay in a deep silence.

One of the constables shouted, "Ho! Open up! Police."

Akitada grimaced. Onlookers were already gathering in the street outside, trying to get a look, but Lieutenant Maeda seemed untroubled. When nothing happened, Maeda tried the door. It opened easily, and they entered single-file, walking along a flagged corridor to a set of folding doors with carvings of orchids on them. Maeda opened these also. Beyond lay a raised room open to a broad veranda and the back garden.

The space was not large but extremely luxurious. It had clearly belonged to a woman of exquisite taste. The reed shades over the doors to the garden were trimmed in green brocade. Silk cushions in deep purples and reds, some with gold embroidery, lay about. Painted screens and rare speckled bamboo book racks stood against the walls, as did red and black lacquered trunks. Lacquered food trays, porcelain dishes, carved braziers, and elegant paper lanterns proved that Fragrant Orchid had entertained lavishly.

Akitada noted the finely painted screens, several musical instruments, and books, and immediately pictured her in their midst. Here, in this enchanting world, Fragrant Orchid had received her lovers, those lucky men whom she had found attractive enough or who had possessed enough wealth to tempt her.

Akitada might have come here himself, and then perhaps she would not have died. He had no proof this was so, only the nagging feeling he was responsible somehow because he had ignored her invitation.

Maeda walked into the middle of the room and pointed at the floor. "We found her here," he said. "She collapsed after vomiting. You can still see the stains." He turned and pointed to a wall. "Over there on the little tray we found a used cup and her folded letter."

Brought back to the ugly reality of such a death, Akitada asked, "Did your coroner identify the poison?"

"Yes. It was *hishima.* Common enough among prostitutes who use it in their cosmetics and in larger doses to cause abortions." Maeda made a face.

"But in this case the dose was very large?"

"Yes. According to Doctor Fujita, it would have killed a horse. Unpleasantly. Violent vomiting and convulsions."

"What about the letter? Do you still have it?"

Maeda pulled a folded paper from his coat. "I thought you might want to see it, sir."

Akitada recognized the tiny flecks of gold and the stiff handwriting. His heart contracted at the memory of her beautiful face. The letter was in the form of a poem:

"Unmindful that ships must wait for high tide, I parted from you too soon . . . oh, for a vermilion boat and a pair of jeweled oars so that I might row across to meet you on the other side."

The words were beautiful and sad. They spoke of lovers parting in this world and of the hope of meeting after death. Not surprisingly, Maeda and others had taken it for proof that Fragrant Orchid had ended her life because she had lost the man she loved. Akitada thought of Governor Tachibana. Was he the man who had broken her heart? Tachibana had planned to leave Kyushu, and he had been a womanizer; it made sense that his affair with the most beautiful woman in Hakata should have been a passionate one. If he had been murdered, had she known something of his death? Was that what she had been about to tell him?

He decided against the broken heart. The woman he had conversed with had not been grieving over the death of a man she loved. In fact, he did not believe for a moment that she had committed suicide.

"Where did you find this?" he asked.

Maeda pointed to a writing box. "It was inside. On top."

"Allow me to keep this a while, Lieutenant," he said to Maeda. "Something about this note puzzles me."

Before Maeda could answer, they heard running footsteps in the garden and turned.

"Go away!" The little girl who had given him the note from Fragrant Orchid rushed down a path and into the room. Her eyes were filled with tears and her pretty face flushed. Behind her huffed an older woman in the clothes of a servant. When she saw them, she stopped timidly on the garden path.

Not so the little one. She dashed up the steps into the room.

"Go away!" she cried again, her small fists clenched as she stamped her foot. "This is *her* house. You mustn't be here. It's wrong to touch her things and stare at them." She burst into loud sobs.

Tora went to her. "Sorry, little one," he said soothingly, bending down and putting an arm around her shoulders. "We've come to make sure the poor dead lady is not forgotten. Who are you?"

She stared at him, sniffling and sobbing, and mumbled, "Umeko. I live here."

Akitada said, "I think she is Fragrant Orchid's protégée. I met her after the banquet."

The girl turned her head to look at him and nodded. "Why didn't you come?" she asked accusingly.

"I'm very sorry."

"She was so worried. She kept saying, 'I hope he comes.'"

Tora straightened up and looked at Akitada. For once, he was not grinning.

Akitada took it hard. Here was the proof. She had indeed wanted to tell him something, something she knew to be dangerous. She had hoped she would be safe by telling him about it. Instead, the risk she had taken at the banquet had brought a killer to her house.

Umeko still looked at him with eyes swimming in tears. He said softly, "I'm so sorry. I didn't know it was important." With unforgivable conceit he had thought

Fragrant Orchid had been flirting with him, had thought him a desirable lover.

Umeko nodded with a small sob. She dabbed at her eyes with a sleeve of the gorgeous small gown she wore.

"You must have loved her," Akitada said, feeling inadequate.

She nodded again.

"We'll find out what she was afraid of," Maeda promised. "With your help. Were you here the day she died?"

A head shake.

"So you don't know if anyone visited her?"

Another shake. "She sent me and Keiko to the dance master when the man came."

"Keiko is her maid?"

She nodded and pointed to the woman outside.

Maeda called, "Come up here, Keiko."

The woman approached and knelt. She had a plain face. Her hair was partially gray and twisted into a knot on her neck.

Maeda said, "So your mistress sent you and the little girl away because she was entertaining a customer that day?"

Keiko giggled. "Not a customer. No more customers after the governor."

"Then who came that day?"

"Nobody. "

"So you weren't here when Fragrant Orchid took the poison?"

"No, Lieutenant." She made him a bow and stared at Akitada and his companions.

"This is his Excellency, the governor, and the two men with him are his officers. You mustn't be afraid. We're trying to find out why your mistress killed herself. Was she sad?"

The maid shook her head. "She was in a temper. She got in a temper when his honor Tachibana left."

"A temper?" Akitada raised his brows. "I because the governor left?"

The maid nodded. "She liked him. My lady did not have many men come into her bed."

Akitada's glance went to Umeko. It was an improper conversation in front of a child her age, but Umeko was a courtesan in training. No doubt she was wise beyond her years in the ways of men and women together.

Maeda must have thought the same, because he began to question the maid Keiko about Fragrant Orchid's suitors. He asked about her affair with the ex-governor, and the men before and since. There were few names. Keiko explained that Fragrant Orchid's rank among the courtesans meant she could pick and choose who she slept with. She chose rarely, but whoever it was paid well.

Akitada did not recognize any of the names. Maeda did, however. Two of the men were local nobles, while two others served in high-ranking positions at Dazaifu. None had visited since her affair with Governor Tachibana. Fragrant Orchid had apparently been celibate since.

Maeda and his men searched Fragrant Orchid's house without finding anything helpful. Akitada trailed along. Only the main room and the garden could be called luxurious. The other rooms, and there were few, were at best utilitarian. Fragrant Orchid had spent her money where it would do most good. It also explained why she had kept no servants except the maid and Umeko.

Keiko was a country woman and not particularly quick-witted. Umeko had to translate some of Akitada's and Maeda's questions. The maid had no idea why they were being asked, nor was she very upset by her mistress's death.

"What will happen to you and Umeko now?" Akitada asked, feeling vaguely responsible for them.

The maid chuckled. "We go away. To another lady."

In the end, they left with more questions than answers.

Outside, Maeda said to Akitada. "I think you suspect she was murdered, sir, and perhaps it is so, but would you explain to me what makes you think so?"

Akitada considered how much he should tell Maeda. He thought it best not to publicize the disappearance and probable murder of Lord Tachibana yet, but in the end, he decided to trust the man. He could not manage this search on his own. He said, "After the mayor's banquet, Fragrant Orchid sent me a note because she had something to tell me. I ignored it, thinking it merely a device to increase business."

Maeda blinked but he kept a straight face. "Fragrant Orchid had no need of new business," he said. "She was quite a wealthy woman. You think she knew she was in danger?"

"Yes, but I didn't know that. There's another matter. Lord Tachibana never arrived back in the capital."

Maeda's eyebrows shot up. "Great gods!" he muttered. "Don't tell me. More trouble, and this time it's big."

Akitada nodded. "Since Fragrant Orchid had been the ex-governor's lover, and since Umeko said her mistress was very worried, I thought perhaps her death was convenient for someone."

Maeda said nothing for a moment. Then he nodded. "If something has happened to Lord Tachibana, the people responsible would do anything to protect themselves. Now and in the future. They will be dangerous. If Fragrant Orchid was murdered, this proves it."

Akitada looked at him uncertainly.

Maeda flushed and added quickly, "I'm not sure how to proceed. I don't know who is involved in this." He paused and added, "I'm afraid nothing is as it seems in Hakata."

Akitada weighed the policeman's words. "Yes. I suspect you are right. We must find out who this silent killer is, and how he operates. We can guess what made him kill Fragrant Orchid, but why did they attack Lord Tachibana, if that's what happened? It's a very serious crime to lay hands on a government official of his rank." He frowned. "Do you always have so many murders here?"

Maeda looked puzzled. "So many murders?"

"Tora kept me informed about the Mitsui case and the neighbor woman's murder. He seems to think the man Hiroshi killed her *and* his step mother. Fragrant Orchid died around the same time."

"We know who killed Mrs. Mitsui, but we'll take another look at Hiroshi if you insist." He sighed. "Do you believe they are all related, sir? That seems unlikely."

"I don't know, Lieutenant. I'm just trying to understand how much crime there is in this province. Or rather, in Hakata."

"Murders are somewhat rare here in the city, sir. But the harbor area is rough. There are many knife fights. We've had a few bodies wash up in the harbor or a sailor knifed in a drunken brawl. Still, I cannot believe . . ." He broke off and bit his lip.

"I wondered if my arrival has perhaps stirred up a nest of vipers."

Maeda flushed. "Surely not, your Excellency. It's probably just coincidence. There is no connection between the three women, and I don't see what a doll maker can possibly have to do with the tribunal."

Akitada sighed. "Well, investigate Fragrant Orchid's death as murder. I have a notion that she sent Umeko and the maid away on purpose because she was meeting her killer. Perhaps he had offered to buy her silence. Otherwise I doubt she would have admitted him. My people and I will look into the ex-governor's disappearance. Something is bound to turn up, and we may see the connection in time."

Akitada dismissed his escort and turned to Saburo. "I want you to return to the tribunal now. Tonight you'll grow your beard again and find out about the man with the missing fingers. I want to know what he does at the harbor. But be careful. Tora and I will call on Merchant Feng and then check ship departures with the harbor office. Report to me in the morning."

19

The Chinese Merchant

Akitada was convinced that the ex-governor was also dead and that Fragrant Orchid's murder proved this. Much as he blamed himself for the courtesan's death, it was clear she had played a dangerous game. What she had known had almost certainly cost that beautiful woman her life.

He wondered briefly if they had been overheard at the banquet. Certainly the mayor had been close enough, and possibly also Feng and Hayashi. But anyone in the room, anyone with a guilty conscience, could have suspected Fragrant Orchid might talk. Moreover, a spy might have been placed among the waiters, musicians, or the other women. There had been no need to overhear anything at all. Later, the girl Umeko had approached him with the note from her mistress, signaling an assignation. Fragrant Orchid had become a marked woman.

They must find the killer, or killers, or perhaps become the next victims.

After parting from Maeda and his men, he walked with Tora to Feng's store. There they were greeted by the same pale young salesman who had waited on Akitada before. He made them several very deep bows, but in spite of this show of respect, he was not pleased to see Akitada. In fact, he looked positively nervous.

Ignoring the man's fears, Akitada said, "I'm the governor and have come to speak to your master. He offered to show me some of his treasures."

The young man blinked. "He's not here, your Excellency. It's early. He usually arrives toward evening." He bowed again.

"Where is he at this hour?"

"A-at home, your Excellency. I think."

"And where is his home?"

Panic flashed across the pimply face. "I . . . he may not be there. P-perhaps if you were to return later? Or I could give him a message?"

Tora stepped forward. "Look here, you little weasel," he snapped, "answer his Excellency's question and be quick about it."

The young man stammered some directions, and they left.

Feng's home was built of plaster in the Chinese style and had a blue-tiled roof. It was a large compound with outbuildings, perhaps stables or more likely warehouses. The man clearly had money and standing in his community.

The gate was heavily carved with Chinese symbols for good luck and Feng's name. It opened readily enough to their knocking. A servant, wearing Chinese clothes, bowed them in politely. Akitada tried his Chinese, asking if his master were home. The man either did not speak the language or was mute. He shook his head but beckoned them on.

Puzzled, Akitada and Tora followed him toward a two-story house across a neat paved courtyard which was enclosed by one-story buildings on either side, giving the whole complex the look of some huge bird of prey with its wings extended, hovering to embrace and devour them. The black-lacquered double doors in the center of the main house opened like a maw.

The house was not raised above ground, like Japanese houses of the better class. Only a stone step led to the doors. The walls to either side and above had ornately carved grilles over the windows.

Ignoring the feeling of being swallowed alive, Akitada walked through the black doors with Tora at his heels. In the dark interior, corridors branched away, leading to dimly lit spaces trimmed with painted and gilded lacquer carvings. The air was heavy with some alien incense.

When the silent servant stopped and gestured, they entered a mid-sized room with one window set high in the wall. Its carved grille let in very little daylight. Several chairs made from some heavy, dark wood stood about, with small, long-legged lacquer tables next to them.

Akitada shook off his unease and went to sit down in a chair facing the door. Tora came to stand protectively behind him.

"This gives me the shivers, sir," he muttered. "Who would want to live in a place like a tomb?"

A door opened, and Merchant Feng came in on soft soles. He had a smile on his round, smooth face with its small mustache and chin beard and wore a black silk robe, slit at the sides, with pale green trousers underneath. The robe's sleeves were narrow and ended at his wrists, revealing fleshy hands and fingers with many rings on them. On his feet he wore embroidered slippers.

Akitada took all this in and raised his eyes to the man's face again. Feng's smile was fixed. It was unpleasant, even when accompanied by a most servile bow, and the exclamation, "A signal honor, my Lord! I'm deeply moved by your gracious visit to my undeserving home. Forgive me, if I'm completely overcome. I had hoped to have a suitable entertainment prepared when your lordship deigned to pay me a visit."

"Not at all, Feng." Akitada was brusque. "This isn't a social call. I have some questions to ask you and hope you'll be able to assist in a matter that's just come up."

Feng folded his body into another deep bow. "Certainly, your Excellency. If you are quite comfortable here, perhaps this poor room is as good as any?"

The strong scent of incense was giving Akitada a headache, but he said, "Of course. Sit down."

Feng bowed again and moved another chair up for Tora.

"I'll stand," growled Tora. Akitada knew from his tone that he did not care for Feng any more than he did.

Feng bowed again and sat down himself. "May I call for some refreshments? Wine? Tea? Sweets? Or something savory?"

Akitada waved this aside. "Nothing at all, thank you. It has been brought to our attention that my predecessor, Lord Tachibana, who left Hakata more than a month ago, never reached his home in the capital. Neither did he take ship as planned, it seems. We are forced to assume he is still here. Naturally, this raises concerns both here and with His Majesty's government in Heian-kyo."

Feng's eyes opened wide. "You don't say. How very troubling! Please continue."

"I am told you had a longstanding relationship with Lord Tachibana. Is this correct?"

"His Excellency honored my store with his business during the time he was here. It was, of course, a business relationship. I'm merely a humble shopkeeper."

"He was a good customer?"

"Yes. Lord Tachibana had a great admiration for the arts of my homeland. Let us say, our dealings were mutually rewarding."

"About how much gold did he spend on art while he was here?"

The directness of the question gave Feng pause. He had been very much in control of himself so far. Now he hesitated. "I would have to consult my accounts. Alas, I do not keep them here."

"Come, Feng, you must have a rough notion."

Feng spread his beringed fingers. "Forgive me, but your questioning suggests an investigation. Since you tell me Lord Tachibana has disappeared and therefore cannot speak for himself, I would like to be precise. I can consult my accounts and transmit my answer to your Excellency in writing."

The tone of the conversation had changed subtly. It was not unlike a first meeting between two armed warriors trying to gauge each other's weaknesses. Behind him, Tora shifted. Perhaps he, too, recognized the tension in the room.

Abruptly, Akitada rose. "It is regrettable that I cannot get the support of the local people," he said coldly, "but my duty is clear. I take it you have no information about Lord Tachibana's whereabouts?"

Feng was also up, bowing deeply. "None at all, Excellency. If his Excellency took a small detour to some pleasant island, I trust he turns up soon. His unaccountable disappearance throws suspicion on many."

Akitada stared at him. The man was very clever. "Send me a list of Lord Tachibana's purchases from you or through you, dated and with the descriptions of the items and the payments." He turned and walked out, followed by Tora.

As they crossed the forecourt to the gate, Tora muttered, "We're being watched. I can feel it."

"Of course, we're being watched," Akitada said irritably. "Word has spread the governor has called on their master."

"And without an escort. You really shouldn't take such chances, sir. Especially when the last governor has disappeared.

Akitada did not comment. Tora was right, and he had a family to consider. But he detested traveling with pomp and circumstance, having his every move observed and being stared at by crowds of people.

"And that reminds me," Tora said. "Mrs. Kimura saw just such a man as Feng with Governor Tachibana. It may have been the day he disappeared."

"How sure is she?"

"Well, it was getting dark."

Akitada humphed. He had little faith in the memory of old ladies.

"What next?" Tora asked as soon as they were on the city street again.

"The harbor office. I want to see their records."

Their arrival and demands caused consternation among the clerks and scribes busy among their ledgers and documents. Their supervisor, an official appointed by Lord Tachibana, turned out to be stubborn. He had never laid eyes on Akitada, doubted his assertion he was the rightful governor of Chikuzen, ignored Tora's angry threats, and withdrew to his office, leaving them standing among the rest of the staff and assorted merchants and ship owners or their representatives.

Tora was for calling Maeda and his constables, but Akitada shook his head. "Time enough for other methods later. It may make the supervisor more cooperative if he fears repercussions."

He turned to one of the clerks and asked, "Would you be willing to explain the workings of this office to me? I've seen the reports sent to the provincial tribunal as well as those in Dazaifu, but I'm wondering if you keep track of arrivals and departures for any of the boats traveling the Inland Sea."

The clerk cast several glances over his shoulder toward the back, perhaps hoping his superior might reappear and relieve him of making a decision. Akitada's mention of having seen harbor office reports made him uneasy. In the end, the possibility that this stranger with his glowering attendant might indeed be the new governor won out.

"Yes, sir, er, your Honor. We do keep track of who comes and goes by listing the owners or captains of the boats and their home port."

Akitada gave him an encouraging nod. "Excellent! Could you check to see what ships departed the same day as the former governor's ship. It would have been the middle of the second month."

After a slight hesitation, the clerk left. Akitada turned to study the people and their dealings with various clerks and scribes. They had lost interest in him. Evidently whatever business had brought them here was foremost in their minds.

One man was the exception. He had apparently come in after them and now lounged against the wall next to the door. Akitada had the impression he had been watching them and turned his head away only a moment before Akitada looked at him. Turning back, Akitada said to Tora, "The man by the door. See where he goes when he leaves."

The clerk returned with a fat ledger. This he opened and held toward Akitada. "The fourteenth day of the second month, sir. As you can see, there were four ships leaving Hakata harbor. His Excellency's ship was the Phoenix. Its captain is called Ueda."

Akitada peered at the ledger and saw one of the ships was indeed the Phoenix. "How do you know this was the ship?" he asked astonished.

"I served His Excellency's captain myself. I know him. He was very angry when he got the message to go on without his Excellency and came here to ask what he should do."

"You're a remarkable man," Akitada told the clerk with a smile. "By any chance, do you also know who brought him the message?"

"No, sir." The clerk closed his ledger. "The captain said it was one of the governor's own men. Still, he thought it strange and waited for his Excellency until the last moment before the tide turned."

"I see. Thank you. Your memory does you credit."

Akitada studied the ledger again and asked about other boats Lord Tachibana might have taken passage on. There were only two, and both had since returned and left again. Apparently neither captain had mentioned giving passage to the ex-governor. And that was unlikely.

When Akitada turned to leave the harbor office, he saw Tora was gone. So was the man who had stood beside the door. Outside, it was turning dark. Suddenly a strong feeling of danger seized him. It was not altogether irrational. For all they knew there might be more than just one man watching them. If the last governor had met with a violent end, he could well be next. The faces of his family flashed before his eyes. He had no right to take such risks. He had come to Hakata without armed men, and now he had sent Tora after someone who had probably been watching them. He wished he had at least worn his sword, regardless of propriety.

For a moment, he debated what to do next, then he walked away from the harbor office as quickly as he could without attracting more curiosity. He reached police headquarters safely, though out of breath and ashamed of his panic.

There he left a message for Tora to return to the tribunal, swung himself on his horse, and left Hakata.

20

The Carter

When Tora had not returned by nightfall, Akitada was concerned but not overly so. He mentioned the watcher in the harbor office to Saburo, who stopped by before leaving on his own assignment.

Saburo listened and said, "Tora knows how to handle himself. He may have decided to have another look at the willow quarter to ask questions about Fragrant Orchid." He smirked. "He was really interested in her."

Given Tora's past among the flowers of the floating world, it was likely, so Akitada nodded, dismissed Saburo, and went to bed.

This time Saburo had taken pains with his preparations. Not only was his homemade beard in place, but he had opted for his patched and stained black clothes with the clever pouches for assorted weapons and tools. The brown jacket he wore over it to hide its peculiarities was new. He had lost its predecessor in the capital, but a seamstress he knew had constructed a new one to his specifications. It was also brown, since he had a fondness for that color. The previous jacket with its full sleeves and loose fit had to be taken off before making a climb to a roof and into someone's house. This was how Saburo had lost it.

The new jacket was an invention of his and did not have this disadvantage. It had two sides. The outer brown side was fuller than the inner black one. All he had to do was to turn the jacket inside out, and it became black as the night and fitted snugly enough not to snag on things when climbing.

He looked like a poor working man as he made his way on foot into Hakata. It was a nuisance to have to walk so far before reaching his objective, but like his master and Tora, he needed the exercise to get in shape. Tired and footsore by the time he reached Hakata harbor, he surveyed the craft tied up at the docks. The ship where he had first seen Fingers was gone.

He next turned down the street to the wine shop where Fingers had met with his cohorts before following the children. He hoped it was their regular meeting place. It was unlikely they would recognize him. Bearded men were common here, and last time he had worn his good clothes and a hat. Now he looked like the regular customers.

The Dragon's Lair was crowded, and the smells of smoke, oil, and sour wine were thicker than last time. Saburo stopped at the door and scanned the room. His quarry was not here, but to his surprise he saw the pimply-faced salesclerk from Feng's shop. He wore old clothes, and Saburo might not have noticed him if he had not raised his head to look toward the door. He gave no sign of recognition, however, and lowered his head again. He sat alone in a corner near a torch light, reading a book of some sort and sipping from a cup of wine.

Saburo found a place as far away as possible from Feng's clerk while still within sight of him. The man had looked to see who had come in; this suggested he was waiting for someone.

A waitress appeared by Saburo's side. He ordered some cheap wine and relaxed. Like last time, the crowd consisted of rough laborers and sailors. Feng's clerk definitely did not belong. Saburo decided to have a closer look at the store later on.

Just before it became necessary to order another flask of the sour wine, another man entered and looked around. He was young, clean-shaven but dirty, and of the same laboring class as the rest of the Dragon's Lair's customers. When he saw Feng's clerk, he grinned and went to join him.

Well, he was not Fingers, but Saburo decided a meeting between the clerk and this laborer was still interesting.

The young man sat down uninvited. The clerk frowned at him, wrinkled his nose, and turned down the corners of his mouth. He asked a question, got another smile, and an emphatic nod. The young man leaned closer and spoke at some length. The clerk nodded and reached into his robe to pull out a small but weighty bag. This he pushed toward the young man, who snatched it up and peered inside. He looked very pleased, tucked the small bag inside his dirty shirt, and called for wine. The clerk, looking disgusted, rose and left the Dragon's Lair without another word to the laborer. He had done what he had come for and had clearly not enjoyed the errand.

Not long after, the young laborer paid for his wine, gulped it down quickly, and also left.

Saburo had been so engrossed in the meeting he had not noticed the waitress hovering by his side with another flask of wine.

"No, thanks," he growled, getting up. "Your rot gut has given me a belly ache."

Outside, the young man was just picking up the handles of a handcart. Without a backward glance, he trotted off down the street toward town. The cart made enough noise to drown out footsteps, and the effort of pulling it meant he could not easily turn his head to look behind him. Saburo followed. Possibly the man's errand had involved nothing illegal after all, but there had been the bag of money, large enough to suggest Feng's clerk had paid the man for more than a simple delivery.

The cart was nearly empty. As they passed a lighted doorway, Saburo saw it contained only some ragged blankets that had perhaps been used to protect an earlier cargo.

Gradually they left behind the gaudy lights and noise of the harbor dives and brothels and passed through streets with shops that were shuttered at this hour. It was quiet here and the wheels of the cart seemed very loud. Saburo kept in the shadow of buildings, but the carter did not pause to look behind him. Soon they were crossing the river and heading into a residential quarter. The man and his cart made for a rundown area. Some of the houses had been abandoned and were falling to ruin. Saburo guessed they were near the shrine where the children had kept their birds.

The cart came to an abrupt halt next to a broken wall. Saburo melted into the shadow of a large tree. For the first time, the carter seemed to become cautious. He looked all around and listened. When he was satisfied he was alone, he reached under the rags in his cart and pulled forth a bundle. With this under his arm, he climbed over the rubble of the broken wall and disappeared.

Saburo approached the opening but could see nothing. Hearing the receding footsteps of the man, he scaled some of the rubble to reach the top of the wall. In the dim moonlight, a deserted courtyard lay before him. All around were more ruins and remnants of buildings. It had either been a small temple or monastery once, or perhaps an official's house. No one had lived there for a long time.

The carter had not gone far. In the center of the courtyard stood a group of trees and under the trees seemed to be more rubble. Saburo could not see what the man was doing because the darkness was dense under the trees. He heard a strange scraping noise, a pause, and more scraping.

The carter emerged from the darkness, wiping his hands on his clothes, and strode back toward the street. He no longer had the bundle.

Saburo jumped down and hurried back under his tree just in time to see the carter emerge, look up and down the street, then take up the handles of his cart, and trot off.

There was no time to inspect the ruined courtyard, but Saburo thought he could easily come back later. He followed the cart to see where it would take him.

It took him to the quarter where the children now lived with the kind Mrs. Kimura. Saburo had visited and knew the quarter. His quarry pulled the cart down a dark alley. When Saburo reached the alley, he had disappeared into one of the houses, leaving the cart next to a fence.

Now what?

His suspect's proximity to the children made Saburo unhappy. While he was not Fingers or one of his cohorts, he might have some connection with them. After a moment's reflection, Saburo felt his way down the dark alley to the cart. It was too dark to see much. Houses and trees blocked whatever little moonlight there was. He felt around in the bed of the cart, but found nothing but stinking rags.

Leaving things as they were, he followed the alley to the street. There he walked to the next corner and looked down the line of houses backing onto the alley. And there, in the middle, was Mrs. Kimura's house. If he had counted correctly, the carter had gone into the house next door.

This was very worrisome, but as it was the middle of the night, and Mrs. Kimura's house was dark, Saburo turned back and retraced the route to the abandoned ruin.

There he made his way to the clump of trees and looked for the bundle the man had left. He did not see it, but while groping about, he caught his toe on a loose board and heard the same scraping noise the carter had made. Reaching down, he found the board was part of a wooden rectangle and heavy, since it was weighted down with rocks. He removed these and flung the board back, nearly tumbling head first into a black, stinking hole the board had covered.

He had found an old well, and the bundle must be down there along with rotting garbage. It was much too dark to investigate further. That had to wait for daylight. He replaced the cover and the rocks, and left.

Somewhere a watchman called out the hour. He had another two hours until dawn. By now he was very tired and his feet hurt quite badly, but his master had expressed an interest in Fingers, and Saburo had not found him yet. He made his way somewhat painfully toward Feng's store.

To his surprise, he saw a faint light behind one of the grilles covering the windows. It seemed to come from somewhere far in the back of the store. His spirits lifted. Having surveyed the lay-out on his recent visit, he guessed someone was in a backroom kept for storage or paperwork. He slipped around the building, took off his loose jacket and turned it inside out. Putting its black version back on, he smeared a handful of dirt over his face, then climbed the tall wall at the back of the premises and jumped softly down into a yard. This service area was filled with boxes and packing materials but otherwise empty. He studied the building. No light at all showed on this side. The back wall of the store had only one opening, a pair of wide doors. The tiled roofs clearly defeated even the cleverest burglar or spy.

With a sigh, he crept up to the door. It was heavy and well-made. The lock looked massive and well-oiled. What he was about to do was dangerous, but he had no other options. Saburo felt through the various pouches of his clever garments and extracted a small set of metal hooks and slides. With these, he began to work on the lock mechanism, cringing at every scrape and click. It was a mechanism foreign to him, so it took trial and error before he finally heard something move. Tucking his implements away, he used his fingertips to move the left panel of the door very slightly. To his relief, the person who had installed such a fine and complicated lock had also oiled the hinges on the door. The heavy panel moved softly and silently.

Saburo opened the door only a little and put his good eye to the crack. He saw an empty corridor and could hear faint voices. There was some light, but it came from under a closed door. He was about to risk opening his door a little more when the other one was flung wide, spilling light into the corridor as someone came from the room.

Saburo's instinct was to run, but something made him hesitate. The person who had stepped into the dark corridor also paused. His silhouette was outlined against the bright rectangle beyond. He was a man, heavyset, and dressed in the Chinese fashion. When he turned his head, Saburo saw he had a small chin beard.

Master Feng, himself.

Feng said to someone in the room, "You're getting greedy. Let's hope you haven't caused trouble. Don't forget what may happen then." Then he switched to Chinese, which Saburo did not understand.

It probably meant there were at least two other people inside. And Saburo's time was running out, because now Feng turned and came toward the backdoor.

There was no time to scale the wall, so Saburo dashed behind some of the boxes, and cowered there, saying a quick prayer.

Feng reached the door and found it open. He cursed in his own tongue and called out to the others. Two people joined him, one very tall and bulky, the other shorter and slender.

Fingers and the clerk.

An argument ensued. The clerk at some point protested, "It wasn't me. I came in through the front. Perhaps you didn't close it properly, Master."

Another curse and the sound of a slap. Then Feng started across the yard toward the small gate in the wall. The clerk, holding his cheek, ran to open the gate, bowed deeply, then closed it behind Feng, relocking it carefully.

He trudged back to the store, muttering, went inside, and slammed the backdoors. Saburo heard the lock click into place and grinned.

He had been lucky. Better not test that luck again tonight. He waited until all was still, then scaled the wall and went home.

21

The Trap

Tora took an unobtrusive glance at the man lounging against the door jamb. He wore a workman's rough clothes, and his hair was tied up in a colorful piece of cloth twisted into a rope. He was big, with coarse, scarred features and fists the size of sledge hammers.

A thug, Tora thought, and Chinese, so perhaps this was the man his master had encountered in Feng's store. He sidled across the room, pretending interest in a loud argument that had broken out between a man and one of the clerks, and risked another glance. The thug's attention was on Tora's master and his interest in a ledger the clerk was holding up for his perusal. Both of the thug's hands were in sight. None of his fingers was missing.

Nevertheless.

Tora turned and strolled toward the door as if he had become tired of the harbor office and was taking a look at the ships instead. The thug saw him coming and ducked out.

Well, this promised to be an interesting quarry after all. Tora intended to find out why he was watching them and who had told him to do so.

The man was big enough to be easily seen above the smaller people milling around. Besides, the colorful cloth twisted about his head waved like a flag. He walked with a lumbering gait, looking back only once.

Very odd. It was broad daylight, and the man knew he was being followed. Let him try to run. Tora felt quite confident he would catch him. The thug carried too much weight in those broad shoulders and chest.

They strolled into the Chinese quarter. Tora grew somewhat less confident: if he had to tackle the man, his fellow countrymen might take exception and jump to his rescue. But his quarry left the Chinese quarter behind and made for a warehouse district. Here he slowed down as if he were looking for a specific place. Tora decided it was time and speeded up.

The other man glanced over his shoulder again and ran through an open gate, Tora at his heels.

They were in a wide service yard of some sort. As Tora had known, the man was hardly fleet of foot. He made for one of the low buildings, but Tora snatched at the back of shirt, growling, "Hold it. I want a word."

The man tore himself free and shouted something in Chinese as he ducked into the building.

Tora rushed after him.

After the bright sunlight, the darkness inside blinded him, and he slid to a halt. At that moment, a heavy blow struck the back of his head and sent him falling forward. He passed out before he hit the floor.

Pain. And voices. Dizziness. Nausea.

A strange smell. Of dirt and something else.

Never mind. Let it go. Blessed darkness.

The voices returned and with them the pain and the nausea.

Maybe he was having a dream. A nightmare.

Serves the bastard right. He'll never interfere with me again.

More pain. A laugh.

This pain was fresh, sharp, and lasting. In his side. He wanted to scream but no sound came. Vomit rose to his mouth. He swallowed it down.

What's next?

The convict ship. They can lose him on the way, if you want.

I want. But I'll have a bit of fun first. Laughter.

Two people. The voices were familiar. Well, not quite. It nagged at him, but his head felt like a sponge, and his side burned with every breath.

A very bad dream!

Do what you want, but don't mark him up too badly. He's as good as dead.

Who was that?

Tora's eyes would not open. Had he become blind? Feet shuffled about on the floor. Clothes rustled. Then more pain. A leather strap. He screamed. Trying to twist away, he realized his arms were twisted behind his back, his wrists tied. Then he passed out.

When he came to next, he knew enough by now not to make a sound. Even breathing hurt. He lay still and slipped into semi-consciousness.

But this did not last. He pulled at his bonds. All it got him was new agony. He gasped and almost passed out again. They had kicked and beaten him. One of his ribs must be broken.

Watch out! He's coming around!

This time he knew the voice: Hiroshi!

A hand seized Tora's topknot and jerked his head up. He moaned and opened his eyes. He saw a fuzzy scene of a lit lantern and two shadowy figures.

"You'll be sorry for this, Hiroshi," he gasped.

A moment's silence, and then a vicious slap that rattled Tora's teeth and made his mouth bleed.

Hiroshi's face sneered down at him. "It's you is going to be sorry, dog official. You thought you were so smart. Had it all figured out. Coming to my house and telling the wife I'd killed Yoko."

"You didn't?" It hurt to speak.

Hiroshi laughs. "Of course I killed her. That bitch asked for it."

"How?" mumbled Tora.

"She was coming back from the market and saw me outside the house. She wanted to know what I'd been doing there the night my father's whore died. I went after her, pretending I was after sex."

"You also killed your mother?"

Hiroshi spat. "That Chinese bitch wasn't my mother. She deserved to die. She'd stolen my father's gold. I'd have overlooked it, but the greedy cunt wouldn't share."

"You're a killer, Hiroshi. You're going away for a long time."

Hiroshi burst out laughing. "*You're* going away forever, bastard." He made a fist and struck Tora's temple, and all went dark again.

When he woke next, he was alone and all was silent. He had no idea how much time had passed, but the pain was still with him, sharp and fresh. He lay very still and breathed slowly. He found he could open his eyes, but they saw only darkness, so he closed them again. Under his cheek was mud. The mud smelled of blood. His blood. It was so still he could hear his own breathing. Was he still bleeding? What had Hiroshi and the other one done to him? Had they left him to die?

If he did not move, the pain was bearable. He drifted off to sleep.

When he jerked awake again, the broken rib reminded him this was no dream. They had attacked him from behind, knocked him out, probably beaten him bloody, and tied him up. Later one of them had kicked him and broken a rib, and later again, Hiroshi had knocked him out with a fist to the temple.

He wanted him unconscious.

Correction: he wanted him dead, but first he wanted him unconscious.

But why?

And who was the other man?

Since he could do nothing else, he thought back. The watcher in the harbor office. He had followed the man, and then he had been ambushed.

The watcher was a stranger. Had he followed them a long time? Their visit to Fragrant Orchid's house had attracted a lot of attention.

Tora tried to remember the crowd, but he could not come up with an answer. His mind had been on the courtesan's death and later on the disappearance of the governor. It was not until the harbor office, that his master had noticed the watcher. And there, he had been pretty obvious, leaning beside the door and staring at them.

He had wanted to be seen.

It was a trick worth remembering. The colorful cloth tied around his head had been part of it, and so had his slow lumbering walk. Of course he had been easy to follow. He had made sure he was.

And like a fool Tora had fallen in the trap.

Self-reproach did not help.

He thought of the other voice again. Yes, it had sounded familiar. In an unpleasant way.

Tora concentrated, trying to play back the words in his mind.

He'll never interfere with me again!

He had it! It had been that bastard Okata. He had taken this revenge because Tora's reports had cost him his position. And Hiroshi had been eager to help. A pretty stupid thing to do. It would just make things worse for Okata. He had attacked an officer of the tribunal. It would not help Hiroshi either.

But dimly other words came back to Tora.

What's next? That had been Hiroshi.

And Okata's answer.

The convict ship.

Either way he's a dead man.

It was not good, but Tora did not immediately understand.

Either way he's a dead man.

Then the memory of Sado Island surfaced. His master had pretended to be a convict there and had almost died in the gold mine on that island.

But here?

And then it came to him: Tsushima. Another island with a mine. A silver mine. And yes, they sent their convicts there. Old Mitsui had hanged himself in his jail cell rather than face such a sentence.

Tora shuddered and bit his lip when pain stabbed at him again.

It had been easy for Okata. He had known all about convict ships, had connections who owed him favors, had made sure Tora would disappear without a trace.

He had no idea what time it was, but that did not matter. They would not miss him. Not today, if it was still that, or tonight, or the next day. He was on his own.

And there was nothing he could do. But he tried anyway. He twisted his wrists, gasping with the pain in his side. The effort did nothing but confirm that his ankles were also tied and somehow attached to the bonds around his wrists. Once, a long time ago, when he was younger and tougher and in better shape, he had been bound like this. He had managed to get to his knees and shuffle forward until he could break a jar and saw the rope apart against its sharp edge.

But such things do not repeat themselves. Besides, there was his broken rib. He could not move.

In the end, he rested from his efforts to loosen the rope and dozed off.

He came awake next when he heard the door slam.

It was still dark, but perhaps the darkness was not quite so dense as before, because he could see a darker shape bending over him.

"Help," he croaked and heard someone cursing.

A whispered exchange followed, then a pause.

He hoped against hope.

Next he was turned over roughly and shouted with pain. The light of a lantern blinded him, but he opened his mouth to plead again when a hand shoved some rough fibers into it and then tightened a stinking cloth over his nose and mouth. He could not breathe, jerked violently, and then passed out again.

Night and nightmares. Monsters and ghosts and devils with knives, slashing his body. Hell. He had died and gone to hell.

The constant darkness suggested being underground. Buried. Buried alive? Yes, he felt pain, so he must be alive.

So, not hell. If not, then where?

The floor beneath him smelled of tar and wood and the stench of human bodies and excrement. And it moved, sideways and up and down.

He was lying down, his cheek against wooden boards. His arms and legs were still tied, but more loosely. He could move them a little.

But he also heard something, the sound of water sloshing against the wood underneath him and all around.

And he knew.

He was on a boat, or more likely, a ship. And, as he knew well enough from his last involuntary sea voyage, there was no getting away now, even if he had not been in agonizing pain.

He was on his way to the silver mines of Tsushima.

22

The Hidden Bundle

After returning well past the middle of the night, Saburo slept late. The sun was high already and slanted into their room in the garrison of the tribunal. Saburo stretched and blinked at the lines of sun and shadow which revealed his surroundings.

He shared this large room with Tora, and while it lacked the comforts of home, it was more spacious than Saburo's corner of the Sugawara stables. All this place contained was their bedding, rolled up during the day and placed in a corner, where he saw Tora's now. Not surprisingly, his roommate was already up, though he did not hear the familiar sounds of his men being exercised outside.

He frowned and sat up. Their clothes hung from various hooks, as did two sets of armor. Saburo detested his and wore it only on parade occasions, but Tora was very fond of martial attire and had had his own armor adjusted by an armorer in Hakata. He frequently polished it after polishing his sword.

Saburo was no soldier, nor ever would be. He got up, yawned, and rolled up his bedding, placing it beside Tora's. Then he dressed in his ordinary blue robe and pants, tying the black sash around his waist, and turning his attention to his topknot. The beard he had removed the night before. It itched too much to let him sleep comfortably.

One of the servants had left a bucket of water outside the door. Saburo brought it in. Dipping a cup into it, he rinsed out his mouth, than spat the water out into the yard. Closing the door again, he washed and, peering in a small mirror, he reapplied Lady Sugawara's makeup to his scars. He hoped he could soon grow a beard and mustache. But not yet. Not while they were in the midst of an investigation into the disappearance of the last governor and none too certain that danger did not lie in wait for the present administration of the province.

Satisfied with his appearance, he tossed the dirty water outside and left the empty bucket for the servant. Then he made his way to his master's office to report on his night's adventures.

Lord Sugawara was already at work in the tribunal office, but when he saw Saburo, he said, "Come, I have some work for you in my study," and got up.

On the way there, he asked, "Have you seen Tora?"

This surprised Saburo. "No, sir. He was already up when I woke." He paused. "Though I didn't hear him exercising the troops. Is it possible he spent the night elsewhere?"

His lordship sighed. "It's possible, though I'd hoped . . ." He broke off. In his study, he gestured to a cushion. "Some tea?"

"Yes, thank you. Allow me, sir." Saburo stirred the coals in the brazier and placed the small water pot over them. Then he filled two cups with some ground tea leaves. "I had an exciting night, sir. Wait till you hear."

His lordship took his seat behind his desk. "I'm anxious to hear about it. Useful information has been singularly lacking in this case. Do your activities throw some light on Governor Tachibana's whereabouts?"

"Sorry, no." Saburo poured boiling water on the tea leaves and stirred each cup carefully, then joined his master at the desk. "But it suggests that the merchant Feng has his fingers in some unsavory business." He presented the tea to his master and sat down with his own.

They both sipped. His master said, "Please proceed. I'm all ears."

Saburo began with his visit to the Dragon's Lair. "Aptly named, I think," he observed. "It's where I saw Fingers, the Feng servant with the missing fingers, last time. This time, the sales clerk was there. He met with a young thug, gave him what looked like money, and left. I followed the young thug."

"Excellent," said his master with a smile. "I hope he didn't recognize you?"

"No. Last time I was wearing these clothes. On this occasion, I dressed like the local crowd. Anyway, it turned out the man was a carter, because he took up his cart outside and headed off toward an area of derelict houses and wilderness. There, he took a bundle from his cart and entered an abandoned courtyard. I couldn't follow him in, but when he came back, he was without the bundle. He next went home, and as it turns out, he lives next door to Mrs. Kimura, who took in the children."

His lordship frowned. "Then I think he must be the son of that doll maker who was just found guilty of killing his wife. Very odd. What about the bundle?"

"I went back to the courtyard. It was too dark to see much, but it looks as though he dropped it into an abandoned well there."

Lord Sugawara sat up and stared at him. "Where is Tora? He must hear this. Why is he absent today of all days?"

"No idea, sir. I haven't seen him. He was with you yesterday."

"Yes, and I sent him off to follow a suspicious character. I got the feeling we were being watched. Something must have happened to him."

Seeing his master's worried face, Saburo offered, "Tora knows how to handle himself, sir. He probably discovered a clue he wanted to investigate further."

"Maybe, but I have a bad feeling about this. Nothing has been as it should be here. And now the disappearance of a ranking official! But go on with your report."

Saburo preened a little. "This is the best part, sir. I decided to have a look at Feng's store. As it turned out he was there, meeting with his clerk and Fingers. I couldn't hear what they were talking about, but they must have reported their activities to him. The clerk wanted money for what he'd done, and Feng slapped him before leaving."

"Hmm. That's interesting. I think Feng is playing some sort of illegal game and using those two in it. We need to find Tora right away. Go back into Hakata in your ordinary clothes. You're acting for me. Contact Lieutenant Maeda and tell him about Tora. And you might as well get his assistance checking out that well. I wouldn't be at all surprised to find that Maeda knows about it."

Saburo thought this last somewhat farfetched, but his lordship's concern for Tora was infectious. He said no more and left.

Lieutenant Maeda was astonished to see Saburo.

"You're very welcome," he said with a smile, "but I expected that rascal Tora. What is he up to? Chasing more women?"

Saburo winced. "Umm. Has he been chasing anyone?"

"Not really. He did have an eye for one of our victims, though. What brings you?"

"Tora seems to have disappeared. His Excellency is concerned and asks that you and your men have a look around for him. He hasn't been seen since he followed a suspicious character from the harbor office late yesterday."

"What?" Maeda shook his head. "Surely the governor's concern is premature. It's not even been a whole day. Maybe he got lost and decided to spend the night. It's a long way back to the tribunal. He'll probably turn up shortly."

"Perhaps, but I think it wouldn't hurt if some of your constables asked some questions in the harbor area. I'll start tracing him myself later, but there's another matter I want to check out. The governor suggests you might give me a hand."

Maeda hesitated. Then he said, "Of course. His Excellency has only to ask."

Saburo thought privately that Maeda sounded reluctant. Perhaps acting independently from the tribunal was ingrained in the Hakata police. But he put a good face on it and said, "Last night I followed a carter who hid a bundle on a deserted property. It turns out that this man is the son of the murderer who hanged himself. He lives next door to Mrs. Kimura."

This got Maeda's interest. "That rascal Hiroshi? What made you suspicious of him?"

Saburo hesitated. He had no idea how much his master wanted the lieutenant to know. "I saw him meeting with someone in the Dragon's Lair. Money passed hands. I decided to see where this Hiroshi was going with it."

"Hmm. Yes." The lieutenant frowned. He ran a hand across his chin. "I don't trust Hiroshi. You say he hid a bundle? Where exactly was that?"

"I don't know what you call the area. It's pretty much deserted. Lots of dilapidated houses. He took the bundle out of his cart and into this courtyard. I couldn't see what he did with it, but when I went back later, I almost fell into an abandoned well. I think it's down there. We should try to take a look." He broke off. Maeda stared at him with such an expression of shocked surprise, that he floundered to a halt.

"Abandoned well? No, it can't be."

"What?"

"We pulled a body from a well like that. That very pretty woman Tora had his eye on. She lived across the street from Hiroshi."

Saburo gulped. "Let's go! What if the bastard put Tora down there?"

Maeda was already through the door and did not answer. In the front room, lounging constables came to attention. Maeda barked orders that involved ladders, ropes, and names. Within moments, ten constables assembled outside, some carrying equipment, and the contingent started off at a lively trot, the front man shouting, "Make way!" and swinging a short whip.

Saburo hurried after Maeda. In a surprisingly short time, they arrived at the ruined courtyard. It looked different in daylight, but Saburo had no trouble recognizing it. His stomach turned at the thought of what they might find in the well.

The constables knew their way and had the wooden cover off quickly. They hung over the side, peering down.

"Is it deep?" Saburo asked Maeda. He was trying to get a look.

"Not very. People have been tossing their garbage down there for years. Dead rats, cats, dogs, and the occasional female." He pushed two constables aside and took a look. "Well, don't stand around," he told his men. "Get down there and bring up what you find."

They made faces, but one man tied a rope around his middle and started down while the others held on and shouted encouragement.

Saburo smelled it now, the familiar stench of rotting flesh. "I thought you pulled the dead woman out?" he asked Maeda.

"We did."

Saburo thought of Tora and felt his stomach clench painfully.

But when the constable was pulled back to the surface, all he brought up was a stained and malodorous bundle.

"That it?" asked Maeda, looking at Saburo.

Saburo wrinkled his nose. "It looks like it. Is it just clothes?"

Maeda, braver than Saburo or more used to the stench of death, took the bundle from the constable and undid it. Shaking it out, he held up a blue robe, much like Saburo's, a black sash and black pants, also much like Saburo's. A pair of boots and a soft black cap fell to the ground. He turned pale.

Saburo swallowed and went closer. He looked at the garments, then picked up the boots and hat. "That's what Tora wore," he said tonelessly.

Maeda nodded. "I thought so. But where is he? And why are just his clothes here? What happened to him?"

Feeling sick, Saburo snarled, "Stupid question. Somebody got hold of him. Instead of standing around here like fools, we've got to find him. He told you that Hiroshi was a killer."

Maeda recoiled.

Saburo took a deep breath. "You've got to arrest him. He knows what happened to Tora. You've got to get it out of him. And that clerk of Feng's paid him. Arrest him, too. I don't care what you do to them. We must find Tora. Dear heaven, he may be dead. The governor will be livid!"

"It may not mean what you think," the lieutenant stammered without much conviction. "I can't believe anyone would attack Tora."

Saburo gave him a savage look. Snatching the robe from his lands, he spread it out. "There's blood on the collar in back. It suggests an injury to the back of the head." He took up each garment, one after the other. "The front of both the robe and the pants is dusty. I think he fell or was lying on his stomach." He studied the dirt by lifting the fabric close to his good eye and then smelling it. "I don't know," he muttered. He pushed the garment under Maeda's nose. "What do you smell?"

Maeda stepped back, then sniffed cautiously. "Just dirt and some of what must've seeped from the other body."

Saburo sniffed again. "There's something. I just can't make it out." He folded the robe gently and carefully, keeping the front inside. Then he studied the boots. "Look! Someone tied his legs. You can see the twists of the rope in the leather. That rope was tight." He shook his head. "He was a prisoner, but there are no cuts or rips in the robe, so he wasn't stabbed or shot with an arrow."

Maeda nodded. "They knocked him out. For that matter, he may have fallen and hit his head, and some beggar liked his clothes well enough to steal them."

Saburo gave him a disgusted look. "You mean a beggar went to all that trouble to steal his clothes, and then gave them to this Hiroshi, who promptly dropped them down a well?" His voice dripped with sarcasm.

Maeda flushed. He ran a hand over his face. "Look, I like Tora. I don't want to think that he's been murdered. All we know for a fact is that someone knocked him out and took his clothes."

"So you're not going to do anything? It's been many hours since I followed the carter."

Maeda had had enough. He turned and snapped to his constables, "Cover that well again, and then go to the Mitsui house to arrest Hiroshi and take him to jail."

But Hiroshi was not home. His hard-faced wife said he had gone out, she knew not where. She seemed uninterested in his whereabouts or in the reason the police were looking for him. Maybe she was used to it by now.

Maeda returned to headquarters, Saburo in tow. "I'll organize a search for Hiroshi and talk to Feng's clerk," he told Saburo. "You'd better report to the governor. Tell him we're doing everything we can. Looks like we want Hiroshi for Yoko's murder after all."

Saburo did not find this reassuring. He borrowed a horse, though he could not ride very well and returned to the tribunal, bruised and sore in mind and body from falling off the horse twice and being laughed at by other travelers.

But worst was his fear for Tora.

23

Deadly Passage

He dozed fitfully, waking from time to time to bouts of nausea and the urge to do something, anything. His body would not obey.

He had somehow rolled on his back. Gingerly, he moved his hands. They were tied with rope and rested on his stomach. He tried lifting his arms, but pain exploded in his side hot as fire. He steadied his breathing and rested until it eased. Then he tried moving his feet and legs. They were tied at the ankles.

The stench of tar, human waste, and vomit filled the cold air. The steady slap of water to the hull masked other noises, but eventually Tora knew there were others nearby. Someone wept softly, and someone else mumbled sutras or repeated in an endless murmur *Namu Amida Butsu.*

He opened his eyes. Darkness. A little faint light crept through the cracks of a trapdoor or hatch above him. He was in the hold of a ship, and he was not alone. He could barely make out three huddled shapes near him and guessed they were convicts.

"Hey?" he croaked, surprised he could make a sound at all.

The praying stopped, but the weeping continued.

"Who are you?" Tora asked. His mouth hurt.

Someone gave a snort that could have been a bitter laugh or a sob. "Nobody. We're all dead men, and so are you."

Waves washed against the hull, the boards creaked and the floor beneath Tora lifted, shifted, and plunged. Nauseatingly. Over and over again. And someone still wept. Tora tried to move again. His side told him all was not well. His companion was wrong about his being dead anyway. The dead felt no pain.

It came back to him then: the talk about convict ships and getting rid of him. Well, they had managed it. He was tied up and at sea. The movement of the ship was too violent for a river. How long since they left Hakata? How far to Tsushima?

He could hear muffled sounds above, and faint shouts. They must be deep in the hold of the ship.

The voice spoke up again: "In a little while, they'll come and drag us up on deck. Then they'll slit our throats and toss us overboard. Food for the fishes." He snorted again.

Tora decided it was a laugh rather than a sob. The one who wept was still weeping. A bit more loudly.

"Is that why you're praying?" Tora asked.

"I never pray."

"Oh."

Tora decided his rib did not hurt quite as much as earlier. Though what good it would do him he did not know. His arms and legs were tied. And even if they were not, where could he escape to on a ship?

"I'm Tora," he said. "What makes you think they'll kill us? I thought we were going to Tsushima to work in the mines."

"Same thing. But a lot go overboard before they get there. What crime did you commit?"

"No crime. I was bludgeoned by a couple of devils. Next thing I knew I was here."

Silence.

Tora stretched cautiously again. His rib protested a little, but the pain was bearable. He realized his wrists were tied in front, not behind him as in Hakata. "Don't you believe me?" he asked, testing the bond of the rope. When he pulled, it tightened. Not helpful. His wrists started to hurt.

"If you're telling the truth, then it's pretty certain they'll cut your throat before we get there."

Tora flexed his wrists. He wondered why they'd tied them in front. Theoretically, it was much easier to escape this way. But then they knew he was not going to go anywhere on this ship. The other answer to the "why" also became apparent. He was not wearing his own clothes any longer. He seemed to have on a rough shirt without sleeves and a pair of thin pants cut off at the knee. They had to untie him to change his clothes. He tried raising his feet to see if he could reach his ankles, but his rib gave him another sharp pain, and he desisted.

"What makes you so sure they'll kill me?" he asked the other man. "I'm strong. I'm a good worker."

The other chuckled. "As I said, if you're telling the truth, then your case is personal. Someone wants to get rid of you. Permanently. This is how they do it here."

"I'm not from here. Just got to Hakata a few weeks ago. You say this sort of thing is common?"

"Pretty much. You made an enemy. Fast work. What did you do?"

"Two actually. One's a bastard called Okata. I didn't like the way he was running things and got him fired."

"Okata? *Captain* Okata?" His companion whistled. "How did you manage that?"

Tora was working with his teeth on the hemp rope around his wrists and could not answer.

"What are you doing?" asked the other.

Tora spat out some fibers. "Trying to chew through this rope. When I'm free, I'll untie you."

"Thanks, I'm not tied up."

Tora froze. Who was this man to be left unbound? Probably a guard. And he was chatting away with him as if they were sharing a flask of wine.

"Who or what are you really?" he growled.

A chuckle. "A man like you."

"But you aren't bound? You can move about freely?"

"Yes. See?" A tall shadow rose beside Tora and waved its arms.

Suddenly afraid, Tora said nothing.

It was silent, except for the slapping of the waves and the rhythmic groaning of the wooden hull. The weeping man had fallen silent also.

His companion sat down again. "I'm a prisoner like you. I just started chewing through my bonds while you were having your nap. I thought I might at least take a couple of them with me before they kill me."

Relief washed over Tora, then anger. "You could have untied me," he said resentfully.

"I wasn't sure you were safe. Convicts bound for Tsushima can be dangerous travel companions."

Tora accepted this. His fellow prisoner spoke like a man who had some education, was someone like himself. "Well, how about it?" he asked.

The shadow rose again and came closer. "You haven't made much progress with your teeth," he observed, feeling the rope around Tora's wrists. He found the knot and started working it.

"You still haven't told me your name," Tora observed.

"You can call me Shigeno. It's the name my father gave me, though I haven't used it for a while. There!"

The rope parted, and the relief was huge. Blood flowed into his hands again. Tora massaged his wrists. "Thanks. Can you get my feet too?"

"Get them yourself!"

"One of the bastards kicked in a rib. I can't bend at the waist."

Shigeno muttered, but he worked on Tora's ankles.

"How many are we?" Tora asked. He thought if they freed everyone they might be able to take over the ship.

"Four, with you."

"Only four? How many above?"

The rope on Tora's feet parted. He stretched and winced at the stab of pain in his chest.

"Twenty, maybe more. Sailors and armed guards. There's a policeman among them. Too many. Besides, you can't fight in your condition." Shigeno returned to his place.

Another voice from the darkness asked, "Please untie me, too."

Shigeno snapped, "What good will it do you? Best stay a prisoner."

"But you and Tora are free."

"Not free, just able to do some damage when they come to throw us overboard. You two are safe. You're going to Tsushima. If I untie you, the guards will kill you."

Silence. Then the man began reciting his prayer again. Tora expected the weeping to start next, but the fourth man remained quiet.

Tora held his breath and struggled into a sitting position. The pain almost caused him to black out. He rested for while, propped against the bulwark behind him and started flexing his leg muscles. He was very stiff after being tied up all this time. How long? He had no idea but guessed it was less than a day but more than four hours.

When his chest hurt less, he tried to get his legs under him and rise. The pain came back, but he struggled on.

Impossible!

He had managed to get on his knees, and this position seemed to ease his ribcage.

"Give me a hand," he said.

The hand reached for his and hauled him upright. Tora gasped and stood swaying, waiting for the pain to subside again. He noted with surprise that the other man was nearly a head taller. He was also strong. "Anything we can use for a weapon down here?" he asked when he got his breath back.

"Too dark to be sure, but I doubt it. Let me see where you're hurt."

Tora took the other man's hand and placed it on his lower ribcage on the left side. The man felt around, and Tora snarled, "Watch it."

"Pah. It's nothing," said the other. "You're a crybaby."

Someone laughed. Since the praying man had not stopped his recital, Tora guessed it had been the weeper. Very funny! He took a few unsteady steps. The motion of the ship was no help.

"Here, wait." Shigeno grabbed his arm. "I'm going to tie my sash around you. That should help keep the rib in place." He wound it around a few times, then pulled it so tight that Tora gasped. "Hold still," Shigeno said and tied a knot. "There!"

It did help. Tora still could not bend very well, but he could move both arms without undue pain and even turn at the waist. "Thanks," he said. Then he called out to the other two shadows," Hey, you two. Do you know anything about sailing a ship like this?"

The praying man said, "We both do. We're sailors."

"Let's untie them, Shigeno. They can help."

"You must be mad. I told you, there are at least twenty men up there. Besides, the ship's too big for two sailors to handle."

"What's your solution? A moment ago you planned to let them toss you overboard."

The praying man said, "Hey, stop arguing and untie us."

The other sailor wailed softly, "They'll kill us."

Tora snapped, "Maybe, but I don't think many come back from the mines. If you get away, you can head for the hills and start a new life elsewhere."

There were no more arguments. Tora and Shigeno untied the convicts and searched for something that could be used for weapons. Even though Tora's eyes had adjusted, it was still very dark. Unidentifiable mounds of things were piled in far corners. They felt around among pieces of rough cloth to mend sails, rope of varying thickness, and pieces of lumber too long and heavy to be useful.

A rough ladder led up to the hatch above. Now and then, Tora could hear footsteps up there.

Shigeno hissed, "Sssh! I think they're coming for us. Hurry!"

One of the convicts gasped, but both came to help. They found an iron spike, a broken oar, and a couple of short spars. Shigeno pulled out a grappling hook with a length of broken rope attached, and Tora took the oar, breaking off the paddle end. The rest would make a cudgel or short fighting staff.

Up above, they heard voices near the hatch. Shigeno said softly, "I'll go halfway up the ladder, grab the first of the bastards, and pass him on to you. You'd best kill him quick and follow. Stand ready!"

It was mad. Tora was conscious of being in poor shape even as he gripped the shaft of the oar. When those above realized their prisoners were free, they would simply slam the hatch cover down again until they reached port and could deal with them.

Shigeno climbed up to the hatch, and Tora took position just below him. The other two sailors waited at the foot of the ladder.

Then the latch cover lifted.

24

Regrets

Saburo arrived in Akitada's office out of breath, dusty, bruised, and speechless. Mori and his scribes stared as Saburo gasped and gestured with a filthy bundle of clothes.

Akitada half rose. "What happened?"

Saburo approached and dropped the bundle on Akitada's desk, where it landed with a thud, unrolled, and spilled the boots.

Akitada recognized Tora's clothes. He felt himself grow cold.

With another gasp, Saburo said, "They got him. He may be dead. They got Tora, sir." He sat down abruptly on the floor.

Akitada briefly fingered Tora's robe, sash, and pants, then studied each boot. "Explain!"

Saburo told of taking Maeda and his men to the abandoned well and how they found that the mysterious bundle discarded the night before contained Tora's clothes. "We went immediately to arrest Hiroshi. He's the son of the doll maker who hanged himself."

"I know who he is. Go on."

"Well, Hiroshi's gone."

Akitada glowered. "Gone where?"

"Sorry, sir. I'm upset. His wife said she didn't know. Maeda sent his people out to look for him. I came back here as fast as I could."

Akitada sat staring at him and stroking his chin. Things had progressed from bad to worse. From the tiger's den, they had now reached the dragon's lair. Tora was in trouble—he did not want to think of him as dead—and needed help, but what could he do that Maeda's constables could not do better? This Hiroshi must be found and questioned as soon as possible. Maeda himself had given the man a warning by setting out very publicly for the abandoned well. "Maeda and his men bungled," he muttered.

Saburo

~~Sadamu said~~, "He couldn't have known what we'd find. *I* didn't know."

"This was the same place where they found the woman's body a few days ago?"

"Yes, sir. Strange, that."

"Not strange. It looks like Hiroshi dumped her body there and when he needed to get rid of the bundle of clothes, he went there again."

"That was pretty stupid. He must have known the police found the dead woman."

"Yes. Hmm." Akitada thought, staring up at the ceiling and noting absent-mindedly the number of cobwebs above his head. "He may not have killed her but heard about the well and decided it was a good place to hide Tora's clothes. He probably thought the police wouldn't go back there again."

"Maybe." Saburo looked doubtful. "I think Maeda plans to arrest Hiroshi for the murder."

Akitada stood. "None of this is getting us any closer to Tora. You and I are going to Hakata to look for ourselves."

Saburo blinked. "On horses?"

Akitada ignored the question. He turned to Mori and the slack-jawed scribes. "Mori, send for the sergeant of the provincial guard. I'll be back as soon as I've changed out of these clothes. Come, Saburo. I have more questions."

In his private quarters, Akitada flung back the lid of his clothes trunk and brought out a set of comfortable trousers, his hunting coat, and his boots. As he took off his working attire, he glanced at the dirt-covered, miserable-looking Saburo. "Sorry," he said. "I forgot about your problem with horses. It can't be helped. You'd better change into something more military."

"If you insist." Saburo frowned as he watched his master put on half armor under his hunting coat, and then sit down to put on his boots.

"I have a good mind to have Feng arrested," Akitada muttered, then went to get his sword from its display stand.

"What for?" asked Saburo.

"I don't know, but it's clear the meeting between his employee and Hiroshi has something to do with Tora's abduction."

Saburo nodded. "Yes, I told Maeda. He'll talk to the clerk."

Akitada buckled on his sword and took in Saburo's glum expression. "Come, Saburo! With your background as a spy, you can't possibly be this averse to fighting."

"I can use a sword, but not well. I clearly cannot ride a horse, to judge by my recent experiences. I don't shoot arrows. Most of my assignments have involved a stealthier form of warfare."

Akitada grimaced. "Exactly what I disliked most about your background."

Saburo nodded. "I'll do as you say. The gods know, I'd do more than that to get Tora back." He turned to leave.

Akitada called after him, "When you're ready, meet me outside in the courtyard. I'll try to find a calm horse for you."

It should have amused Akitada, but fear for Tora sickened him every time he remembered that a day and two nights had passed since he had sent Tora after the watcher. Unless they—whoever they were—wanted information, they had killed him already. And if they wanted information, he would wish he were dead.

The worst part of this was that he still had no grasp of the plot that had made the last governor disappear and caused the murder by poison of the beautiful woman Tachibana had loved.

As he walked back to the tribunal office, he pondered the situation.

If Feng was behind Tora's disappearance, what had he hoped to achieve?

If he had interpreted the meeting between Feng and his men correctly, then Feng had paid Hiroshi. For what? Surely not just to get rid of his clothes. But someone had set the man to watch them, and Tora had followed this man. Where had the watcher taken him? What had Tora discovered that had made him a threat?

And again he cringed at the knowledge that he had sent Tora into danger.

He had sent him into the unknown unarmed. Akitada touched the sword at his side and winced. He had remembered the threat they faced too late to protect Tora.

In the tribunal office, the sergeant of the tribunal guard awaited him. He blinked when he saw Akitada with sword and half armor and saluted stiffly.

Akitada wished he remembered the man's name. Another oversight. He said, "Thank you for coming so promptly, Sergeant. It seems Lieutenant Sashima has been attacked in the city. He didn't return from an assignment. You will gather as many of your men as can be spared from watching the tribunal and assist Lieutenant Maeda's constables in searching Hakata. We are leaving for police headquarters as soon as your men are mounted."

The sergeant saluted again. "Does your Excellency expect an attack on the tribunal?"

Good question. Anything at all might happen in this cursed place. "No, Sergeant, but a few men should remain. And please find a docile mount for the *betto.*"

Another snappy salute, and the sergeant was gone.

Akitada turned to Mori who stood beside his desk, looking frightened. "I rely on you to see to things while I'm gone, Mori. Saburo is coming with me." He went to his desk and put away the documents he had been working on. After giving Mori instructions for the day's work, he took a look around, and then walked out into the forecourt of the tribunal.

The mounted guard was assembled, some fifteen armed men. Saburo, wearing half armor and a sword, waited beside a horse, clearly postponing the inevitable until the last moment. Akitada nodded to the sergeant, swung himself into the saddle, watched Saburo climb up, and they set off.

Their arrival in Hakata sent the people in the streets running. Akitada wondered what they were thinking. That it was war? Perhaps it was. His fear for Tora had given him a furious anger at the people in this godforsaken place, at the grand officials who had seen fit to send him here, at the assistant governor general in Dazaifu for leaving him without support, at the late Governor Tachibana for having allowed the criminal behavior which had led to this.

At police headquarters, the constables on duty poured out of the building to stare. Akitada stayed on his horse. "Where's your chief?" he bellowed.

"At the harbor."

Akitada turned his horse and, followed by Saburo and the soldiers, he galloped to Hakata harbor where his arrival stirred up more consternation. Lieutenant Maeda came running from the harbor office.

Akitada dismounted. "Well? Anything?" he demanded grimly.

"Not much, your Excellency." Maeda, looking strained, stared at the mounted soldiers and Akitada's armor. "My men are combing the wine shops and gambling dives asking for information. Most of the reports are unreliable, but a couple of people think they saw Tora following a man with a red rag around his head. The man seemed to be heading for the Chinese settlement. That was on the evening before last. I had a talk with Feng's clerk. He says he paid Hiroshi for a delivery of goods."

Whatever that meant.

Too much time had passed. And already the clouds were streaked with crimson in the west as if they were about to rain blood across the earth. Akitada bit his lip. "It makes sense," he said. "Let's go to the Chinese settlement. I brought the soldiers to help."

Maeda called for a horse and gathered his men. They set out for the Chinese settlement as if they intended to conquer a foreign country.

And perhaps they were.

As soon as they passed through the gates into the Chinese quarter, people started scattering. Mothers dragged their children behind them; a toddler stumbled and fell in the path of the horses; his mother threw herself over him; screams from women and children brought men running. Some shook their fists at them; others herded people inside and slammed doors.

Akitada shouted to Maeda to stop. He did not want this. What gave him the right to make war on women and children because Tora had disappeared? He said as much to Maeda and the sergeant of the tribunal guard.

"Nobody got hurt." Maeda said. "I doubt these people had anything to do with Tora's abduction, but they have eyes to see. I think it best to go from house to house and store to store in the business district. Someone may have some information."

"Very well. Tell your men to be polite." It would take time. A lot of time. Akitada needed to be doing something as his fear ate away at him. It might already be too late.

Maeda gave his orders and the constables dispersed. He and Akitada dismounted to await results.

"Any news about Fragrant Orchid?" Akitada asked to distract himself.

"Nothing beyond the fact that the governor was apparently very much enamored with her. He seems to have been an almost daily visitor in the months before his departure."

"How did she take his leaving?"

Maeda gave a snort. "She received a generous present, I think. The maid said her mistress looked quite pleased and spent lavishly on new clothes."

"I see." It was common enough to pay off one's mistress. Given the luxurious lifestyle enjoyed by the courtesan, he assumed Tachibana had been especially generous. He suddenly remembered the letter she had left. It suggested a passion which was strangely at odds with her behavior. There had been something about its wording. He bit his lip. Tora's fate had driven the matter completely from his mind. "What about the other murdered woman? Is it possible that Tora's interest in the case caused someone to attack him?"

Maeda frowned. "Well, we found Tora's clothes where Yoko's body was for a week or more, and since it was Hiroshi who put them there, it seems reasonable that Hiroshi also put Yoko there. He is wanted for her murder. And yes, if Tora discovered something that proved Hiroshi killed her, he would be likely to try to get rid of him."

More than likely. And Hiroshi would not leave Tora alive. Akitada turned away with a shudder.

Maeda said, "You mustn't think the worst, sir. We didn't find Tora's body, just his clothes. It proves he wasn't killed, doesn't it?"

"Perhaps," Akitada said, "but we cannot be certain." He clenched his hands.

"Hiroshi is a small-time crook. I doubt he could outwit Tora."

Akitada did not answer. It was easy to make a mistake, he knew. And sometimes a small thing might be the last mistake a man made.

The constables were returning one by one. No one had seen Tora or the man he had followed. Akitada looked around at the people who were slowly emerging from their hiding places again. They all looked either hostile or frightened. He sighed.

"What are your orders, Excellency?" asked Maeda.

"Keep asking questions, but not here. I doubt anyone here will give any help to the authorities. You must find Hiroshi. I'll leave you my soldiers. Make use of them. As soon as you have any information, let me know. I'll be staying at your headquarters for the time being."

25

Kill or Be Killed

The light from the open hatch was blinding, but Shigeno tossed his grappling hook and jerked the rope hard. There was a cry; then a man fell past Tora, nearly knocking him off the ladder. Down below, his scream turned into a sickening gurgle.

No time to look or wonder. Shigeno was already through the open hatch. Shouts and screams greeted him. Tora scrambled up and out, cudgel in hand, squinting into the light.

He had a vague impression of running people and of the gray sea and the large white sails above them. Shigeno was swinging his grappling hook by its short rope. Tora got a quick look at his powerful physique and his long hair and full beard, then he saw the guards in their half armor drawing their swords.

An uneven battle at best.

Beyond the figure of Shigeno wading into a hopeless confrontation, sailors were running everywhere in the gray daylight and the spray of seawater.

The two convicts came up beside Tora, one tall and thin, the other short. He doubted he'd done anyone a favor by encouraging them to fight their way to freedom, for here came men with knives and swords.

A sailor with a long, curved knife was in front. He attacked with a shout. Tora raised his oar handle to parry the knife, but the pain in his side shot through him like a flame. He saw the sailor through a haze of agony and desperation, knowing that, in a moment, he would be dead. He would be killed, and so would the others. Already he could feel the blade slicing into his body, but he could do nothing about it.

Then an object flew past him and struck the sailor, who went down on one knee. Tora finally moved, swinging his stick as hard as he could at the other man's head. Even with the noise of sails, sea, and fighting, he heard the crack of the impact and saw the man fall over, blood gushing from his nose.

Another sailor rushed him from the side. Tora jumped away and swung hard at an extended arm. He saw a knife flying through the air and over the rail into the sea beyond. The man screamed, fell to his knees, cradling his hand against his chest, and Tora kicked him hard in the face. A shadow darted past and swung an iron spike. The sailor collapsed.

But already there were more attackers. A sailor went for one of the convicts, and a guard charged Tora.

Tora side-stepped the sword, and parried. The guard was not a very good swordsman, but a man with a sword had little trouble killing another man who only brandished a broken oar.

They danced around each other. Tora slipped on the wet deck and went down just as the other man swung at his neck. Dropping his oar handle, Tora grabbed the man's leg and jerked it out from under him. The sword flew from his hand, slid away, and fell down the hatch opening. The guard kicked with both legs and scored a glancing blow to Tora's chin, but Tora had found his oar and came to his knees, swinging it at the man's face. The guard fell; blood poured from his nose and mouth, and his eyes rolled back in his head. Getting to his feet, Tora looked around desperately. There must be a way to stop this, to convince these men of who he was.

Shigeno was at the other end of the ship, a couple of guards squirming on the deck near him. He still swung his grappling hook and drove forward as sailors backed away from him.

One of the convicts, perhaps the one who had saved Tora's life, lay a few feet away, unmoving, his face in a puddle of blood.

Across the way, more men were advancing on Shigeno. Tora went to his aid, lashing out at the nearest sailor. His oar handle connected with the man's head, and he went down. But another sailor had seized a length of chain and now came for Tora, swinging it much like Shigeno did his grappling hook. Someone shouted, "Kill the bastards!" Tora ducked under the flailing chain and felt pain slice through his side again as he head-butted the sailor in the stomach. The other made an "oof" sound, bent double, and sat down. A vicious slash from Tora's stick finished him off. Tora was no longer trying to spare lives. This was a battle to the death.

More sailors were coming. Someone shouted commands. Through the noise, Tora heard the convict reciting his sutra again; only now there was a fierce rhythm to the sacred words. He saw him, a tall scarecrow of a man, swinging a long knife as he fought to kill or be killed. Even so, the odds were hardly improving.

But Tora found new strength. He met the next sailor near the side of the ship and struck at his knees. The man screamed and fell. Tora hauled him up and pushed him over the side, hoping he could swim. Some object missed his head but struck his back. For a moment he could not catch his breath. When he swung around, he barely parried a curved knife wielded by a huge bear of a sailor. Tora's oar handle had a sharp, pointed end where the blade had broken off, leaving a long splinter behind. Tora ducked and buried the point in the man's side. He screamed, and the knife fell from his hand.

Tora snatched up the weapon, hesitated a moment, then plunged back into battle. How many left?

The skinny convict had disappeared, but near the front of the ship, Shigeno was still laying about him with the iron grappling hook. One sailor was covered in blood. Another saw the vicious, toothed hook coming for his face, shrieked, and flung himself overboard.

Something else hit Tora's right shoulder. When he turned, he saw a sailor with a bloody knife and then felt the pain and the hot blood. He tried in vain to raise his own knife. Gasping, he jumped aside just a moment before the sailor's blade went into his chest. His right arm would not obey, but he kneed the man in the groin, and when his attacker fell groaning, he kicked the knife from his hand.

He clutched his useless arm, dripping blood, and looking for escape. He knew he was done for. To his surprise, Shigeno was beside him. He, too, was bleeding badly; his shirt was soaked and had turned crimson. In spite of his wounds, Shigeno finished off the groaning sailor with the hook, snatched up his knife, and turned to meet new attackers.

"Stop!"

The shout came from the middle of the boat and broke off the fighting.

A red-coated policeman had appeared from somewhere below. Reluctantly, guards and sailors retreated. The policeman looked at Tora and Shigeno. "Give yourselves up and nothing will happen to you," he shouted. His voice was sharp and high. He sounded frightened though he stood among guards.

Tora heaved a sigh of relief. He stepped forward and shouted back, "I'm a tribunal officer. This is an illegal ship engaged in murder for hire. Arrest the captain and put him in the hold. He's in the pay of a criminal gang."

One of the sailors burst out laughing. Others joined in. "Very funny!" the policeman shouted with a laugh.

He had found his voice of authority. "You're a convict. All of you've committed crimes and killed people. Give up, and you'll serve your sentence. If you resist, you'll die."

"There's your answer." Shigeno sounded bitter. He was leaning against the side of the ship, looking pale beneath his tan. Several bodies lay about the deck, but there were still some six or eight men standing with the policeman, and other sailors were elsewhere. Tora did not see the two convicts. Perhaps they were both dead by now. There was a good deal of blood all over the deck.

What if this was a legitimate transport? Tora knew they had killed men. It was no use trying to explain it away. The memory sickened him as his blood still dripped down his arm and onto the boards he stood on.

He glanced again at Shigeno and told the policeman, "We don't want to have to kill anyone else, but neither will you take us prisoner again. Tell your men to go down in the hold now, or this battle will continue."

Brave words. He might be bleeding to death, and Shigeno looked badly wounded and had dropped his grappling hook.

"No," said the policeman and shouted, "Go get them. They're wounded and done for. If they try to fight, kill them."

But his people hesitated. Then one of the sailors threw a knife. Tora jumped aside, and gasped as pain pierced his side. For a moment, he thought the knife had found its mark, but it had struck the rail where he had been standing a moment earlier. The man had thrown it with deadly accuracy.

Another knife flew past and into the sea. Tora thrust his good arm around Shigeno and dragged him behind the big mast.

"Let me at them," Shigeno muttered. "I'll show the bastards."

"Follow me!" Tora cried and ran across the slippery deck, dodging bodies, hearing Shigeno's sharp breath behind him.

Two against overwhelming odds.

Shigeno growled, "Cut them down!" and then they were among them, Tora swinging the long knife with his left hand, feeling it bite, hearing screams, seeing them scatter. "Give up!" he shouted, "or you'll all die." It was a mere croak.

And an empty threat. Shigeno stumbled and fell beside him as two sailors converged on them.

Someone yelled, "Look out! The ship! We're going to strike"

Then pandemonium broke out. People were running everywhere, and Tora stopped to gape at the scene.

Beyond the ship a black mass had risen from the sea. For a moment he thought he was losing consciousness . . . or hallucinating. "Dear gods," he muttered, falling to his knees beside Shigeno who was struggling to get up.

Then Tora realized what must have happened. Distracted by the fighting, the sailors had not paid attention to their ship, and the wind or tide had carried it too close to land. The sudden peril of submerged rocks taking the keel out of the ship outweighed even the threat of two convicts trying to escape.

Tora saw the panic in the sailors' faces. They rushed about, colliding with each other, some running for the rudder, others pulling at the big sails.

The dark shape of the cliff already towered over them like some monstrous sea creature.

Land, he thought. We've reached Tsushima. It was all for nothing. He dropped the knife, and asked Shigeno. "How are you, my friend?"

"Done for," muttered the convict. "My legs have given out. How about you?"

"Not sure. I got a cut in the back."

Shigeno looked at his back. "Can you move your arm?"

"A little, but there's not much strength in it. It's over anyway. We're in Tsushima."

Together they looked at the rocky shore which was still approaching in spite of the frantic efforts of the crew. Their captors no longer cared about them. They worked the ship and the oars, desperately trying to bring her away from the rocks. Even the policeman and guards lent a hand at the oars.

Shigeno chuckled weakly. "The fools. Serves them right. Can you swim?"

"Yes. You?"

Shigeno nodded. He seemed to be regaining some of his strength and was getting to his feet. "It's not far."

Tora reached over to lift the other man's blood-soaked shirt. His chest and side had taken a number of cuts that were still bleeding, some more than others. Impossible to tell how deep they were, but he must have lost a lot of blood. How could they think of swimming? "Are you sure we'll be shipwrecked?" he asked.

Shigeno flexed his limbs, gritting his teeth. "Any moment. Where are the other two?"

"Dead or unconscious."

But as Tora glanced across the deck, he saw one of the bodies move, lift his head, and peer back at him. The thin man. After a glance around, he got to his feet and came to them in a crouching run.

"They'll never make it," he said, pointing at the cliff.

At that moment they struck.

With a grinding noise the ship lifted, sending them staggering. They heard the wooden bottom tearing and the crew yelling. Then the masts cracked and, like giant forest trees, they slowly began to lean and then fall. Timber and rigging snapped, taking spars and the huge sails as well as two sailors with them. A large spar missed Tora by a mere foot. The ship tilted sharply when the masts and sails hit the water and sank, pulling it over on its side. Tora slid, then fell.

He hit the water, ice cold and wildly surging, and went down. Kicking out, he swam for the surface but came up under a sodden sail in a tangle of lines. As he fought free, he thought this would be his grave. He dove again, came up, and found more sail pressing him down into the depths. Once more he dove and struggled back up again using the last of his strength. He reached the

surface just as his chest and head were about to ex-
plode.

26

The Late Governor

The search for Hiroshi—and Tora—continued into the middle of the night. At that point, Akitada, who had been waiting at police head-quarters for news, decided to call it off. Saburo had left already, though he was searching on his own. Akitada thanked the weary constables and the tribunal guard as they returned, and then he and his people went home.

Home?

This place was more and more like the horrors of exile he had dreaded in the capital. Far from his true home, where his wife might even now be struggling to give birth to their child, and while he tried to come to grips with losing Tora, Akitada had nothing but pain to show for this appointment.

As tired as he was, he could not sleep. Instead, he lit as many oil lamps and candles in his room as he could find to keep the menacing darkness away and then sat at his desk to reread Tamako's letters and to smile at the scrawls and drawings the children had included. He missed them all. His utter loneliness overwhelmed him, and he almost wept.

But his despair reminded him of Fragrant Orchid's supposed suicide letter. He rummaged among his papers and finally found the note still in the sleeve of the robe he had worn the day Maeda had given it to him.

Unfolding the scrap, he read again: *"Unmindful that ships must wait for high tide, I parted from you too soon . Oh, for a vermilion boat and a pair of jeweled oars so that I might row across to meet you on the other side."*

It sounded like a death poem. "The other side" was a standard reference to the afterlife. But the words still seemed vaguely familiar. And another thing struck him. It read as if it had been written by the one who had left, yet it was in Fragrant Orchid's hand, and she had not left. It had been Lord Tachibana who had left her.

Biting his lip, he rose to scan the books he had brought with him from home. The poem must be something he had read somewhere. Fragrant Orchid had copied it down, perhaps to send to Tachibana. Women did such things; it proved how well-read they were.

An hour later he found the lines in the *Manyoshu,* that compendium of sadness and loneliness expressed by men and women parted from each other while in

government service. It was not a suicide note but simply
an expression of regret that the lovers had missed a few
more hours together.

Of course, they had already come to the conclusion
that Fragrant Orchid had been murdered, but now he
had proof the note was not what it seemed to be. The
murderer had been a little too clever trying to make her
death appear to be suicide.

Akitada sat back down and stared out the open door
at the night sky. What sort of man was this killer of a
governor and a reigning courtesan?

He wondered briefly if a woman could have killed
Fragrant Orchid. Jealousies among courtesans were
common enough, but in this case it seemed unlikely.
The timing of Fragrant Orchid's death shortly after she
had sent for him linked her murder with that of Tachibana—assuming he was dead.

Where was his body?

Akitada got up again and started pacing the floor of
his room, thinking furiously. Surely Tachibana had
been killed just before he embarked for the capital. He
had disappeared somewhere between the tribunal and
the harbor of Hakata, most likely in the city. His body
might well be in Hakata.

Against all logic, Akitada thought of the abandoned
well. It was too much of a coincidence. But why not?
The tangled web of crimes in Hakata had been marked
by ruthlessness as well as carelessness. He doubted the
killer who had dealt with Tachibana and Fragrant Orchid was ignorant. The ruse he had used to separate
Tachibana from his servants and the message sent to

the captain were the work of a clever and plotting mind. The same mind was likely to leave a poem to convince provincial police that the courtesan had killed herself. But he had been forced to use underlings because he did not want to dirty his hands or thought himself above menial chores. Arrogance had dulled his caution. Yes, such a man existed, and tomorrow Akitada would ride back to Hakata and ask Lieutenant Maeda to investigate the abandoned well more thoroughly.

Feeling slightly less defeated, Akitada went to take his bedding out of its trunk. Under it he saw his flute, and on an impulse, he took it out. He went into the small courtyard outside and sat down on the narrow ledge. The blossoms on his little tree shimmered pale in the darkness. The night air was scented, and the starry sky stretched northward. Far away, above the black band of forest, a faint hazy glow marked the city, and beyond that stretched the Inland Sea with its islands.

He played from memory the songs that had pleased his own family, now far away, and also two that had been Tora's favorites. Perhaps this way he might reach out to them and let them know how much he cared. But tears rose to his eyes again, and eventually he lowered the flute.

It was too much like playing a dirge for the dead. Wiping his eyes, he rose, went inside, closing the shutters, and lay down to sleep.

"I heard you playing your flute," Saburo said the next morning as he came into Akitada's room just as his master was brewing himself a cup of tea. "Here, let me do that, sir."

Akitada handed over the utensils. Saburo appeared drawn and tired. "I'm very glad to see you," he said. "Did you get in late?"

"Just before you finished playing. I didn't want to trouble you, seeing it was late."

"Thank you. I don't suppose either of us got much sleep. Any news?"

Saburo passed Akitada his cup of tea and made himself one. "Nothing, sir. I broke into Feng's store. Nobody was there, and no sign that Tora had been there." He reached into his gown and brought forth a slender book. "I took one of the account books. I hope I did the right thing?"

Akitada stretched out a hand. "At this point nothing matters but Tora. You had a reason to take it, I assume?"

"Yes. My knowledge of the finer points of keeping business records is sketchy, but this was buried under a mass of trivial paperwork in a locked chest in Feng's office."

"Ah!" Akitada opened the slender book. It was in Chinese, but not the type of Chinese characters he had learned in his youth and employed when writing official documents. He frowned as he tried to make out the columns of words and numbers which covered every page. The words must be names, he thought. Customers? Suppliers? Occasional comments were added in smaller, less careful brush strokes. He guessed this had to do with orders, customers, and amounts, but he had no idea what the goods were. He laid the book aside and said, "It may well explain what Feng has been up to, but it will take time to decipher. You had reason to think it contained illegal transactions?"

Saburo nodded. "The ordinary account books lay stacked by date on a bamboo stand. I thought these entries might not be for the eyes of others."

"Yes, why else hide them? Excellent work." Akitada finished his tea, picked up Feng's account book, and rose. "Well, I'm going back to Hakata today. It occurred to me last night that the well may contain other surprises."

Saburo got up also and collected the cups. "Surely the police would have found those, sir. The constables have climbed down there twice."

"I don't have much faith in the local constables, especially if assigned to an unpleasant task. The body of the woman was apparently well advanced in decay, and Tora's clothes positively stank of death." He suppressed a shudder and bit his lip. "They would not have stayed down there any longer than they absolutely had to. You know how most people feel about death."

Saburo stared at his master. "You are thinking of your predecessor, sir?"

"It wouldn't surprise me, given that all the murders and abductions seem to be connected to a handful of the same people."

In the tribunal office, Akitada asked Mori if he had any knowledge of the Chinese spoken by the immigrants. To his satisfaction, the small clerk nodded.

"We have to work with registers and reports from Chinese merchants and local businessmen," he explained with a smile. "Their Chinese writing bears little resemblance to our own official documents. I've often wondered if that is because they are poorly educated, or if official Chinese dates back to a long time ago while the people now speak differently."

"A very acute comment, Mori. I suspect it's a little of both. But in any case, will you have a look at this?" He passed Feng's private account book to the old man. "I'd like to know why Feng kept this well hidden."

Mori blushed with pleasure and bowed. "I'm honored, your Excellency. Who would have thought I might be asked to provide assistance in such a difficult case?"

Lieutenant Maeda looked as weary as Akitada and Saburo, but he listened with raised brows to Akitada's request. "The men would have mentioned such a thing, sir," he said dubiously.

"Don't forget they had little light to see by and were sent down for a very specific thing, the body of a woman in the first instance, and a bundle of clothes in the second. Also, some time had passed. For all we know, other debris may have been dumped there."

Maeda nodded. "Yes, it's possible. But the murder of a high-ranking government official? Surely it will bring the army down upon us."

"Frankly, Maeda, that's the least of my worries. With a string of murders and the disappearances of a governor and my assistant, Hakata and its inhabitants deserve no less."

The police chief hung his head. "I'll get to it right away, sir. Do you care to witness the search?"

"Certainly."

They set out for the abandoned well, followed by a group of disgruntled constables carrying ropes, pulleys, shovels, and lanterns and pulling a cart for anything of interest they might find.

The well was only wide enough to allow one man to work with a shovel. The rest of the constables crouched in a circle above, peering down and shouting encouragement. Now and then, they lowered a large basket to remove dirt and garbage. Nothing else happened for a long time. They dug in shifts and brought up the basket filled with assorted debris many times. Not only garbage was down below, but also rocks, broken tiles, and other building debris. Akitada was about to call the effort off. It had been too far-fetched. But before he could admit having made an embarrassing mistake, there was a shout. He and Maeda pushed into the circle of constables and looked down.

The upturned face of the unfortunate constable, who had been sent down by the luck of the draw, was a pale circle with shock-widened eyes. "Another corpse, Lieutenant," he reported. "And this one's wearing a fine silk robe."

Maeda said heavily, "It seems you were right, sir."

Akitada nodded grimly. "Bring him up."

But first the constable who had made the discovery emerged, looking green and walking away a few steps before vomiting into a bush.

Akitada peered down into the darkness of the pit. He thought he saw some faint colors below, a bit of white and some green, and a pale round object that might be a skull.

Two more constables descended the ropes with a large piece of cloth. A short while later, a shout from below caused those above to start pulling on the rope. Slowly the body rose to the daylight, wrapped in the cloth and tied securely. They swung it out and lowered it to the ground, where one of the constables untied it and opened the cloth. The smell of decomposition was strong and nauseating.

Both Maeda and Akitada looked at the partially decomposed body of a nobleman. The type of clothing the dead man wore made that much certain. Identifying him as a particular person was no longer possible. The features had lost any resemblance to a living human being. Apart from a few patches of moldy, darkened skin, the face had become a skull, its bones showing pale against remnants of black hair and the folds of a green, shell-patterned silk robe. The formerly white silk trousers were stained and clung loosely to the bones beneath.

Given the clothing and the fact that no other member of the nobility had gone missing, it must be Tachibana. It seemed shocking that a powerful and fortunate man at the height of his career and in the full enjoyment of a privileged life should end up like this.

Not only had much time elapsed since the governor's death, but the recovery of the body had involved clumsy handling by the constables. Akitada and Maeda both knelt beside the body for a closer look. Akitada refrained from touching anything, but Maeda lifted a fold of clothing here and there, searching for signs of wounds. He pointed to dark stains and tears in the outer robe and matching black stains on the white silk undergarment. These were on the front and left side of the body's chest area.

"Knife wounds, I think," Maeda said softly. "He was stabbed."

"They cut off his hair," Akitada commented, looking at the short strands. "Possibly he was also tortured. Someone enjoyed killing him."

The constables had all come to stare at the corpse. Contact with the dead made them all ritually unclean and prohibited their taking part in certain Shinto observances. Their profession should have inured them to this, but they looked morose and muttered.

Maeda asked the two constables who had been in the well, "Did you find a weapon?"

They shook their heads. One of them said, "We looked good this time, Lieutenant."

Akitada rose. "Will your coroner be able to confirm the cause of death?"

The police chief nodded. "I think so. He's a good man. What will happen next, sir?"

Akitada glanced at the corpse of Lord Tachibana. "Identification of the body as that of Lord Tachibana. It should be easy, given his clothing. People will have seen him and remember. It was murder, and the murderer is here in Hakata. He must be found. I shall report to the assistant governor general and to our government in the capital. You carry on with the investigation."

But as they loaded the ex-governor's corpse onto the cart and gathered their tools, another of Maeda's men arrived at a run. He was flushed with exertion and gasped, "We found Hiroshi."

Akitada asked, "Where is he? Did you arrest him?"

The man was breathless and just shook his head.

Impatiently, Akitada turned to Maeda. "Come, we must question him at once. This is about Tora."

But the constable finally managed, "He's dead, your Excellency. Murdered."

Akitada's disappointment was staggering . With Hiroshi dead, chances of Tora being alive had just shrunk to nothing.

27

The Island

The green water boiled around the black rocks, tossing men and parts of the ship mercilessly against the sharp teeth of the island. Most of the men were already dead, drowned or killed by the battle on board.

Tora swam by instinct only, breathing when his head happened to emerge briefly from a wave and fighting against the dark pull of the sea that battered the rocky shore. Eventually he managed to cling to a rock much like barnacles did. Here he rested, his eyes closed, feeling the rush of the cold water hit his back, then pull at him as it tried to suck him back into the hungry sea.

He thought of nothing except resistance to the pull of the water until he heard his name called.

He had to hear it twice before he managed to open his eyes and peer around. Another wave washed over him, but he had seen enough of the open water to know the ship lay impaled on rocks, its masts gone and its body breaking apart. The sea was littered with debris, but he saw no living human beings. A dream, he thought, as the wave receded.

But the shout came again. And this time he looked the other way, toward land. And there on a rock lay a man, looking down at him from a bearded, shaggy face.

Shigeno?

It was Shigeno. He was waving and shouted, "Swim ashore. Hurry!"

Tora was afraid of releasing his rock. The next wave would pull him back out to sea, and he did not think he had the strength to swim. But he could not stay here forever, and there was another rock only some ten feet away. Each time a wave hit, the water would spout up from between the two rocks before receding and leaving for a few moments a calm surface.

He watched the next wave and trying to time it carefully, let go of his rock and plunged into the water. It instantly sucked him out again and he struggled desperately, but then, quite suddenly, he was free and reached the next rock. From there it became easier. The waves did not come in with as much force and he made his way to the shore where his feet met rough sand. There he collapsed, lying prone and exhausted.

Shigeno seized his arm. "Get up! You can sleep later."

Tora spat out some sea water and sat up. His side protested with a sharp pain that left him gasping. He found that Shigeno's sash, sodden with water, had slipped to his waist. Looking at the big convict, he said, "By all reason you should be dead, yet here you are and in better shape than me."

Shigeno snorted. "I'm a better man than you. Besides, I grabbed hold of a hatch cover and let the sea carry me ashore. But no time for chit-chat. We've got to get away before they notice us."

Tora looked at their surroundings. A rocky shoreline extended in both directions. Up ahead toward the west, forest had crept down almost to the water. In the other direction, debris from the capsized ship lay washed up on shore, along with some of the crew. They lay about, exhausted, unconscious, or dead.

Shigeno extended a hand and pulled Tora to his feet. Tora groaned, but Shigeno said again, "No time for that. Head for the trees."

Together they staggered toward the line of green that showed beyond the black rocks and pale sand. It seemed miles away.

Once there, they paused to peer back at the scene of the shipwreck. Shigeno had been right. Here and there, men stirred. Tora hoped they were too stunned by the disaster and their survival to wonder about the escaped convicts. He sat down cautiously, feeling his ribcage. The cut on his shoulder mostly itched. He hoped the sea water had cleansed the wound so it would not get infected.

"How are your wounds?" he asked Shigeno.

The big man had lost his shirt. He looked down at his broad chest. The knife wounds had stopped bleeding and looked pale. He touched them, one by one. "Mostly superficial, except for this one." He showed his upper arm where a deep cut to the flesh still oozed a little.

Tora unwound the sodden sash from his waist. "Here, let me make a bandage with this. My side feels fine," he lied. "Maybe the exercise was good for it." He hoped this was true.

Shigeno nodded.

As Tora wrapped and tied the makeshift bandage around Shigeno's arm, he asked, "What next? We aren't much better off, having landed on a convict island."

Shigeno grinned. "We're free. All we need is a boat."

Tora stared back. "A boat? Is that all?"

"Well, we should have held on to our weapons. Those knives would have come in handy."

"We have no boat and we no longer have anyone to sail it," Tora reminded him. "I guess the others didn't make it."

"Wrong. Ito didn't make it. Takeshi's looking for a boat."

"Which one's he?"

"The one that prayed."

"You're kidding."

Shigeno chuckled. "Goes to show, doesn't it?"

Tora shook his head. "He was good with a knife."

"Sailors use those long knives all the time. They can do some damage to thick hemp ropes as well as to people's bodies." He regarded his arm with a frown. "Well, let's move on up the coast. There's nothing for us to do here."

The broken wreckage and the few—very few—figures on the distant beach seemed a lifetime away. The survivors were beginning to pick through the flotsam, perhaps searching for their friends.

"Terrible!" muttered Tora, shaking his head.

"You're a softy." Shigeno chuckled. The big man's face wore a broad, happy smile, his teeth glinting from his bushy beard. At Tora's expression, his mouth opened even wider and he laughed out loud.

Tora clamped his hand over the other man's mouth. "Are you mad? Do you want them to hear you?"

Shigeno stopped laughing and nodded. Tora removed his hand. "How can you laugh?"

"Because I'm alive, Tora. Because I'm filled with joy to be alive to see the beautiful world around me. How can I not laugh?"

The beautiful world was cold, gray, and windy. The sea looked choppy, and a few rain drops struck their faces.

Tora shivered. "Postpone your happy dance," he said sourly. "We're still in trouble."

"You're right, but I can't help how I feel. Let's go then and find Takeshi."

They started walking along the shore, away from the wreck. It was hard going, because the terrain was rocky and took them up and down, forcing them to trudge inland to skirt small bays and offering little but desolate land with occasional glimpses of the slate-gray sea.

Whenever they rested, Tora asked questions.

"Do you know this place?"

"No."

"Any idea where they keep the convicts?"

"Near the mine, I'd think."

"Where is it?"

"Don't know."

It was not helpful. And there was no sign of Takeshi who might have been a better source of information. Dusk fell as they approached the sea again. Seagulls circled above, their harsh cries as inhospitable as the weather and the land. Tora was exhausted, and Shigeno had slowed down and stopped often to rest. When they reached a small mossy knoll, Tora suggested a rest. Shigeno nodded and collapsed on a rock.

For a while neither spoke. The seagulls came to look them over, screaming their disappointment at not finding food, and swooped away again.

"This place is uninhabited," Tora said wearily. "I wish I had something to eat. It's been at least a day, maybe two."

"I wish we had some water," said Shigeno.

They fell silent again. Tora shivered and looked at his companion. If he did not have that scruffy beard and tousled hair, Shigeno might be good-looking. His remaining clothes were mere rags by now, but he was slender, muscular, and not much older than Tora. More interesting were other aspects, not visible to the naked eye. Shigeno was no illiterate thug. He almost seemed wise at times, and his speech was that of an educated man. In addition, he was a formidable fighter and had shown great courage on the ship. How could such a man end up a convict?

But Shigeno had his own doubts about Tora also. He broke the silence first. "Was it the truth that you used to work for a governor?"

Tora smiled. "I still do. I wonder what he'll have to say about all this." He paused. "Not just any governor either. I work for Sugawara Akitada, the new governor of Chikuzen province. He's a famous man in the capital for solving crimes." He paused again. "I help him," he added modestly.

"So what happened?"

"We-ell, we barely got to Kyushu, and all hell broke loose. The former governor had been recalled, you see. He left without paying his people. They stole everything they could lay their hands on, and we found an empty tribunal. That bastard Okata refused to investigate, and my master dismissed him."

Shigeno's eyes widened. He whistled softly. "I like it so far. Go on."

"Turns out the former governor never reached home, and we had an investigation on our hands to see what happened to him. I was making some progress with that when Okata and his hired thugs jumped me, beat me up, and left me trussed up like an animal. Turns out that bastard Okata told them to ship me to Tsushima. And that's how we met."

"Okata did this just to get back at the new governor?"

Tora pursed his lips. "Well, not quite. I was the one who reported his mishandling of an investigation and his methods. It was personal all right."

Shigeno laughed and stretched out a hand. "Shake, brother. I'm one of the ones who suffered from his methods."

They shook hands, and Tora said, "All right. Your turn. What did you do?"

Shigeno's smile disappeared. "I killed a man, was tried, and sentenced. I'm a convict by rights. The story doesn't matter."

"It does to me."

Shigeno gave him a searching look. "It's complicated."

"We have time."

Shigeno turned his face away. "I don't like to remember. It's easier to be no one."

"I doubt it. How can you wash away the past? It lives with you."

Shigeno lowered his hands. "You're right. Since you insist, I grew up in Osumi province. My father had land there, quite a lot of land, but it was poor, so we were poor. There were my father, my mother, my sister, and me. Because we were poor, another man offered my father money for some acres in the mountains. My father refused to sell. It was rough land. Nothing would grow there, but my father and I liked to hunt in the mountains. It was beautiful. You could see for miles." Shigeno's eyes misted over as he looked out over the sea.

"What happened?" Tora urged.

"We discovered some men digging on our mountain and sent them away. My father thought they must be searching for silver or gold. Then the same man came to us again. This time he claimed the land belonged to him. Our mountain is on the border between Osumi and Higo. The man was the district prefect on the Higo side. The case went to Dazaifu to be resolved by the assistant governor general. We won. Then, within a month, my father was attacked on the road and left for dead. When he didn't come home, I went to look for him. He was barely alive and told me the men who attacked him had worn the prefect's colors. He died in my arms. I carried him home and left immediately for the prefect's house. There, I killed him in front of his family. I was arrested, tried, sentenced to exile, and our land was confiscated by the government. So, there you have it."

Tora shook his head. It wasn't all that rare an occurrence, he thought. Everywhere in the country such things happened, and men in power always ended up getting what they wanted. "I'm sorry," he muttered. "Was there silver in your mountain?"

"How should I know? I never got to see my home again. I spent months in the prison in Dazaifu until they moved me to Hakata for transport to Tsushima."

Silence fell.

Shigeno frowned. "I wonder," he said and stood up to look around. "I don't think we were at sea long enough to reach Tsushima. This might be some other island. Ikishima maybe."

"So we're lost?"

I. J. Parker

"Well, yes, but we may be much closer to Kyushu than we thought."

Tora brightened. "Come, let's walk again. There must be some fishing village on the coast. We can borrow a boat. And once we get home, I'll have my master look into your case."

Shigeno received this promise with a snort of derision. "Forget it. He'll have no chance against the Dazaifu. I bet he won't even try. I'm fed up with officials. As for borrowing a boat, how will you accomplish that? Fishermen need their boats. They won't let you have one without getting paid extremely well."

He had a point, but Tora waved it aside. "We'll think of something when we get there."

To their surprise, they found a house very soon after this. It clearly belonged to a fisherman, because a sturdy boat with a mast lay on shore. Smoke curled from a kitchen shed next to the house.

Tora laughed. "Look, they are even cooking our dinner for us." He started down the hill toward the house, Shigeno on his heels. They had covered half the distance when they heard the screams.

Tora cursed and started running, Shigeno at his heels. Somehow, they both guessed what was happening. Tora was the first to burst through the door of the small wooden house. The room was barely large enough for the three people it held, and Tora stumbled over the legs of an unconscious man on his way in.

The rest of the floor space was taken up by a woman and the convict Takeshi who was raping her. With one step, Tora reached him, seized him by his hair and pulled him off the woman. Then he hit him. Takeshi screamed. Blood spurted from his nose and trickled into his mouth.

"Here," snarled Tora to Shigeno. "Tie up this bastard. He just lost his bid for freedom."

He tried to help the woman up, but she scurried into a corner, looking at them fearfully. She was still young and not unattractive. The unconscious male on the floor was at least twenty years older. Apart from having been knocked out by the disgusting Takeshi, he seemed all right.

Tora sighed. "Well, that settles it. He'll hardly agree to lend us his boat after this. We'll have to borrow it without permission."

Shigeno grinned. "Steal it, you mean?"

Tora turned to the woman. "Your father's all right. He'll come round in a little while. I'm sorry about what happened."

She looked from him to the man on the floor. "My husband," she whispered.

"Oh, sorry. I'm Tora, and my big friend is Shigeno. The other animal is called Takeshi. We were shipwrecked."

She relaxed a little.

Tora asked her, "Where are we? I mean, what's the name of this island?"

She giggled at the question. "Ishida."

Tora grinned at Shigeno. "You were right. This isn't Tsushima."

She rolled her eyes. "No, not Tsushima."

"Well, we need to borrow your boat. And maybe some food?"

The mention of food startled her into action. She jumped up, stepped over her husband with barely a glance, and ran to the kitchen shed.

Shigeno had found some rope and trussed up the unconscious Takeshi. "What shall we do with him? Leave him here?"

Tora considered. The fisherman looked sturdy enough, but he was short. "It would serve him right, but he might get loose and start all over again. No, he's under arrest. We'll take him back to Hakata and put him in jail."

Shigeno snorted, but he followed Tora to the kitchen shed.

The young woman was stirring a large pot suspended over a charcoal fire. A wonderful smell came from it. Tora snatched up a couple of chipped bowls and held them out to her. "Please," he begged. "We're very hungry."

She glanced at him, smiled briefly, then used a ladle to fill both bowls with the fish and vegetable stew.

They ate hungrily, sipping and slurping the food, burning their mouths, and shoveling in the rest with their fingers. She watched them.

"You can't have the boat," she finally announced. "My husband needs it for fishing."

Tora returned his bowl and flashed her his best smile. "I know. I wish I had money to give you, but we have nothing. We need to take the boat to get back to Hakata. Afterward we'll return it. With payment."

She looked anxious. "Are there more men coming? Like that other one?"

Tora thought of the survivors they had left behind. It was very likely they would come this way. He eyed the fishing boat. It looked sturdy and large enough. "I tell you what," he said, suddenly inspired. "We'll take you and your husband and our prisoner with us. Your husband can handle the boat, and you'll both be safe. In Hakata, we'll pay you, and I'll buy you the prettiest gown you can find."

She looked toward the house. "My husband, is he really all right?"

"Let's go see!"

The fisherman was already stirring when they got back. He was sitting up, holding his head in his hands. It took a while to explain to him. Fortunately, he did not know Takeshi had been raping his wife, and nobody told him. They apologized that their escaped prisoner had attacked him and proposed the boat journey.

The man's wife said, "They'll pay good. Fifty pieces of silver." She shot Tora a sly glance.

"Fifty pieces of silver?" echoed the fisherman, looking stunned.

Tora nodded. "Fifty pieces of silver."

28

Conspiracy

Tora's fate overshadowed everything else. Even though the discovery of Governor Tachibana's body ranked as a political incident of the first order, Akitada did not travel to Dazaifu to report and receive instructions. Instead, he and Saburo stayed in Hakata to view Hiroshi's corpse. The weather had turned cold and wet again, and the doll maker's son had washed up in Hakata harbor. According to the coroner, he had been strangled.

Immediately afterward Akitada used Maeda's office to dictate to Saburo a terse account of Tora's presumed abduction and the recovery of the ex-governor's corpse.

"Address it to Lord Fujiwara Korenori, Assistant Governor General, Dazaifu. The subject is 'murder of

Lord Tachibana Moroe.' Write, 'The body of His Excellency Lord Tachibana Moroe, was discovered today in an abandoned well in Hakata. I await further reports from the Hakata coroner, but it appears the former governor was murdered about a month ago, probably on the day of his intended departure for the capital. The case is being investigated by Lieutenant Maeda of the Hakata police force since all crimes are handled locally in Chikuzen province.

"I must also report the disappearance of my retainer, Lieutenant Sashima, known as Tora. Since he was investigating the disappearance of Lord Tachibana at the time, I shall pursue this matter with all the vigor at my disposal.'"

Akitada paused. Saburo cast a glance at his master and said, "I'll have Maeda's staff make copies for our files."

Akitada nodded. "The usual superscription and conclusion. As soon as it's written out and copies have been made, it is to be taken immediately to Dazaifu by a tribunal guardsman."

"The assistant governor general won't like it."

"It's the way the Dazaifu administration set up the system of law enforcement in the Kyushu provinces; let them live with it now."

Akitada could well imagine that complaints about him would be dispatched to the court, but he did not care. He had made up his mind to ignore the assistant governor general until Tora was found. And Feng must have the answer.

He would deal differently with the merchant this time. On the last visit to the man's house, Tora had been with him. They had both felt palpable danger there, and Feng had been much too sure of himself. Since then, Feng's employees had been seen engaging in suspicious dealings with Hiroshi and with foreign ships docked in the harbor. Feng's clerk had paid off Hiroshi, and Ling had been present when Feng had vented his anger on the clerk later. Akitada had already suspected the Chinese merchant of having had a hand in Tachibana's murder, but most importantly, he was now his prime suspect in Tora's disappearance.

He thought about what Tora and Saburo had reported to him during the past month. It had all begun with the murder of Mitsui's wife. The Mitsuis were both doll makers, and her husband had confessed to killing her and had then committed suicide. Still unexplained was where and how Mrs. Mitsui had earned the five gold coins which had enraged her husband. The business with the dolls was also a puzzle. Why had the brute Ling stopped Akitada from buying or handling some of the dolls on the shelf? Something had been wrong with those dolls.

Hiroshi had probably been killed to keep him from talking to the police. As soon as they had found the bundle of Tora's clothes in the well, Hiroshi had to disappear. Next Feng's clerk had disappeared and might also be dead. Akitada felt he had waited too long to arrest the merchant.

An overlooked aspect affecting all those tangled cases was that both Hakata and Hakozaki were shipping ports. Lord Tachibana had been killed before he could board his ship in Hakata harbor. Hiroshi had worked for the privately owned port of Hakozaki, but his body had been dumped into Hakata harbor. Mitsui senior had delivered his dolls to ships docked in Hakozaki but had been sentenced to be transported to the Tsushima mines in a police boat from Hakata. Those who committed serious crimes were commonly dispatched to Tsushima, an island where they worked in the silver mines. Tsushima was very much like Sadoshima where Akitada had been imprisoned in a gold mine. Tora had come to find him then. Could it be Tora this time who had been condemned to the mine? They should have checked with the harbor authorities about recent departures from both ports.

Lieutenant Maeda returned to his office, and Akitada shared his concern. "I think we should check both here and in Hakozaki."

Maeda nodded. "Yes, of course. A convict boat left with prisoners two days ago, but there were only three convicts, two sailors who got in a fight and killed someone, and a man from Osumi province who had killed a prefect. A police sergeant and guards were on board."

"Not a likely conveyance then." Akitada got up from behind Maeda's desk. "Saburo is busy with a report to Dazaifu. I'd like you to accompany me to arrest Feng. We'll take some of the constables and soldiers. There may be trouble."

Maeda looked surprised but did not object. He left instructions to check on shipping, and then joined Akitada.

"By the way, sir," Maeda said as they rode in a drizzle into Feng's compound, followed by the tribunal guard, "when I sent for Feng's clerk again, my constable returned and said the shop was closed. I think the clerk may have become frightened and run."

"Either that or he's dead," Akitada said dryly, looking at the many deep wheel ruts left in the gravel of the courtyard.

Maeda was shocked. "Surely not, sir. I don't know what things are coming to. Is Feng behind all of it?"

"I don't know, Lieutenant, but I hope to find out." He dismounted. Leaving constables and soldiers in the courtyard, Maeda and Akitada knocked on the door.

The same aged servant admitted them. The house was as silent as last time, but there was a subtle difference. Last time, Akitada had had the feeling of being watched by many eyes. Now the place felt merely empty.

"We are here to see your master," Akitada said.

The old man bowed, but that was all.

Maeda asked in Chinese, "Where is your master?"

The old man bowed again and said nothing.

"We're too late. He's gone," Akitada said. "I think he's taken his goods and his family with him."

Maeda stared. "What? Why?"

"I noticed tracks of many wagons in the courtyard."

"The sly devil! We'd better search the house." Maeda pushed the servant aside and walked in.

"The men can help you," Akitada said, and turned to issue commands. He asked the servant, "When did your master leave, and where has he gone?"

The old man bowed, again silently. His behavior frustrated Akitada to the point where he wanted to shake him, but he reminded himself that such loyalty deserved respect. Feng might be a criminal and a murderer but he had inspired devotion in this old man. As he followed the soldiers and Maeda, the old servant brought up the rear, watching everything they did.

The house showed signs of having been left hurriedly. Gaping trunks stood about with some of the fine clothes still inside, a beautiful lacquer screen had been knocked over and broken, and papers covered the floor in what must have been Feng's own room.

Akitada stooped to look at these, but they were in the same puzzling writing as the account book. He suddenly knew they were wasting time.

"Does Feng have a country estate?" he asked Maeda.

"Not allowed, Excellency. Merchants, especially those of foreign descent, are not permitted to own land."

"Then I think Feng has escaped to the harbor. Are any Chinese ships in Hakata?"

"Also not allowed. Foreign ships dock at the *korokan.* But I think there's one in Hakozaki. Lord Akisuki has a special permit. I wish we knew when Feng left. We'd better hurry."

A break-neck gallop of nearly an hour through Hakata to Hakozaki brought them to the wharf where boats were still ferrying trunks and bundles across the gray, white-capped water to a large ship with a finely carved dragon writhing from its bow.

"Low tide. It's too shallow for big ships to dock," said Maeda with a grin of satisfaction. Now we shall see." He dismounted and walked quickly to the wharf. "You there," he shouted to some boatmen. "We need a couple of boats. Stop loading. The ship's not going anywhere."

On board the Chinese ship, their arrival had been noted. People were shouting and the sailors ran to raise the anchor and the big sails.

"They're trying to make a run for it," said Akitada. "Hurry, or we've lost him."

Maeda laughed. "They'll never make it. Wind and tide are against them, and it takes too long to get out of the harbor."

Akitada and Maeda were in the first boat across. With them were four constables and four of Akitada's soldiers. It was a joint operation.

The Chinese sailors had given up their efforts to get under way, and Akitada and the others boarded well ahead of other boats, bringing more support in case the Chinese made objections.

Feng and a man who must be the ship's captain awaited them on deck. In the background, several women and children huddled under a canopy. Feng was white-faced.

As it turned out, his pallor apparently was due to furious anger rather than fear.

He ignored Maeda, who confronted him with the words, "You're under arrest," and addressed himself to Akitada who had followed more slowly.

"This is an outrage, Governor," he shouted. "My family and I were taking our annual journey to worship at the tombs of our ancestors. This is a deeply spiritual journey for us and we had prepared carefully for it. This rude and disrespectful interruption is upsetting my women and children. Please take your men off this ship. If you insist, I'll come ashore to answer whatever questions you may have."

Maeda was about to respond equally angrily, but Akitada raised a hand. "Let it be so," he said. "We do not make war on women and children. Come with us now, and you may return to your family as soon as you have satisfied the investigators. Lieutenant Maeda will stay on board with his men to look for a fugitive."

Maeda stiffened into a salute, but from his set features, Akitada knew he did not like the order. Akitada not only hoped the search would turn up the thug Ling, but he needed to make certain the Chinese ship did not leave Hakozaki harbor without causing a political incident with China.

Akitada took Feng back to Hakata. There, in Maeda's office in police headquarters, with Saburo and a police scribe in attendance, he began his questioning.

Having been treated with a modicum of courtesy, Feng relaxed. "It is my pleasure to help your Excellency and the police in every way I can," he said. "I've said so before. You had but to ask."

Akitada smiled coldly. "Good. You may recall my assistant, Lieutenant Sashima, from our recent visit. Where is he?"

"I do remember him indeed. A very impressive young man. Alas, I have no idea where he might have got to. I never saw him again."

"You may not have seen him yourself, but people who work for you may have done so on your orders. He has been abducted."

Feng's eyes widened with shock. "Certainly not. Why would I do such a thing? I see that someone has blackened my character. People hate me because I'm of Chinese descent and have been very successful in this great country. I assure your Excellency that I'm a loyal subject, pay my taxes, and support my community. My reputation is excellent. You may ask the mayor, or the chief of the merchants' guild, or even the shrine priest. I honor the laws and customs of your country."

Akitada bit his lip. The man was very smooth. "Where are your employees Ling and your store clerk? What is his name?"

"His name is Masashi, but I could not tell you where they are. Because of my journey to visit my ancestors, I have closed the store and given them time off to see their families."

"Ling and Masashi appear to be involved in Lieutenant Sashima's disappearance. I want you to produce them as quickly as possible."

Feng started to rise. "Of course. I'm sure they are quite innocent, but I'll see to it right away."

"You'll stay here. We'll send a constable."

Feng's face fell. He subsided. "My personal servant is still at my house. He will know how to contact them. Allow me to write a note."

Akitada nodded, and Feng wrote something on a piece of paper. After glancing at it, Akitada gave it to the constable to deliver.

"Now then," Akitada continued, "there's also another matter. You may be aware the body of the previous governor has been recovered from an abandoned well?"

For a moment, it looked as though Feng would deny all knowledge of this, but then he nodded. "I heard a rumor but could hardly credit it. Is it true then?"

"Yes. We are trying to find out who was the last to see Lord Tachibana."

There was another hesitation, then Feng said, "I gave myself the honor to bid his Excellency farewell and wish him a safe journey that day. I went to the tribunal to see him off."

"Ah. And when did you leave him?"

Feng's face twitched. "As it happened, we left together. I went home and his Excellency continued to the harbor."

"What if I told you a witness saw you and Ling take Lord Tachibana to your home?"

Feng grew very still, but the twitch was still there. He said, "Is this the same person who accuses me of abducting your Lieutenant Sashima?"

"You deny taking Lord Tachibana to your house?"

"Absolutely. His Excellency was anxious to go on board. He would not have accepted an invitation to my house."

"How was it that Lord Tachibana went unaccompanied by his people on his way to the harbor?"

"I cannot tell. I think there was a last minute delay and he expected to catch up."

Akitada had made no progress. He switched subjects abruptly for the second time. "On my visit to your store I saw some very pretty dolls. Your clerk said they were made locally. By any chance were they made by Mrs. Mitsui?"

Feng frowned. "The name's familiar, but my clerk handles such matters. Once he gets here, he will be able to tell you. He said you bought two dolls for your children. Quite exquisite for such trivial things, aren't they?"

"Yes. And they were very inexpensive for something that must have taken many hours of work. I intended to get the plainer versions, but Ling was quite rude when I reached for one of those."

"Alas, I did not know this. My apologies. Ling has not been in this country long. It was a misunderstanding, I think. I would be pleased to send you several of those dolls at no charge whatsoever to make up for the unpleasantness. Or perhaps a painting would be more acceptable?"

"Thank you, no. Mrs. Mitsui received five pieces of gold for a special order just before she died. Did she get this payment from you?"

"I don't deal with craftspeople in person. My clerk does."

Feng looked positively pleased by now, smiling expectantly as he waited for the next question. Akitada was casting about for inspiration when Maeda finally returned from the harbor.

He came in and closed the door behind him.

"We found twelve strongboxes in the hold. They were very heavy. I had one of them broken open. It was filled with gold and silver coins."

Feng lost his smile.

"Thank you, Lieutenant," said Akitada. "Your property, Mr. Feng?"

"Not mine," Feng managed through clenched teeth. "You must ask the captain. It's probably money he earned engaging in legal trade."

"Somewhat rich for a short visit to our country, I would think," Akitada commented. "As for legal trade, Hakozaki harbor belongs to Akisuki Masanobu according to provincial records. His trading powers are restricted by the court. I think we'll confiscate the strong boxes, Lieutenant Maeda. An investigation into illegal trade with a foreign nation is indicated."

Maeda saluted and left.

Feng said nothing.

"I'm afraid I must cancel your planned journey while we are investigating," Akitada informed him.

Feng nodded and prepared to rise.

"Your family may return to their home, but you'll remain here in the Hakata jail until these matters are resolved."

"In jail?" Feng collapsed again. "But that's unjust," he protested. "I have done nothing wrong. You cannot keep me without cause. I shall complain to Dazaifu. No, I'll complain to the government in the capital. There are many powerful men there who know me and my family. We have served this country's noble families now for three generations. Such things are not forgotten."

Akitada thought of Tora. Feng's threat, though probably well-founded, meant nothing to him. "There's no more to be said," he snapped and called for a constable.

When the man appeared, Akitada ordered Feng bound and taken to jail.

On the way out, Feng cried, "Wait. I may have information about your Lieutenant Sashima."

"Speak then, and make it quick."

"I heard the former police chief, Captain Okata, held a grudge against the lieutenant."

Akitada stared at Feng. Could Okata have been behind Tora's disappearance all along?

Feng pleaded, "I can help you find your lieutenant, but I must be free to do so."

"No. Take him away, Constable."

Feng departed, muttering.

Saburo and Akitada looked at each other. "Captain Okata?" Saburo asked. "Do you think it could be the answer?"

"It's as likely as anything. Let's go get him."

Akitada went in search of Maeda. He found him in the courtyard, giving instructions to a group of constables about removing the strongboxes from the ship and placing a guard on it to make sure it did not depart for its homeland.

"Do you know where Okata is?" Akitada asked.

"Okata? Not really. His family owns land near the *korokan*. Why?"

"Feng says Okata is behind Tora's disappearance. I think I'll take Saburo and some soldiers from the tribunal and arrest Okata." Akitada was both angry and miserable. Maeda and the assistant governor general had warned him that Okata might take revenge. He had brushed their warnings off.

Leaving Saburo behind, he gathered his soldiers and, still wet and chilled from the ride to Hakozaki, climbed back on his horse.

They had not yet left Hakata on their journey west when a constable on a lathered horse caught up with them, shouting and waving his arm. They stopped.

"He's back," shouted the man. "He's safe. Lieutenant Maeda says to tell you Lieutenant Tora just got back."

They crowded around him. "What happened?" Akitada asked, scarcely believing the good news.

"Lieutenant Tora says Captain Okata and his men caught him and sent him to Tsushima on the convict ship. Not sure about the rest, Excellency, but the lieutenant thought you might want to come back."

Of course, he was going back. The gods had been kind once again. Tora was alive—and apparently well. Akitada was too overcome to speak.

29

The Skein Unravels

Tora looked wet, filthy, and battered, his face bruised and covered with stubble, his ragged clothes torn, and his legs and feet bare. Beside him was another man, a big, shaggy-haired and shaggy-bearded fellow. Saburo hovered by their side.

When Tora saw Akitada, he gave a happy shout and they embraced.

"I've never been so glad to see anyone," Akitada said, holding him. Tora used only his right arm to return the hug. "What's the matter? Are you hurt?"

Tora still had his irresistible grin. "Just a little. We've been to war, both of us." He turned. "This is Shigeno. Show 'em your chest, Shigeno."

The big man lifted a ragged and blood-stained shirt. The crowd gasped at the many stab wounds and slashes. Shigeno sat down quickly.

"We've sent for a doctor," Saburo supplied.

"Coming!" cried a voice from the door. "Let me through." A very short monk appeared with his medicine case. He nodded to Maeda and looked the two patients over before crouching beside the big man and taking his shirt off. Shaking his head, he said, "Amida! I need to sew you up," and produced a long, dark needle and some silk from his case.

Shigeno grew a shade paler.

Akitada asked Tora, "How badly hurt are you?"

Tora grinned. "Only one small cut that's stopped bleeding. I want to get that bastard Okata. He's the one set his thugs on me and bundled me off on a convict ship. Him and Hiroshi." Tora put a hand on Shigeno's shoulder. "But we showed them, didn't we, brother?"

The big man nodded.

"Hiroshi?" Akitada asked.

"Oh, yes. And he killed both his stepmother and Yoko. Seems Yoko confronted him with being at the Mitsui place the night she was stabbed. Hiroshi hated her and thought she'd stolen gold from his father."

"It explains a lot, sir," Maeda said.

"I told you, Maeda. You should've listened." Tora returned to his story. "Anyway, I woke up in the hold, but Shigeno and I and two convicts, we got out and we fought them all, guards and sailors both. They got distracted and wrecked their ship on Ikishima. We escaped, all but one of us, found a fisherman and hired him to bring us back. I owe him fifty pieces of silver, sir." Tora paused to give Akitada an apologetic grin.

"I can hardly believe it," remarked Akitada, shaking his head. "You fought them? Why didn't you identify yourself to the person in charge of the transport?"

"I tried to, but they just laughed. I have a notion the policeman and the guards work for Okata."

"Ah." Akitada glanced at Maeda. "You'd better look into this."

Maeda nodded. He looked stunned.

Akitada spoke to the fisherman and his wife and paid them the promised sum. The couple seemed to regard their visit as a great adventure and the astonishing reward as a miraculous event. They kept bowing and muttering thanks.

When Tora and Shigeno were able to answer more questions, Maeda, ever the policeman, started with, "You told us three convicts escaped. What happened to the other two?"

"One died, I think," said Tora. "The other didn't trust the authorities and took off."

Maeda glowered. "No surprise."

Shigeno began to look very uneasy, and Akitada asked him, "But you decided to put your faith in us? Or did Tora make more promises?"

The big convict flushed. "It's true that Tora said you'd fix things but, frankly, I didn't believe he could do anything for me. I decided to take the risk of making my case to you."

Akitada raised his brows. The man was educated, not your run-of-mill convict. "What were you sentenced for?"

"Murder. Of a prefect, I was told," Maeda snapped.

Saburo gasped. "You killed a prefect? That's hardly an insignificant crime."

Tora frowned at him. "Just wait till you hear his story. The prefect was a crook who had Shigeno's father killed so he could steal their gold mine."

"Gold mine?" Akitada stared at Shigeno.

"Well, someone found either gold or silver on our mountain," explained Shigeno. "Not sure if there's a lot of it. We never had a chance to look."

"But you killed a prefect?" Akitada shook his head. "There are better methods of settling land disputes."

Tora pointed out, "If Okata can be a crooked police chief, then Shigeno's prefect can be a murderer or worse."

It was true; not all officials were honest. And this was Kyushu. Akitada said, "You're right. Very well, we'll look into it. Meanwhile Shigeno will be my guest at the tribunal. I want his word he won't run."

Shigeno smiled. "You have it, your Excellency. And thank you."

"Has Maeda told you, Tora? A lot has happened since you disappeared."

Tora nodded. "They found my clothes in the abandoned well where Yoko's body had been. That bastard Hiroshi! He was there, working me over. And Okata was, too. I recognized his voice. He's the one set it up for getting dismissed. I expect Hiroshi took me to the ship on his cart. He had to get rid of my clothes. Much too official-looking on a convict. Too bad he's dead. I was looking forward to meeting him again."

Maeda asked, "Are you sure he admitted killing both of them?"

"Yes. He was pretty cool about it, too. Killed his father's wife for stealing from his father. My guess is he found the gold coins, and she refused to give them to him. Hiroshi had gambling debts that went away after her death. As for Yoko, she apparently saw him at the house the night of the murder and asked him about it."

Maeda shook his head. "Yoko was the type to confront Hiroshi. She'd mention seeing him even if she didn't think it important."

"Poor Yoko."

Akitada cleared his throat. "As it turned out, the well seems to have been a popular burial place. My predecessor was also down there."

"Maybe Hiroshi had a hand in that, too. And to think you'd never have known any of this if it hadn't been for me." Tora grinned.

"We found Yoko before you disappeared," Maeda objected.

Akitada added, "We certainly can't pin the governor's murder on Hiroshi, busy fellow though he was. It's not the sort of crime he would commit. But at least we can be certain of his killing his stepmother and Yoko."

Tora nodded. "The boy Kichiro said Hiroshi got very angry when he saw him looking over the fence. That must have been right after Yoko was killed. I expect Hiroshi got rid of whatever was in that hole. Best do some more digging, Maeda."

Maeda made a face. "Well, I'm glad you left me something to do."

"If you like, I'll help you."

You're going to bed," said Akitada. "Both of you, since Shigeno has agreed to be our guest."

They returned to the tribunal, where their arrival caused gratifying pleasure. Akitada cut all questions short with a brief statement, and Saburo saw to it that Tora and his new friend had baths, food, and a rest.

In the tribunal office, Akitada asked Mori, "Did the report to the assistant governor general get off?"

"Yes, sir."

Akitada next filled Mori in on some of the other news. The secretary was dumfounded. "Lord Tachibana was murdered?"

"Yes, Mori. Right after he left here. Do you recall the day?"

"Yes, your Excellency." The old clerk showed little grief. He merely shook his head in amazement. "His Excellency was irritable. He didn't look forward to going home. Most of the officials sent from the capital hate Kyushu, but Lord Tachibana made friends here and bought many beautiful things. Of course, there was the matter of the recall."

"Yes, indeed. If you recall what the governor was wearing, you'd better report to Lieutenant Maeda. It will help identify the body."

"Yes, sir." Mori sighed. "It's hard to believe. Merchant Feng made a lot of money from him and must have hated to see him leave."

"I don't doubt it in the least."

"Merchant Feng was a frequent visitor here and came to see his Excellency off. They left together. His lordship, Merchant Feng, and that Chinese servant of his."

"Feng admitted as much. By any chance, were you aware that Lord Tachibana had a relationship with a courtesan called Fragrant Orchid?"

Mori blushed. "Oh, yes. We all knew. He was very taken with her. Merchant Feng introduced them." Mori paused. "I've had a look at Mr. Feng's account book."

Feng's secret account book must hold the key to Tachibana's death, and they badly needed evidence against Feng. The recalled governor's very close business relationship with the merchant had ostensibly been based on his obsessive acquisition of Chinese art, but such a fixation was a weakness that could be exploited by unscrupulous men. If Tachibana had indeed engaged in illegal and treasonous dealings through Feng, then his departure for the capital, where suspicion of malfeasances would have brought interrogation by the censor's bureau, was a mortal danger to Feng and possibly others.

Akitada gave Mori an encouraging nod. "Excellent! And what have you found out?"

Mori went to his desk and returned with the book.

"I am not quite sure, your Excellency. Mr. Feng used colloquial Chinese, but I also believe some of the names and objects are disguised by other words."

"Very likely. Have you learned anything at all?"

"Yes. Merchant Feng has been ordering pictures and some carved figures in exchange for certain sums or unspecified favors. He listed expenditures also, in one case, in one of the last entries, he mentions children's toys. Since the pictures and so forth were for Lord Tachibana, possibly the moneys and favors might have been supplied by Lord Tachibana in payment?"

"Probably. I hate to think what favors Lord Tachibana did the Chinese merchant." Locking away the account book, Akitada thanked Mori, adding, "We'll let Lieutenant Maeda ask one of the Chinese merchants to translate this."

Akitada went to his study for a cup of tea and a brief rest before returning to Hakata. The distance between the tribunal and police headquarters was becoming a nuisance. At least the rain had stopped. To his surprise, he found the houseboy Koji squatting on the floor. The boy shot up and immediately prostrated himself.

"Askin' pardons, zir. Is a message."

Irritated to be kept from his refreshment, Akitada snapped, "What message? And why didn't you give it to Mori?"

Koji shrank. "Very private. Only for governor's ears. I promise on my mother's grave." The boy eyed him anxiously. "You're angry. I cannot tell you if you're angry." He turned to go.

"Koji!" thundered Akitada.

The boy froze, his back to him. Akitada said more gently, "I'm not angry, but I have much to do, so please say what you've come to tell me."

Koji did not turn. "I waited 'cause I promised."

"It's all right. I appreciate your patience."

"Someone's here," Koji offered, looking at him over his shoulder. "He won't come out if you're angry."

Come out? "Who is here?"

Koji shook his head. "I cannot tell if you're angry."

Akitada controlled himself with an effort and managed a smile. "Did you ask his name?"

"Yezzir. I ask many times. No name."

Akitada sighed. "Where is this person?"

Koji walked into the adjoining eave chamber and pointed at one of the trunks standing in a corner. It had held Akitada's books and papers but was now empty.

Or so Akitada had thought. He crossed quickly to it and flung back the lid.

A man cowered inside. He was on his knees and had his head tucked under his arms as if he expected to be beaten.

"Don't hurt him, zir," Koji cried. "He's afraid."

"Get out," snapped Akitada.

After a moment, the slight figure of Feng's clerk Masashi unfolded its thin limbs and stepped out of the trunk. He was sobbing. He stood for a moment, then fell to his knees and knocked his head against the floor. "Save me, your Excellency," he cried. "They are going to kill me."

Akitada nearly smiled. This was a stroke of luck and should fix Feng for good. He said in a reassuring tone, "Don't worry, Masashi. You're quite safe here. Koji, this is Masashi. Go and get us some wine and something to eat. Masashi looks worn out."

"Good!" Koji clapped his hands, grinned, and ran out.

"Now then, Masashi. Sit up and explain."

The clerk did indeed look pitiful. He was pale and trembled uncontrollably. His stringy hair hung into his face, and his clothes were torn and dirty. He wept again, quite noisily.

"Calm yourself now, "Akitada said a little more firmly. "There is nothing I can do for you unless you speak freely."

Masashi nodded, hiccupped, and wiped his blubbered face with a dirty sleeve. "Ling came to kill me," he managed. "I got away, but he's looking for me." He pulled the shirt from his neck and pushed his hair back. Masashi's neck was covered with huge bruises. There were other bruises on his arms and on the side of his face.

"Why did he do this?"

"The master sent him. Just as with Hiroshi. Ling kills people for the master."

No surprise there. Akitada regarded the clerk with an encouraging smile. Surely Masashi was about to give him more proof of Feng's crimes. "I suspected as much," he said. "Why did you come here?"

"Where else could I go? Nobody in Hakata would help me. They're afraid of Feng or owe him money."

"Hmm. I take it you know we found the governor's body?"

The clerk nodded.

"Did Feng kill Governor Tachibana?"

Masashi looked frightened. "I don't know. I wasn't there. Surely not even Ling would have dared touch one of the good people."

"What about the courtesan Fragrant Orchid?"

"Feng bought her house and set her up. He introduced her to Lord Tachibana."

"Did Feng have anything to do with her death?"

Masashi gave him a startled look. "They said Fragrant Orchid killed herself out of grief over Lord Tachibana leaving."

"She was poisoned because she wanted to speak to me. What sort of secret might she have had knowledge of?"

Masashi became agitated again. "Oh, this is terrible," he moaned. "That Ling is a monster."

"He is Feng's monster. Did Feng send Ling to kill Fragrant Orchid?"

"Maybe. Feng told Ling, 'The woman is going to talk. Take care of her.' And he gave him something wrapped in paper. I thought it was gold and he meant to pay her off to keep quiet. The governor must have told her about Feng's business."

Koji came back with a tray of food and a flask of wine. Giving Masashi an encouraging nod, he set these down before him and left.

Akitada thought back to the alleged suicide letter. It did not fit. He decided he had been wrong about the killer leaving it. Ling was not clever enough. Perhaps it had been something Fragrant Orchid left lying about, something she had saved from her affair with Tachibana.

But the rest was falling into place. Feng's business indeed! Masashi was a godsend! "Go ahead! Eat and drink," Akitada urged.

Masashi eyed the bowl of rice cakes hungrily, but settled for a gulp of wine instead. He was not shaking quite as badly as before.

"And what was Feng's business exactly?" Akitada prodded.

But here Masashi was no help. "I don't know. He didn't trust me. I don't think he trusted anyone, not even Ling. He did a lot of business with China, but this is permitted."

"In his case, probably not. What about those dolls Ling wouldn't let me touch?"

"Ling was very rude. Feng really doesn't like him waiting on customers. The dolls were a special shipment meant to go on the ship to China. I couldn't see it myself. The other dolls were much better made. These were careless, as if the Mitsuis had rushed the job."

"Did Feng ask you to pay Mrs. Mitsui five pieces of gold for them?"

"Five pieces of gold? No. That would have been crazy."

No doubt Feng had dealt with Mrs. Mitsui personally. There was no proof, of course, but Akitada thought about it and decided Mitsui had not been involved in the special dolls. Feng had spoken to his wife, probably because she was also Chinese and could be trusted to keep the secret from her abusive husband. Too bad Hiroshi had found out about the gold.

Masashi had nothing else to tell him. Like Shigeno, the clerk would stay at the tribunal under guard. Masashi was grateful. Akitada did not tell him he would still have to face charges, though he seemed to have been kept in the dark by his master. He made him repeat his tale for a scribe and sign his statement.

Akitada finally changed his clothes and brewed his cup of tea. He sipped it while reading through Masashi's statement. Then he rode back to Hakata, where Maeda received Masashi's testimony with great excitement. "All we need now is Ling!" he cried. "And we'll get him. There's no place he can run. The Chinese ship isn't leaving Hakata until this is settled. And look what we found on the ship." He pointed to a box beside his desk. In it stood nine plain dolls beside the shards of a tenth. And among the shards lay a handful of gleaming gold nuggets.

Akitada touched them. They looked just like the gold he had seen and touched on Sado Island. He remembered Shigeno's story and said, "So Feng hid this gold in the dolls and was sending it to China. I wonder why. The convict Shigeno was involved in a land dispute over mining a mountain in Osumi. What happened to that land after he was sentenced?"

Maeda looked blank. "No idea. Okata handled the case."

"Well, since Shigeno was sentenced to transportation here, get me the trial notes. I think Feng planned to sell information about the gold mine to the Chinese. He was sending the gold in those dolls as proof. We need Okata. You have enough to charge him. Why hasn't he been arrested?"

Maeda flushed. "I sent my sergeant with some men. I thought I'd better stay here, what with Feng and the Chinese ship."

"Yes, of course. I didn't mean to snap at you. Too many things are happening; it's hard to keep everything in mind."

Maeda grinned. "It's exciting, though."

Akitada really liked the man.

An hour later he had the paperwork on Shigeno's trial. It confirmed what Shigeno had told him. Of even greater interest was the fact that Captain Okata had played a significant role in the investigation and that he had managed to lose three witnesses whose information would have confirmed the prefect's involvement in Shigeno's father's death. Akitada would see to it that these witnesses would be called. This time Shigeno would fare better.

They brought in Okata toward evening. He was full of outraged bluster until confronted with the charges against him. These ranged far beyond what he had done to Tora. Akitada informed him of Feng's arrest and then revealed his intentions of reopening the case against Shigeno with particular attention to Okata's involvement in Feng's plot to exploit the gold of Kyushu. He might well have brought about an invasion by China.

Treason of this magnitude carried the death penalty. Okata started talking.

30

Yesterday's
Cherry Blossoms

L
ing was not caught until a week later. By this
time Akitada no longer cared. When Maeda
informed him, he only said, "Do whatever it
takes to make him talk." Ling confessed quickly. He
died on his way to Tsushima.

When Feng was confronted with the evidence
against him, he took poison, having been supplied with
the means either by accident or design. Akitada did not
care about this either.

The Chinese ship was released with a warning, and
Korenori, the assistant governor general, congratulated
him on solving the murder of governor Tachibana and
stopping a dangerous plot against the nation.

Okata was condemned to death and transported.

Matters of much greater importance had happened after Okata's arrest.

Akitada had returned to the tribunal in the knowledge that he had stopped a dangerous man and a possible invasion by the Chinese. He looked forward with considerable complacency to making his report to Fujiwara Korenori.

But first there were letters from home.

Tora and Saburo were already waiting anxiously for him to open the thick package of official and personal mail. They sat in his study as he undid the oiled cloth that covered mail sent by ship. Laying aside official documents and some letters from friends, Akitada opened a separate package, lovingly tied with a scrap of silk ribbon.

Letters and drawings from the children fell out first. Then he saw a letter from his sister Akiko. Akiko was willful and too conscious of status, in his opinion. Lately she had begun meddling in his work. He laid her letter aside with those of the children. Hanae's handwriting he recognized and passed to Tora. There were also some missives for Saburo. Finally there was nothing left but a disappointingly thin sheet, folded somewhat badly. It had no superscription, but when he unfolded it, he saw it was from Tamako. The writing was oddly uneven, a mere scrawl, and the letter was only a few lines long.

"My dear husband—we had a son—alas, he died. Forgive your loving wife."

The death of the child was an unexpectedly painful blow. It was, of course, a common occurrence that newborns died, and this child had been born before his time to a mother who was no longer young. He had not expected to grieve for a creature he only knew from feeling its movements inside its mother's womb. How like Tamako to ask his pardon in her own grief. There was nothing to forgive. Fate frequently opposed human hope. He sighed and reminded himself that Tamako had already given him two beautiful children—no, three. Yori had also fallen prey to the cruel hand of fate. It was the human lot to suffer such losses. He would write to Tamako. He did not need more children to find happiness in his marriage. She was all he had ever wanted and needed.

He laid her note aside and started to tell Tora and Saburo about the death of the baby. To his surprise, they looked stricken. He said, "It was a boy, but he died."

Saburo shook his head and wiped away tears. Tora said in a thick voice, "Read the other letter, sir."

Later he would not be able to say when he knew. Was it Saburo's face when he had smeared Tamako's make-up by wiping tears from his eyes, or Tora's choking voice?

Akiko's letter explained it. It was a short letter for her. He read it and felt the room spin. He read it again, and his hand started shaking so badly that the letter fell from it. He did not have the strength to pick it up.

"I'm very sorry, sir," Tora said in a half-stifled tone.

Saburo wept openly now. "Me too, sir. We'd both give anything to undo this."

Akitada could not speak. He nodded and waved a hand, and after a moment they rose and left the room.

Tamako was dead!

Her short note had been her last words to him. An apology. She had barely had the strength to hold the brush; Hanae had helped her. And then she had died. Without him by her side. He had been chasing after villains who meant nothing to him. For a government that had demanded the ultimate sacrifice from him.

Now he was alone and would remain alone. Tamako was such an essential part of him that her place could not be filled—not by the children, though he loved them—not by Tora or Genba or Saburo, though they were his closest friends.

He was alone and nothing mattered any longer.

After a long time, he got to his feet and walked outside. The ground beneath the little tree was white. Snow, he thought. Snow, as pure and cold as death.

But it was not snow. The little tree had shed all its blossoms overnight, and beauty had left the world.

Historical Note

Kyushu—the name means "nine provinces"—is the southernmost of the large Japanese islands and closest to Japan's neighbors, China and Korea. Historically this is significant because Japan took much of its cultural identity from China, either directly through embassies and an exchange of travelers or via contact with Korea. This included, for example, Buddhism, the structure of its administration, its official language, its art and architecture, and much of its learning.

Diplomatic wrangling required that both China and Japan consider the other nation as a vassal and exchange gifts that were received as tribute. In time, Japan tired of the exchange and closed its borders to foreign visitors. All shipping and travel between Tang China, Korea (Koryo), and Japan was strictly regulated and had to stop in Kyushu, where the Tsukushi Lodge, a reception area for foreigners (*Korokan*) was built near Hakata. Kyushu was heavily fortified against invasions, and its government center was located inland at Dazaifu behind a massive dyke or water fortress (Mizuki) and numerous mountain fortresses guarding its access road. Frontier guards guarded Hakata Bay.

The administration of Kyushu was from the beginning a particularly sensitive one. It was a long distance from the capital so that it took weeks to transmit reports and instructions; it was settled by land-owning nobles frequently hostile to the central government; and it was close to both China and Silla, an enemy on the Korean peninsula. Thus it was administered by a type of viceroy, called a governor general (*sotsu*), from a heavily protected administrative center located at Dazaifu. The governor general was always an imperial prince, who remained in the capital while the business of Kyushu was handled by the assistant governor general, a high-ranking nobleman. He supervised foreign trade and travel, military facilities, and the eleven governors who administered the individual nine provinces of Kyushu and the two island provinces of Tsushima and Iki.

Early on, merchants from Korea and China came in numbers, but in the ninth and tenth centuries formal relations with China and Korea stopped, and trade diminished. Foreign pirates ruled the seaways. In the late tenth century, Kyushu was invaded by the Toi, ("barbarians"), from Mongolia and Northern China. The defense of Kyushu as the gateway to Japan became a priority. The system of importing frontier guards from other parts of Japan was abandoned and local forces were used instead. This strengthened local landowners greatly and led to their gaining power and influence in the administration at Dazaifu. Military control in Kyushu passed to them, and they filled both military and administrative positions where they pursued their private interests.

By the eleventh century, some restrictions against trade with China and Korea loosened because of demand for luxury goods by the ranking nobility and the court, and because of efforts of Buddhist centers to acquire religious documents and art. Foreign merchants managed to bypass government controls by dropping anchor in privately owned harbors to load and unload their goods.

It is against this background that Akitada's assignment to the office of governor of Chikuzen province must be seen. Chikuzen included Hakata, a major port city on the Inland Sea, Dazaifu, where government headquarters were located, and the Tsukushi Lodge (*korokan*), where all foreigners stayed. The headquarters at Dazaifu, a smaller version of the Greater Imperial Palace (*Daidairi*) in the capital, severely restricted the powers and independence of Kyushu governors. To add to these problems, Hakata had attracted settlements of Chinese and Koreans who had arrived during more favorable times and stayed, while local nobles had usurped certain powers and frequently served in administrative positions. Meanwhile, the central government in the capital was extremely nervous about the erosion of trade restrictions and the threat of new invasions from China or Korea.

As the central government in the capital tried to control distant provinces of the country in order to levy rice taxes and corvee labor, provincial administrations were headed by court nobles from the capital. These men brought their own small staff, but most of the bureaus in the provincial headquarters were headed by local men. Provinces were further subdivided into prefectures (*gun*) and the prefects were again local men. In time, the system eroded further in that governors were absent, leaving the work to the local appointees, or letting a lower-ranking member of the central government substitute. This was certainly the case with the Dazaifu office.

Akitada would have found a poorly staffed headquarters or tribunal, probably lacking the usual amenities, such as military barracks, jails, granaries and storehouses for tax goods, a tax office, and provincial archives. He could not expect help from an assistant governor, an executive officer, an inspector, and a chief magistrate, not to mention tax grain chiefs, corvee directors, scribes or a minimum of four servants for each of these. He could also expect local appointees to be uncooperative.

The manufacture of elaborate dolls is a more recent development in Japanese history, and Hakata dolls are famous. This suggested the idea of the doll maker and the hollow dolls. However, dolls certainly existed long before Akitada's time. By the eleventh century, they were made both as toys for children and as ritual objects intended to protect a child from evil spirits, either by confusing them or by drawing them into the doll which could then be disposed off.

In the early years, Japan was poor in both silver and gold. As these metals were needed for trade, there was always a great interest in discovering deposits. Silver was being mined in Tsushima early on, but in the Heian period, the only gold came from the north of the country. The gold mentioned in this novel is a fiction, though a rich gold mine was eventually discovered in Osumi province in modern times.

As for details of the location of the places mentioned here, modern archeological digs have confirmed Dazaifu, the *korokan*, the elaborate dam protecting Dazaifu, and the mountain forts that protected it and the Kyushu coastline against foreign invasions. The rest of the historical facts comes from documents dating to the time. Bruce L. Batten's book *Gateway to Japan: Hakata in War and Peace, 500-1300* is a good source of information about the area in early times.

About the Author

I.J. Parker was born and educated in Europe and turned to mystery writing after an academic career in the United States. She published her Akitada stories in *Alfred Hitchcock's Mystery Magazine,* winning the Shamus award in 2000. Several stories have also appeared in collections (*Fifty Years of Crime and Suspense* and *Shaken).* The award-winning "Akitada's First Case" is available as a podcast. Many of the stories have been collected in *Akitada and the Way of Justice.*

The Akitada series of crime novels features the same protagonist, an eleventh-century Japanese nobleman/detective. It now consists of eleven titles, with the early ones published by Penguin. *Death of a Doll Maker* is the latest. Most of the books are available in audio format and have been translated into twelve languages.

Her historical novels are set in twelfth-century Japan during the Heike Wars. The two-volume *The Hollow Reed* tells the story of Toshiko and Sadahira. *The Sword Master* follows the adventures of the swordsman Hachiro.

The Akitada series in chronological order

The Dragon Scroll

Rashomon Gate

Black Arrow

Island of Exiles

The Hell Screen

The Convict's Sword

The Masuda Affair

The Fires of the Gods

Death on an Autumn River

The Emperor's Woman

Death of a Doll Maker

The Collected Stories

Akitada and the Way of Justice

I. J. Parker

The Historical Novels

The Hollow Reed I: Dream of a Spring Night

The Hollow Reed II: Dust before the Wind

The Sword Master

The Left-Handed God

For more information, please visit I. J. Parker's web site at http:www.ijparker.com. You may write the author at heianmys@aol.com.

Books may be ordered from Amazon and Barnes&Noble. Electronic versions of the novels are available for Kindle and PC. The short stories are on Kindle and Nook. Please do post Amazon reviews. They help sell books and keep Akitada novels coming.

Thank you for your support.